JANIE BASKIN

This book is dedicated to Flo who lives in my heart, and to Ruth who illuminated my path with her wisdom.

Scarlet Voyage, an imprint of Enslow Publishers, Inc.

Library of Congress Cataloging-in-Publication Data

Baskin, Janie.
Paint me a monster / Janie Baskin.
pages cm
Summary: Rinnie relates a childhood marked by privilege but also abuse, which steadily increases after her parents' divorce and remarriages, emotionally crippling Rinnie until a school counselor helps her begin to heal.
ISBN 978-1-62324-018-9
[1. Mothers and daughters—Fiction. 2. Family problems—Fiction. 3. Emotional problems—Fiction. 4. Psychotherapy—Fiction. 5. Eating disorders—Fiction. 6. Family life—Ohio—Fiction. 7. Jews—United States—Fiction. 8. Cincinnati (Ohio)—Fiction.] I. Title.
PZ.7.B29228Pai 2014
[Fic]—dc23 2012051040

Future editions:
Paperback ISBN: 978-1-62324-019-6
EPUB ISBN: 978-1-62324-020-2
Single-User PDF ISBN: 978-1-62324-021-9
Multi-User PDF ISBN: 978-1-62324-022-6

Printed in the United States of America

112013 Bang Printing, Brainerd, Minn.

10 9 8 7 6 5 4 3 2 1

Scarlet Voyage
Box 398, 40 Industrial Road
Berkeley Heights, NJ 07922
USA
www.scarletvoyage.com

Cover Illustration: Shutterstock.com

Part One
The First Ten Years

YAH, RINNIE

"You girls draw me something pretty," Verna says, handing us paper and what she calls a rainbow-in-a-box. "Just be sure to keep those colors on the paper. Lord knows your mama's given me enough house-cleaning to last a lifetime."

"Thank you, Verna," we say. "We promise to be sure."

"1958—you'd think Mrs. Gardener never heard of Abraham Lincoln," Verna mumbles.

I love the smell of waxy crayons and their jiggy jag lines.

"When all the colors slide over each other, it makes a rainbow out of the box," I say to my sister, Liz.

"That's scribbling, Margo," she says. "I don't scribble. My picture is our house. 61 Peregrine Avenue, Cincinnati, Ohio." Lizzie underlines the letters with red zigzags. "Here're the thorn bushes, our tree house, and our sandbox." She sits back on her knees, chest out like she's about to sneeze.

I don't care what a Cincinnati, Ohio is. "Scribble scrabble, scribble scrabble, scribbly scribbly scribble scrabble." The words pop out of my mouth. They are hard, soft, and sweet at the same time.

"Scribble sounds like chocolate caramels or ice cream," I tell Liz, drawing more wiggly lines. She colors a yellow sun in the corner of her picture.

I push my crayons away so I can watch television.

"Yah, Rinnie," yells a man on TV. "Yah, Rinnie, get the child out of the house."

A big dog with a fluffy tail runs into a house on fire. When he comes out, his fur is dirty. In his mouth, he drags a boy by the pants.

"Good work, Rinnie. You're the smartest, fastest, strongest dog in the world!" says the man, clapping his hand on Rinnie's back.

I want to be Rin Tin Tin.

"Lizzie, if you call me Rin Tin Tin, I will do anything you ask. Say, yah, Rinnie."

"What?" Lizzie asks.

"I'm Rin Tin Tin," I say.

"OK. Rin Tin Tin, get me an oatmeal cookie. YAH, Rinnie! Go see if Verna's made lunch yet. YAH, Rinnie! Hand me the coloring book on the chair. YAH, Rinnie!"

I am the strongest, fastest, smartest dog in the world. I see myself run across the brown grass waiting for it to turn green—and to save people.

MONKEY BUSINESS

"The door to the extra bedroom has to be kept shut," Verna says. Her whisper is so soft the sound almost tiptoes past my ears. The gold tooth on the side of Verna's mouth winks at me. It shines like the slicked-down black hair she calls a wig. It matches her clothes.

There's a secret on the other side of the door. My three-year-old feet creep, creep, creep forward.

The upstairs hallway is lit from below. I take off my shoes so no one can hear me. Downstairs, in the den, the ladies in Mommy's bridge club play cards and laugh. They sound like the birds outside, tweeting loudly for the same worm. No one can see me. My toes are so close to the crack where the light peeks from under the door. I'm almost inside the room with the secret. I reach for the knob, and turn it slowly—slow-ly so it doesn't make one squeak. *Push.* The door opens.

Light from the morning sun blinks through the blinds and makes stripes where I stand. Tiny white dots cover the green carpet like snowflakes on grass. The walls used to be white. Now they are painted with giraffes, monkeys, and elephants. It looks like a monkey is climbing into the old crib I used before I became a big girl. I look up and see a familiar shape, like an upside-down cereal bowl stuck on the ceiling, but it is the light.

"Heee," says a voice. I turn around. The "heee" came from the crib! It came from under a green blanket. It heeed again, gurbled, and moved.

"Margo," Verna whispers.

"I'm Rinnie. Rinnie, Rinnie, Rinnie! Please call me Rinnie, Verna."

"Get out of the baby's room. If Mrs. G. catches you, you'll get a spanking . . . Rinnie."

"A baby is in there?" I ask. "I didn't know we had a baby. Why do we have a baby, and how did it get in?"

The baby starts to whimper. Mimi comes in and picks the baby up. Verna shoos me into the hall. Muscles make little brown hills on her arms when she turns me away.

Why is my nurse holding that baby? "Mimi, is that your baby?" I ask. She shakes her head.

The laughter from downstairs gets closer. The bridge club follows Mommy into the baby's room. A lady shuts the door. The hallway is quiet.

"A baby," I say to Verna. "What will we do with a baby?"

ANGEL BABY

I listen to the giggles and coos in the baby's room. *The baby must be doing tricks*. Why else would the grown-ups laugh and give it so much attention? I can't think of anything the baby does that I can't do. I can roll in a ball and stretch my arms. I can smack my lips. I can do things the baby can't. I know how to zip. I practice my tricks and want to show Mommy.

Verna opens the door. "Mrs. G, do you want the pastries put out now?" she asks Mommy. "I have the porch tables set with the pink linens."

"'Scuse me," I say, squeezing my way in and through too many legs. "Mommy, look." I pat the round tummy above me. "Mommy look at *my* funny face," I say, pointing my face in her direction. Mommy touches the top of my head and says we'll talk after the company goes home.

"But Mommy, look how high I can reach."

Mommy's big hands brush mine to her sides. "Later, Margo. Later."

"It's Rinnie, Mommy. Call me Rinnie." I try to get small, and I squish my way through the forest of legs to find Verna.

"What are you doing, girl?" she says.

"Tricks, like the baby," I say, curling my head under my legs until I feel like a roundish bump.

Through my legs, I see white nurse's shoes.

"Look at my trick, Mimi," I call.

She makes her super-d-duper smile and points her thumb up in the air before she turns the other way.

I see Mimi pull something from the crib that looks like messy laundry. Mommy's bridge club is around her, still talking, talking, talking.

Mimi takes the bundle and sits in the chair with a high back. *My hide-and-seek chair.* She pulls a bottle out of her pocket and sticks it in the laundry mess. The bridge club doesn't stay. They go to the room with candies and nuts and the table with cards.

I put my thumb in my mouth and move toward Mimi without picking my feet up off the floor. I put my head on Mimi's bony knee. "Are you holding a baby in your lap?" I ask.

"I'm holding your brother," Mimi says. "Can you see him?"

I dig my toes into the carpet and rise high enough to see a little blue-pink face. His eyes are closed. "Why are his cheeks moving in and out, in and out, in and out?"

"He's sucking milk from the bottle," Mimi says.

"Can I try it?"

"You have already tried it. When you were a baby, I held you and fed you just like this," Mimi says.

I put my head back on Mimi's bony knee. "Now I'm big, but I would fit in your lap."

"I think so, too," Mimi says, shifting the baby.

I climb onto Mimi's leg. "How do you know it's a brother, Mimi?" I say.

"The angels told me."

BABY IDEAS

The baby's name is Evan, and he doesn't do much. Mimi feeds and rocks Evan and shushes him when he cries. Lizzie and I watch as Mimi moves her arms in the air like a whirlybird and makes sounds like the wind. Evan opens his mouth and smiles. Plop, goes a spoonful of baby mush into Evan's toothless grin.

"Bingo!" Mimi says.

"You're like a mommy bird dropping a worm in her baby's beak," Lizzie says.

"Mimi, watch us," I say, and I take my sister's hand. We twist and turn across the kitchen, our arms flapping like crazy birds. Flap, hop, flap, hop. "We're whirlybirds! Look, Evan, look!" we shout. I open my mouth and eat a pretend spoonful of mush.

Evan's eyes pop like a jack-in-the-box.

"I know what babies are for—they're 'sposed to watch us!"

A MAID, a NURSE, and SLEEPING BEAUTY

"Wash up, lunch is ready," Verna says, wiping her dirt-colored hands on the white apron covering her uniform. She reminds me of a penguin only instead of being round she is long. Verna doesn't have extra padding anywhere.

I crawl onto the wooden bench dragging my baby doll, Dollie, to the table. Croquette, our dog, sits at one end waiting for something to drop. Next to Lizzie, she is my best friend because she sleeps on my bed, next to my legs, every night.

"Move over, Rinnie. I'm the big sister," Liz says. "I get to sit next to Evan and help Mimi feed him."

I scootch across the bench with Dollie.

"Hootchie kootchie, here comes the wind," Mimi sings, twirling in front of Evan's high chair. "Here I come," she says, pushing a spoonful of yellow into his mouth.

"BRZZZZZ," I say, flying my grilled cheese sandwich. "BRZZZZZ, open your mouth, Dollie, here I come."

"Rinnie, put that sandwich in your mouth. Lizzie, sit down and eat your lunch," Verna says. "Mimi's the nurse. She'll feed Evan."

Liz sits and pulls on the melted cheese dripping from her bread.

"Ta da," she says, licking her lips. "I made the cheese disappear."

Dollie and I eat my sandwich, and Verna says I can have a cinnamon graham cracker for dessert.

"Lizzie, when you finish your lunch you can tickle your brother's toes and make him smile, so he'll open his mouth," Mimi says.

"You can tickle Evan's toes tonight," Liz says, pointing to me.

"Okie dokie, pinokie," I say, putting Dollie on the floor for a nap. "Verna, will you play with me?"

"Good Lord, girl, I have to wash dishes, polish the candle-sticks, vacuum the third-floor bedroom, dust every room up and down, and wake up your mother. It's past noon. Then I have to see what special chore she has me doing this afternoon. The only thing this house is missing is a moat. You and Lizzie play on the swings," she says, holding the screen door open. Croquette zooms past us and we follow.

On the swings, we pump our legs harder and harder and go faster and higher. We can see over the top of our neighbor's apple tree. Croquette barks when the swings get close to her. I think she would like me to take her flying with me.

"Liz, why doesn't Mommy make breakfast or lunch?"

"Because she's getting her *beauty* sleep," Liz says, holding her legs out to fly with the swing.

"Why doesn't she make dinner?"

"Because that's what Emmy is for," she answers again. "Verna takes care of us in the day, and Emmy takes care of us when Verna goes home."

"Who takes care of Verna and Emmy?"

"We do. We make sure they have someone to love."

"Do we take care of Mimi, too?"

"Yes, and we've done a good job, because when Mommy has a baby, Mimi always comes back to us."

I think of Mommy waking up so late. Now I know why she is beautiful.

VACANCY

I am four years old. My mother holds my hand. Her white cotton glove covers my fingers. Lizzie is on her other side.

We are in a roomful of people waiting to see someone who is important. He's a friend of Daddy's, and he teaches football for Ohio State University. His name is Woody Hayes. We have gray and red party ribbons in our hair.

"Are the girls twins?" I hear people ask.

"Almost," Mommy answers.

Lizzie and I are dressed in our pink organdy dresses. Starched crinolines hold the skirts of the dresses out like open umbrellas. I am admiring the freckles on my arms and legs and how small and round they are. The only things I can see are legs and shoes. I practice balancing on one foot by putting one black patent shoe on top of the other.

Mommy bends and whispers fast and hard, "I don't want to tell you again. Stop twitching. Be still like Liz."

"I'm prettier than Liz, aren't I?" I whisper back and suck my top lip inside my mouth.

"No. Pretty is what's inside you. Pretty girls listen to their mommies."

What does that mean? Can Mommy see inside me? I didn't listen. Mommy must think I'm ugly. I suck harder.

Liz is on the right side of my mother, and I am on the left.

GAGA

When Gaga's big red car stops in the driveway, we hear the brakes and watch her head poke forward and back and forward again like a chicken's. Pop Pop says her head moves that way because, "My wife's just too damn short to be driving a Ford Fairlane."

The first thing I see when Gaga gets out of the car are her galoshes. "Everyone needs galoshes," she says, but I don't have any. I have boots. Before Gaga rings the doorbell, I whoosh open the door and yell extra loud, "Gaga's here!" so Lizzie will come downstairs.

"Lizzie and Margo what good hugs you give!" she says and hugs us back.

"It's Rinnie. Rinnie like Rin Tin Tin," I say, frowning.

"So it's still Rinnie is it? Then Rinnie it will be." Gaga's mouth pushes her cheeks and eyebrows up. "Well, I'm glad to see you, Rinnie."

"Yay, Gaga's here," Lizzie and I jump in circles around her. Croquette barks and joins the jumping. Gaga bends, to kiss us and leaves the smell of baby powder and red lipstick marks on our cheeks. Croquette gets pats on the head.

"Evan's taking a nap," I say.

"Well, I have something special for you two, darlings," Gaga says.

Magic words! We hold our breath. We know "I have something special" means we're going on an adventure.

Verna comes from the kitchen. "Can I take your coat, Mrs. Samuels? You just missed your daughter. She's at the beauty parlor and won't be back for who knows."

"Thank you, Verna. I dropped by to see my grandchildren."

Gaga places her coat and cap across Verna's arms. I don't know why one side of Verna's hands are so much lighter than the other side. Maybe it's because she's tall and there isn't enough brown to cover all of her.

Gaga moves to the steps, sits next to us, and reaches into her shiny red purse. Out come pieces of paper the same size as her thumbs.

"Tickets!" she says very fast. "We're going to the Paragon to see a movie, *Swiss Family Robinson*. It's about resourceful children like you."

The hurry in Gaga's voice makes resourceful sound like a good thing.

The Paragon! The Paragon! We've never been to the Paragon or anywhere to see a movie.

"Is Mommy coming?" Lizzie asks.

Gaga shakes her fluffy hair side to side. When it flies around it looks like one color, but when it stops, her hair is the color of a chipmunk married to a squirrel.

"Will Daddy and Pop Pop come?" Lizzie asks.

"Nooooo," Gaga stretches her arms around us. "Just us. It's the perfect outing for grandchildren and their grandmother on an autumn afternoon."

"Yippeee," we shout. "When, when, when do we get to go?"

"I can't stay until your mother gets home, so I'll call her tonight, and we'll decide," says Gaga. "Now I have to get to the groceries. It's Thursday night, and Pop Pop expects fish for dinner."

She stands and gets her coat behind the mirrored closet doors. Gaga's head doesn't reach the shelf above the coats. She has to stand on the footstool we keep in the closet, in order to reach her cap.

"Help me balance while I put my galoshes on," Gaga says.

A key clicks in the front door and Emmy shivers in. Raindrops pitter-patter from her short coat.

"Seemed like an extra-long walk from the bus stop today. The temperature dropped! Hello, Mrs. Samuels," she looks at Gaga. "Are you stayin' for dinner? I can always find something to add."

"No, Emmy, whatever you're cooking for the family tonight will be just for them. Is it four o'clock already? I've got to be scooting." Gaga looks outside. "The leaves are blowing inside out. That means more rain tomorrow. Maybe Verna needs a ride to the bus. . . ."

"I hear you, Mrs. S. I can be ready in two shakes. I appreciate the ride."

Daddy calls four o'clock the "Changing of the Guard." The bus drops Emmy off and picks up Verna. After dinner, when the dishes are washed and put away, the bus comes back for Emmy, and tomorrow the bus will return Verna. It's like Verna says, "Good things always comin' and goin.'"

KINDERGARTEN

The kindergarten room is big. It has tables and chairs, a rug, and a huge wooden jungle gym. Along the walls are pictures of balloons with signs that say things like RED, BLUE, GREEN. I can read them. A brown paper tree with cut-out orange and red leaves stuck to it is glued to the window. "Fall" is written in yellow letters under the tree. A calendar almost as big as me leans on the wall under "Fall." In the corner is a fuzzy rug jumbled with dolls. Two girls and a boy play house and laugh.

Mrs. Grayson is my teacher. She is tall. Her voice is tall also, and her face is pretty. I like her very much. She pats my head, smiles, and tells me to come inside the room. I play with everyone and climb on the jungle gym. It is my favorite thing to do. One day, Mrs. Grayson tells us to sit in a big circle so we can play a game. I sit with my back to the door. When I look up, I see Mrs. Grayson's happy face across from me. It has a big smile that makes little holes in her cheeks.

"Someone is going to hide a toy in their lap. We will guess who it is. Cover your eyes with your hands," she says.

While our eyes are closed, she hands a plastic doll to someone in the circle. I spread my fingers the tiniest bit so I can see what is going on.

“Rinnie, you’re peeking,” Mrs. Grayson says. “That’s not how we play. You are cheating.”

I don’t know what cheating is, but I can tell it is bad. Mrs. Grayson’s happy face isn’t in her tall voice anymore. I am ashamed of cheating. I scrunch the shame into a little ball and stuff it way down inside me, so no one will ever know I am a cheater—maybe not even me.

ENCOURAGEMENT

"Mrs. Grayson tells me you need a little encouragement following directions," Mommy says, knocking ashes from her cigarette into a tiny china bowl. "It's important to do what you're told in school. No one likes a troublemaker."

"OK, Mommy."

THE BASEMENT

Mommy yells, "OK, kids, get in the car. We're going to Gaga's. Emmy, plan to serve dinner about thirty minutes later than usual. Mr. Gardener is working late."

The butterscotch candy in my mouth lasts all the way to Gaga's house. When we arrive, Lizzie and I peel out of the car and race to ring the doorbell. Evan's chubby legs totter side to side as he tries to keep up with us. Gaga smears our cheeks with red lipstick.

"I put fresh nuts in the candy dish in the living room," she says and heads toward the reading room with Mommy.

We push each other out of the way to get to the nuts. Gaga hates that we pick out the cashews and salty walnuts. She hates that we leave the long nuts that look like cocoons and the little round ones that taste like they're rotten in the crystal dish.

"Next stop, the basement." I dash to the door near the front entrance. Lizzie takes a shortcut to a second set of stairs that leads to the basement and beats Evan and me.

"I got here first. I'm the soda man," Lizzie says. She lifts a piece of the bar top and ducks under it. Behind the bar are glasses and clear bottles filled with stuff the color of maple syrup. We aren't allowed to touch them. The stools in front of the bar are too high for Evan to crawl on, so the two of us stand next to each other on wood crates that Gaga brought home from the grocery store.

"I'd like a soda, please," I say.

"What kind?" Lizzie asks.

"A big one please."

"How about you?" Lizzie looks at Evan.

"I want one with a straw," he says.

We drink our pretend sodas and jump on the sofa with the hole that Pop Pop swears "those rambunctious children made." Because the paint on the legs of the sofa is scratched up and the seats fall in when we sit, I think the sofa is just old.

"I wish Pop Pop would let us turn the light on. It's too shady in here," I say.

"I wish he believed that we'd remember to turn it off," Lizzie says.

Except for the bar, it's kind of an unfriendly place. Before we give up making the basement fun, we turn all the knobs as far as they'll go on the unplugged television and on the big radio next to the sofa. We talk into the drain on the floor and listen to how loud our voices sound.

Evan tugs the handle to the door under the stairs.

"Noooo, Evan!" Lizzie and I yell. "No!"

"That's the stink room." We hold our noses. "Get away. That's where the suitcases are, and they're stuffed with moth balls."

"What's a moth ball?" Evan asks.

"It's white and you need a nose clip to get near it and gloves to touch it. Let's get out of here," Lizzie and I say.

"Next time, Evan," I say. "We'll explore where you can open all the doors."

WOOD CHUCK HOLLOW

Gaga doesn't have to tell us going to Wood Chuck Hollow is "another something special for her darlings." We already know it.

"There used to be hundreds, maybe thousands of woodchucks living here, but now there is only one family left, and it's good luck if you see one," Gaga says.

I don't think we'll see one today because the snow is too deep.

"Why are we here in winter?" Evan says. "There aren't any animals in the cages. I want to see the skunks, garter snakes, rabbits, and foxes."

"Me too. I want to walk on the trails and look for turtles and frogs in the pond," I say.

Liz is rubbing her hands together. She left her gloves at home.

"Here, Lizzie, you can wrap my scarf around your hands and pretend they're gloves." I unwrap the scarf tied around my hood. It's my favorite scarf. Mommy knit it, and it's fuzzy and squishy.

"Thank you, Rinnie," Lizzie says. "You're a good sister."

"Yes you are," Gaga says, patting my purple hood. "Winter is a special time. Most people stay inside and miss the wonders of the cold. You can still find animal tracks—more easily, in fact. The tracks tell the story of where the animals live and how far they travel. Today, Evan, we will follow a trail. You can lead us. We're going to the picnic tables under the big trees."

Evan stomps ahead of us to the splintery post that marks the trail we've taken so many times and starts making footprints in the snow.

"We're on a treasure hunt," Gaga says. "Before we go home, let's see if we can find a bird's nest, rabbit tracks, deer tracks, and a hole an animal might have used for a home."

"Look!" I say, holding out a pointy stick.

"Look at what?" Liz asks.

"My wand. Can't you see? It's part of my treasure collection. Abracadabra." I circle the wand above my head and hit myself in the hood. "It's not tamed," I laugh. "I have to train it."

"That's a good idea," Liz says, giggling.

"Tracks!" Evan says. "They're little so they must be rabbit tracks."

"Aha. Have you ever seen a rabbit with little feet?" Gaga asks. "Whose tracks could these be?"

"Deer tracks," Liz says. "Deer are big but have small feet, like Bambi."

Gaga pats her head with a gloved hand. "Good observation, Lizzie. That means you used your eyes and your memory well."

"It's easy to spot bird nests in winter," I say, pointing to two nests on one tree.

"There's another!" Evan shouts. "Across from the log with the big hole."

"You found another part of the treasure," Gaga says.

"Maybe a raccoon lives in the hole," I say.

"Or a bear," Evan says.

"We've found everything except rabbit tracks. Let's stop at the picnic tables and measure how deep the snow is," Gaga says. "Follow the wall of evergreens, Evan."

"Can we dance on the tables like we do in the summer?" Lizzie asks when we get there. She sweeps snow from the table with my scarf and climbs onto its top.

Evan finds a snow bank and steps in it. "It's up to my knees," he grins and splashes snow into the air and into his eyes.

Gaga sits on the bench, her arms out ready to catch Lizzie if she falls.

"Oh, what a beautiful morning. Oh, what a beautiful day," Lizzie shouts in her best singing voice. Her arms look like angel wings.

Gaga claps and stands up and claps some more.

"Lovely, Lizzie, just lovely."

Liz hops a little and curtsies.

For my turn, I crawl on the table and say, "Knock, knock."

"Who's there?" Gaga says.

"Ach," I say.

"Ach who?"

"God Bless you!" I say, standing while Gaga claps for me.

"You three are the best treasure of all."

FRANCHONS

The light turns green. "Hold hands, girls. It's a busy street." Mommy puts my gloved hand in hers, and I take Liz's. It takes 37 steps to cross the street. The red fish on the bottom of my dress swim between my legs as the wind hurries them like a wave.

"F-R-A-N-C-H-O-N-S," I spell.

Liz reads the black letters on the window, nods and adds, "Fine Clothing for Young Girls and Boys." We open the door and shiny silver bells jingle above our heads.

"Good to see you again, girls. March is coming in like a lion," the saleslady says. "Time to buy spring clothes, Mrs. Gardener?"

Mommy picks out what she likes. I hold a dress up to my chin.

"Oh look at the layers of gold and silver net. This is a queen's dress! I love this dress!"

"It is a beautiful dress," the saleslady says, "and the net is called Royal Woven Mesh. It's from France. There have been many queens from France."

A little skip happens in my chest. "Mommy, can I try on the Royal dress? Mommy, please can I try on this dress? It's every good thing I can think of."

Mommy touches her lips with her finger, hands clothes to the lady, and points Lizzie and me to a padded sign with the letters F-i-t-t-i-n-g R-o-o-m sewn in gold thread.

"Mommy, did you remember the Royal dress?" The silent swing of a curtain is my answer. In the corner, the huge pile of clothes reminds me of a fairy tale Daddy tells. "Look Lizzie, I'm the princess from the *Princess and the Pea*, except instead of mattresses, there are layers of puffy dresses." I smoosh my body into the fluffy layers of clothes.

"Rinnie, you're crushing the dresses. You're going to get into trouble."

I float my head up like a balloon filled with the smell of new clothes.

"Stop goofing around," Liz says.

We model everything for Mommy and she says, "We'll take the blue, green, and yellow cotton print dresses in both sizes, the dresses with the rhinestone belts, the blouses embroidered with parrots, and the polka-dot skirts I called about. Oh, and will you add six pairs of white socks for each of the girls."

"You've selected lovely merchandise," the saleslady says.

I watch as she folds our new clothes. Dress by dress is fed into a shopping bag. Dress by dress, the bags get fatter.

"What about the Royal dress?" I ask. "Please, Mommy. It's so beautiful."

"Not today, Rinnie. You have other pretty things."

"But it's the prettiest."

"Not today."

"Here you go," says the saleslady. She hands each of us bags. Her smile is so big I can count the teeth in her mouth. She opens the door, and out we go. I don't care about the other pretty new things. I want the Royal dress.

WHAT IS a WHILE?

"Today is once in a while," Mommy says after we put our new clothes in the car. "Let's go across the street and have lunch at the Windsor. Let's make this a real day downtown."

We wait for the light to change, and I watch a man talk on the phone in a telephone booth. The seat is too little for him, and he looks like he's going to fall off.

The light changes and we hold hands to cross the street again. I *love* the Windsor, and the tall skinny windows with squares of colored glass, the dark high-backed booths with seats so slippery we have to sit on our knees to keep us from sliding onto the floor. Gaga calls it "an experience." The best part of lunch is when we finish. On the counter next to the cash register is a silver tree. Instead of leaves, little see-through boxes hang from the branches. They're filled with tiny treasures, no bigger than my fingernail. Across each box in curly letters are the words "World of Miniatures." I reach for one that has a hammer, nails, wrench, and tape measure inside, like the ones on Daddy's workbench. Then I take one filled with mommies, daddies, children, and a perfect doggie. They are so perfect I can hardly breathe.

"Don't touch anything," Mommy says. "I mean it!"

Does she know how hard it is just to look?

We pay for lunch, cross the street, and walk to the car. I reach to pull myself in when a thing in my armpit drops. Mommy stoops to pick it up.

"What is this? Where did it come from?"

"It's from the silver tree," I say.

"In-the-restaurant?" she says in one long word as she shoves the box in front of my face.

I watch Mommy's hands. One speeds toward my leg where there is no dress and bites me above my sock. Mommy's other hand drops the box of treasures and tugs my coat collar. I hear the cry of material coming apart as it scratches across my throat. Then I am outside the car.

"I'm sorry Mommy, I'm sorry," I say, covering my bottom with my hands.

"Rinnie, you march yourself right into the Windsor and tell the clerk you took the box! What you did was terrible."

Mommy and Lizzie walk me to the Windsor and make me go inside by myself. The inside of my mouth feels full of spiky bubbles.

"I took this," I say and hand the family in the plastic box back to the lady behind the counter. The bubbles burst in my mouth and the spikes sew my lips together.

"Oh my," she kneels down in front of me and lifts my chin with her fingers. "You must have wanted this very much to take it without paying for it. Bringing it back must be very hard."

My head nods up and down and tears fall on the floor with every nod.

"I won't do it again, I promise and—I'm sorry."

"I believe you," she says and hands me a tissue. "How would you feel if someone took something that belonged to you?"

"Mad."

She shakes her head like she knows.

I think of the Royal dress, the little family waiting in the see-through box, and I feel sad.

"I just wanted something special and perfect," I say.

She kneels in front of me, and I look at her eyes.

I want to give her a hug, but I don't. When I come out Mommy makes me open my hands and raise my arms above my head to show I gave the treasure back.

"Monster," she says.

WHERE IS THERE?

"Let's go Mommy, I'm tired. Let's goooo!"

"Just a few more things to try on, Rinnie. Sit in the corner and tell me if you like the pattern on this blouse."

I squeeze between Mommy's shopping bags and the mirror but don't look at Mommy. Instead, I line up pins that are stuck under carpet fuzz. The plain pins turn into a house with a chimney and smoke. The ones with smooth round tops, like crowns, are kings and queens. They live in the house. It's a castle-house, and it has a playground.

"Rinnie, move away from the mirror. I want to see if this blouse is too dark for my brown skirt."

I spread out like a starfish, so she can see over me.

"I want to go home."

"Do you like the blouse?" Mommy asks. "I do."

She smiles and twists, first to my side, then the other.

"I like the tiger top you wore here. Zzzipzzippp," I make the sound of the pants Mommy puts on.

"Houndstooth is a nice change. I'll take these, too."

"I'm hungry," I say and stick the queen inside the chimney.

"Shhh, I can't think when you whine, Rinnie." Mommy takes off the barky pants, puts on a pair the color of mustard, and pulls a dark orange sweater over her head. "Hmmm," she hmmms and wiggles out of the clothes.

"Rinnie, please get up. The floor is dirty."

"I'm a starfish."

"Starfish live in the ocean. Are you in the ocean?"

"No, Mommy, you're silly."

She puts her tiger top on and tucks it into her brown skirt. "Up, Rinnie. Time to go."

I wave good-bye to the queens and kings and scramble to my feet. I want to hold Mommy's hand, but it's lost under the pile of clothes in her arms. They are the same colors as the leaves on our trees.

"You look like fall," I say.

At the pay counter, we have to wait for two ladies who are in front of us. Their clothes look like autumn, too.

"How much longer, Mommy? I want to go. I'm hungry."

"Hush."

Mommy's voice isn't nice. It feels like being stuck by the queen pin. I squat like a jack-in-the box waiting to pop out and count, one, two, three, four. . . . When it's our turn, the lady behind the counter won't stop talking, and Mommy won't stop listening. She doesn't feel my tugs on her coat, and when I pinch her ankle, her happy blouse smile is gone. The lines between her eyes frown.

"What is it you want? Can't you be still for a minute? All these pretty things to look at and you have to misbehave."

"I want to go. I'm hungry."

"Then go. Find a place to play over there," she points. I look to see where there is, but Mommy's talking again.

Across the aisle, a man plays a piano and pushes pedals with his foot. Maybe he'll let me play. When I get close, he winks and makes his fingers run from one end of the piano to the other, pressing only the white parts. Plink goes the last white note. Plink, plink, plink.

"Can I do that?" I ask and hold up my pointer finger.

"When you get bigger you can take piano lessons, and then you can do this, too." He zips his fingers across the white keys. "It's time for my break."

I watch him zipper past the long dresses. He stops and looks at a tag on one of them. The dress sparkles like a glitter star with a necklace of feathers. This is what the pin-queen would wear if she were real. I squeeze my eyes as tight as I can, hold my breath, and make a wish on the glitter star dress. *I wish I were a queen. Then Mommy would have to listen to me.*

I open my eyes. The piano man floats by going higher and higher until he disappears. *Where did he go?* I march behind a wall of clothes and see the moving stairs that floated the piano man away. *Mommy and I rode the stairs when we came to the store.* I take a step before the stair moves too far away and squat on it. I have never done this without Mommy. Up I go and then down. And up and down again. I have to show Mommy I found the place "over there" to sit and play. Her pin voice will unstick. On the down floor, I look for the lady at the pay counter.

"Where's Mommy?"

"Who is your Mommy?" the lady asks. She bends down. The air smells like old oranges and cinnamon.

"She's the lady you talked to for a long time. She smells like flowers."

The pay lady holds my hand, asks my name, and makes a phone call. I hear my name run across the air.

“Your Mommy will be here soon. Why don’t you draw while we wait?” She hands me a pen and some paper. I kneel on the floor and draw the moving stairs.

When Mommy comes, her hands tighten white under my shoulders. Up I go, then down. Mommy presses me hard, squishing my head into my neck. When I land, my school shoes pinch my toes.

“But Mommy,” I say when I catch my breath. “I found the over there place to sit and play!”

GRANDMA GARDENER

Grandma Gardener has a fire in her house.

"Don't go near this, girls," she says to Liz and me. "It burns up little children like you."

The fire is in her kitchen, and she calls it the incinerator. The drive to her house is long, but we don't mind. It's our last fun summer thing before first grade starts. We count trains, tracks, and bridges, and wave good-bye to Ohio when we cross into Pennsylvania. When we finally arrive, Grandma gives us shiny dimes to stack and spin.

"Thirty dimes for three children, how many dimes do each of you get?" She asks. Lizzie and I make three piles of dimes and count out the dimes and then help Evan make his piles.

"Ten," we shout.

"Well done," Grandma says.

Behind Grandma's house is the School for the Blind. I can see it from the bedroom I share with Liz. At night, the lights in the spooky brick building of the blind school stare at us through the window. I hear the soft music that rides the sky all the way from the blind school to my ears.

At bedtime, Grandma doesn't say much about the school when we ask. Instead, she hands us each a glass of milk with a piece of chocolate in the bottom and tells us to drink for sweet dreams. Liz and I always drink the milk.

Evan is in a different room, but I think he drinks his milk, too.

"Charles, Charles," Grandma Gardener calls when she wants my father. Everyone else calls him Chuck. Her words are sharp like her laugh, and she mostly talks to Mom when something has to be done. "Rose, bring in the suitcases. Rose, take the children to wash their hands."

Mommy said one time Grandma visited our house. It was very late at night and she heard Grandma call, "Rose, Rose, I need a towel." Mommy pretended to be asleep, but Grandma Gardener wouldn't stop calling, "Rose, Rose."

Finally, Mommy got up and asked Grandma why she didn't call her son.

"What, and wake him?" Grandma said.

Mommy got Grandma the towel. "Witch," Mommy grumbled.

Grandma Gardener looks like the witches in my fairy tale book, with her black eyes, long gray hair, and big curved nose. But I don't think witches give money to kids.

GETTING READY

"Liz, Margo, Evan, this is Ward Brenner. He's a student at the seminary college. Ward will drive you to school and pick you up. Ward, these are my children."

"It's Rinnie, not Margo! My friends call me Rinnie," I say, bending my neck up as far as it will go to see Ward's face.

He sticks his hand out to shake mine and a silver bracelet with a fish on it slides to his palm.

"Nice to meet you, Ma . . . Rinnie," he stutters.

Ward unfolds a piece of paper from his pocket. "Looks like after I pick you three up I stop at the Myer house a few doors down and pick up Marty, Maddox, and Marcie June."

The Myers have five kids, but the other two are too old for our school. Marcie June Myer is my best after-school friend because she lives so close to me. She wears her hair in a pony, too. Everyone in her family has a name that begins with the letter M, including her dogs, Moses and Max. Even her maid's name starts with an M. I like that in my family we have different letters for our names, and I get two if I want. One letter for Margo and one for Rinnie.

LOOKING

Today at Gaga's, Lizzie and I play our special kind of hide-and-seek. We seek what's hiding in the cabinet above the toilet in Gaga and Pop Pop's bathroom. The cabinet is built into the wall. It's so deep I can barely reach the back of it even when I stand on the toilet and stretch my body.

"Be careful to put everything back just where you get it," Lizzie says as she watches me pick up a handful of hair clips and a ruffled shower cap.

I hand her bottles of nail polish, a used-up emery board, and squares of cotton.

"Maybe Gaga will give us manicures," Lizzie says.

I shrug my shoulders and move to a higher shelf. There are long stretchy bandages rolled up, boxes of gauze, scissors, a gold razor, egg-shaped bars of soap, and a container of pink perfumed powder.

"Mmmm, smell this," I say and pass the round box of pink powder to Liz.

"Smells like jelly beans taste," Liz says.

"How 'bout these?" I hand Liz a basket filled with medicines for stomach discomfort, headaches, and "Loose Stools."

"No thanks," Lizzie says. "Looks too doctor-y. Can you see what's on the top shelf?"

I stretch my legs as far as I can and reach inside. In the very, very, very back under a flattened handkerchief is a package of cigarettes and a silver lighter. I pull them from their hideout.

"Why does Gaga keep cigarettes and a lighter way back in the corner? She can't even reach them," I say.

"I'm not sure," Lizzie says. "But I don't think we should remember them. Anything else up there?"

"Red mouthwash."

"Well," Lizzie says slowly, "like Verna says, 'if you look hard enough you'll find what you don't want.'"

"What's that mean?" I look over my shoulder at Lizzie and scrunch my lips sideways.

"I'm not sure," she says. "But it sounds like a good thing to remember."

FIRST GRADE

The big room at the end of the hall is my first grade room. A sign on the door says *Mrs. Lindermann—Teacher.* Her nose looks like a chubby crayon, and her lips are cracked like a dry mud hole. Her hair is pulled back tightly. Streaks of gray and brown cover her head like a spider's web. Her clothes look strict and uncomfortable, and her skirts are so tight she can't take big steps. There is hardly enough room for Mrs. Lindermann in her clothes. I never stand too close to her. I am afraid she might explode. I want first grade to be over.

There is a girl named Lola in my class. She is almost as tall as Mrs. Lindermann. I can hardly take my eyes off Lola. She looks like a giant peach, all pinkish and pale, and round. There is someone else in the class I watch. His name is Asa Mitov. His house is in back of my Gaga's house. I like him, and he likes Lola. Their desks are next to each other. Every day, I wonder what I would say to Asa, if he talked to me.

GAGA'S HOUSE

Green cement oozes out of the cement mixer and fills the hole where the front walk used to be. We want to stand by the cement mixer and watch the lumps of thick gunk plop into the long hole between the sidewalk and the house. But Gaga says it isn't safe. Instead, Evan, Liz, and I lean over the rail of the balcony built above the front door.

"Why Pop Pop thinks we need a green walkway is beyond me," Gaga says. "But it is pretty isn't it . . . the color of mint leaves."

"It reminds me of a shamrock," Lizzie says. "Maybe Pop Pop will want the house to be green instead of stone."

We step onto the blue iron curlicues that decorate the bottom of the balcony railing to get a better look. The ivy growing over the blue shutters by the balcony has climbed on the curlicues, too.

"Can we step in the cement?"

"If it were only up to me, you could, Evan, but Pop Pop wants it exactly as it is, undisturbed. He always thinks his ideas are the best."

"Except when you disagree with him. Pop Pop changes his mind for you," Lizzie says.

"Yes, he does do that." Gaga spins her wedding ring and leans on the balcony between us. "Children, there's something new in the playroom for you. Do you think you can find it?

It's small enough to fit on the bookcase, but too big to fit inside the cookie tin that holds your crayons."

"Bye cement mixer!" we yell. Past the landing to the second floor, we chase the winding banister up the stairs. It ends near the playroom. The playroom is our make-believe room. It has a carpet we pretend is magic like Ali Baba's. Around the carpet is the river. It's made of wood and looks like the floor, but it's the river. If we step in it, our feet get wet and then we have to take our shoes off.

Gaga told us, "This carpet is from Persia. It's very good, but very old. If we spill on it we don't have to worry too much." I feel the worn-out places with my fingers. I think this carpet is older than Gaga and Pop Pop.

Lizzie jumps over the river and walks to the middle of the room. She looks under the wooden desk in the corner, the phonograph, and a little metal table holding dried-up plants.

"Not there," Lizzie says. "Where are you, surprise?" she sings.

Evan checks inside the block firehouse he built and behind the heavy curtains. "I found a dead fly," he says, opening his hand to show us.

"Put it in the jar with the other dead flies," I say. We save them to feed to the squirrels that tightrope walk across the telephone lines.

"I'll check the closet," I say, "But I may need help."

The closet is the same size as the entire bathroom. A huge drawer is filled with girdles and nighties and lacey bags of underwear. Another drawer is stuffed with extra blankets, and one more drawer holds tablecloths and napkins. I climb on top of a long, wide shelf and crawl past piles of *National Geographic* magazines, round fabric boxes with hats inside, and rolls of toilet paper.

"What are you doing in there?" Lizzie yells.

"Help me," I answer, pushing my way through hanging dresses and shoe-bags filled with high-heeled shoes.

"Did you find the surprise?"

"Not exactly." I lug a fat book of photographs to the table. "S. SAMUELS INC. Suppliers of Restaurant and Kitchen Equipment Nationwide," I read.

"You better put that back. It's one of Pop Pop's business books," Liz says.

I open the first page and there is a picture of Pop Pop. Under it is the word "President." There's a picture of Daddy, too, with the words "Vice President." Behind them is a sign that says "Forty years of Unrivaled Service."

There are pages and pages of photographs of "appliances": refrigerators, ovens, stoves, dishwashers, and sinks, and even more pages of shelving, carts, glasses, plates, scales, counter-tops, lights, and furniture.

"Let me see," Lizzie says, grabbing the heavy book. "Wow, there are even fireplaces like in the olden days. I want one of those."

"I'm thirsty," Evan says. He spreads himself on the floor, faceup, as if he's floating on a raft in the swimming pool Pop Pop had built so Mommy could swim and exercise her bad back. Evan's eyes are wide open and his tongue is out.

"I found it! I found it!" He pops up and points to the wall with a shelf above a photograph of the American Indian, Sitting Bull.

On the shelf with our books are three new yellow ones tied with yellow string. Next to them is a monkey and a man wearing a hat the same color as his clothes.

"*Curious George and The Man in the Yellow Hat*!" Lizzie and I say at the same time.

Lizzie stands on a chair and reaches for the new books, and I grab the stuffed toys.

"I'm still thirsty," Evan whines. "Maybe Beulah will give me a drink."

"Good thinking, Evan," I say. "Maybe Beulah has finished the housework for Gaga, and she'll make lemonade for all of us."

We head downstairs holding the curvy banister, except for The Man in The Yellow Hat. He slides down the banister with George on his back.

TERRIFIED

Last night, when I closed my eyes, I saw a monster blow across my bed, back and forth—slowly, going nowhere. It breathed cigarette ashes into my nose and tapped a finger without skin on my heart.

"I'm gonna getcha. I'm GONNA GETCHA!" It hissed.

I know it is real—when I wake up, my throat burns.

WOOLY WILLY

Doctor Ron is in Evan's bedroom. It's been two days since I talked to Evan. Verna says he's "quarantined."

"Don't open Evan's door," Mommy says. "He has bad germs, and I don't want you to catch his fever."

"I wish I had a fever like Evan's. You and Mommy are with him all day," I say to Verna.

"Girl," Verna says, "as soon as Evan feels a little better, you and I'll make sugar cookies together, and we can have a tea party with your dollies."

"Can I have a cookie now?" I say.

"You sure can, you don't have no ills. Evan can't. He can't hardly swallow anything," Verna says. "His throat is too sore, and his tongue is fat and red as a ripe strawberry."

"Is he going to die?"

"Lord, no!" Verna says. "But it's going to be a while before his fever and rash go away."

"I have something for Evan. Will you give it to him?"

I get Wooly Willy out of his special place in my toy box and smooth out the hard plastic cardboard that covers Willy's face. Before I give Willy to Verna, I drag a clump of black bits to Willy's head with a magic stick.

"Now he has hair," I say. I move the red stick with the magnet inside, and it picks up more dark clumps that look like a bunch of ants stuck on a piece of sucking candy.

"Look. Willy has a mustache, an eyebrow, and hair in his nose." I show Verna. "Be careful not to shake him, and tell Evan it's from me."

Verna takes the piece of cardboard with Willy's decorated face into Evan's room.

I miss Evan. I miss teaching him his ABC's. I miss showing him how to draw cats. I miss holding his hand and bump bumping down the stairs on our tushies.

"Evan's sleeping. Let's go downstairs and get you and Lizzie some lunch," Verna says.

Mommy and Doctor Ron follow Verna, and I follow them to the bottom of the stairs. The doctor gives Mommy a slip of paper and tells her to go to some place called the "farmfac'try" for medicine. Why is the doctor giving Evan animal medicine? Does he think my brother is a cowboy?

"Rinnie, that was very nice of you to give your game to your brother," Doctor Ron says. "You must love him very much to give him something you can't have back."

"I didn't give it to him. I let him borrow it," I say.

"It has sick germs on it. When Evan is well, Willy has to be thrown away," the doctor says, putting on his coat.

"But it's mine. Evan's borrowing it," I say. "He can't keep Willy."

"He's not keeping it," Mommy says. "Willy will be thrown away."

"No! You can't throw Willy out. He'll miss me," I cry.

No one listens. Verna is frying baloney; Mommy and Dr. Ron are saying good-bye.

I sit on the bottom step with my fists on my cheeks, and rock, back and forth, back and forth. It's not fair. Willy's mine.

SECOND GRADE

Second grade is serious business. My teacher, Mrs. Hipshell, jiggles when she walks and doesn't smile. Her orangey brown hair is wavy and the same *every* single day. Maybe it's a wig. She is old and has tan spots on her face. Some spots are buried in her wrinkles. Last year, she was Liz's teacher, and Liz says she *really* is a witch and cast a spell on one of the boys to make him keep quiet.

We pull our chairs into small circles for reading groups. Soon, I will move up to the top reading group. The chairs are just the right size for seven-year-olds. The varnish on them makes them shiny, like a just-licked lollipop. I sit by the window and the sun warms the smooth wood. My hand likes to rub the varnish and feel its slickness. I could sit in my chair all day rubbing the varnish and reading about Dick and Jane and Spot. Everything about them is rosy and friendly. Spot looks soft and squishy like my mother's fur coat. I'd like to hold Spot and bury my face in her fluffy fur and kiss her.

FUN

Fingers fly, hands flap. Mommy and Daddy are going out tonight. Emmy's gone home. She left right after dinner. She never baby-sits. She just cooks dinner and cleans up the mess. Verna hardly ever stays late because she's married, and her husband wants her home. But tonight she's here. Hooray! This means popcorn and pillow fights and staying up late, late, late.I love Verna, and she loves me back. After dinner, Liz, Evan, and I put on our PJs. The smell of hot buttered popcorn lures us downstairs. We grab the pillows from our beds. Croquette is in her kennel so she won't get hurt.

"Whoever gets the Old Maid kernel, the last of the bunch, washes the bowl," Verna warns.

"'Cept me," Evan says. "I can't even reach the soap."

The salty popcorn dissolves in my mouth. Mmmm. This is so much fun. I never take the last handful, and Liz has to clean the bowl.

Sneak attack. I smash Evan on the head with my pillow.

"Hey!" he grumbles from the floor.

"Whamo Bamo, two tushies in one blow," he brags and tries to knock me over.

"Wap-a roni!" Liz cheers a direct hit.

Evan's been beaned and his pillow trips Liz. She drops on top of me. Verna has us pinned with her knees, and I tickle Evan who grabs Liz and tickles her.

"Time out!" Lizzie says.

"I have to breathe," I say and sit up. Evan swipes at Verna's legs and misses.

Whack! Whack! Whack! Verna's pillow lands on us again and again. "Do you give?" she says. "Quit now, and you get to watch TV before bed."

"We quit, we give up, we quit." Our pillows mark our spots in front of the television, and we scramble upstairs to brush our teeth. I squeeze a gob of blue on my toothbrush and wonder if Verna would like to live here with us all the time.

"Last one downstairs is a rotten egg," Liz yells.

Three toothpaste spits hit the sink at the same time. The clock in the hall cuckoos eight times and then, before we know it, ten times. Our screen door squeaks open. Uh oh. "Shhhhh." We scramble up the stairs and shush into bed.

"Did you have a nice evening? I'll get my jacket, and I'm ready to go, Mr. G." Verna's words skip the stairs and fly straight to our ears. They're code for close your eyes and get to sleep.

THE OTHER SITTER

Mommy and Daddy are going out again. Verna has to be with her husband. This time a nursing student will stay with us. Mommy calls me into her bedroom while she dresses. I watch her brush on eye shadow.

"One, two, three, four, five, six, seven," she says, stroking her eyelid with blue powder.

"Are my eyes even?" she says. "Is the color the same on both sides?"

"A little more on the left lid," I say and listen to a three count. "That's good."

Mommy puts on her dress and spiky high-heeled shoes. She is so pretty. I wish I could look like her.

"Hurry up, Rose!"

Daddy looks at his watch and rubs his forehead. "Why is your mother always late?" he says. "We can't be anywhere on time."

Before leaving, Mommy goes over the rules with the sitter. "Bedtime is eight o'clock, and be sure the kids brush their teeth." She tugs on her fur to make sure it is on straight. "No fighting," she says to us.

The sitter makes Liz, Evan, and me play while she watches her television program and does homework. When eight o'clock comes, we are in bed, lights out, no noise anywhere. I miss my parents. Maybe if I look out the window I will see their car. When I stand on my pillow, I see the birch tree outside my window swaying in the wind. A storm is coming. On the lawn, the tree's shadows makes shapes of alligators with sharp teeth and an octopus with twisted arms.

Like fingers, long branches brush the glass. Please, tree, don't crash through the window, I pray.

I stand on my bed a long time, waiting for Mommy and Daddy. I hope they'll be excited when they find out I stayed up to see them. My head rests sideways on the window ledge, and the world looks crooked. I wish Croquette was here, but she's hiding.

Moving lights turn into the driveway. I hear the front door and the coat closet open. "Thanks again. Drive carefully," Mommy says.

High-heeled and flat-shoe footsteps take turns on the wood steps.

The footsteps stop first in Liz's room, then Evan's, and finally mine.

"Hello!" I jump out like a grasshopper. "Guess what? I waited up for you!"

Mommy jumps back. She is beautiful in her fur coat, even though her lips make a big red circle. Daddy's lips press against his teeth. His chin sticks out.

"Rinnie, you should be asleep." Mommy's head must hurt because she holds her forehead in her hand. She bends to me.

I hug Mommy through her coat and hide my face in the cold, thick fur. It's smoother than melted chocolate. I want to lick the softness.

"The sitter said you were asleep. You need your rest," she says and leans over to kiss my forehead. "Sleep tight. Tomorrow is another day."

I close my eyes and listen to the whoosh of Mommy's coat as she turns to leave.

"Was I a good surprise?" I ask Daddy.

He winks and says, "Sweet dreams, Rin."

EIGHT CANDLES

My birthday is in a few days, but I'll be at camp. My birthday wish is to stay home with Verna, Evan, Gaga, and Croquette all summer. I want to ride my bike through the alley next to the Starr's house and stand in their fountain, chalk hopscotch on the driveway, and roller-skate down our slanted driveway. I want to eat Verna's grilled cheese and potato chip sandwiches. I want to play mermaid in Gaga's pool, and I want to break eggs in the gutter. The crack of smooth shell against the ground is a song. It's over so fast. I want to hear it again and again. Inside is a yellow sun, sitting in goo. I pour the sun like melted butter into the gutter next door and think about it never becoming a chick. I hope it looks like our neighbor cracked it so I don't get into trouble.

Mommy and Daddy have a different birthday wish. They think going to camp will be more fun for me. My second wish is that they remember the birthday candles belong to me.

CLOUDS and REDWOOD

The plane lifts itself from the runway and tilts toward heaven. It's my first time flying.

"How high does the plane go?" I ask Lizzie. "Will it know when to stop? How do we get down?"

"Don't worry, Rinnie. I did this last summer, and it's easy. The pilot took a test to make sure the plane won't fall and he uses a compass," Lizzie says. "The plane can even fly in the dark! Those ladies in the blue uniforms are hostesses. They'll get you anything you want."

"Their caps look like cans of tuna fish," I say.

We are on our way to Camp Redwood. Two months sounds like a long time: no Verna to gather worms with, no Evan to tease, no dressing Croquette in her raincoat or baseball cap, no Mommy and Daddy.

Mommy says, "Don't worry. Lizzie will show you the ropes." Liz knows all the kids from last summer.

Daddy says, "You'll celebrate your eighth birthday with new friends." He gives me a velvet box with an angel pin and two coins inside—one for good luck with the year I was born on it and one for love.

They promise Liz will look after me if I need her.

The plane flies through clouds. Where are the angels? From the ground, the clouds look like marshmallows. Clouds aren't solid at all.

"The clouds look like the steam room at the club," I say. A hostess brings Lizzie and me Cokes with straws. The fizz in my Coke spits on my lips.

"They're not steam, they're cold," Liz says. "Things inside the earth are hot. Things outside the earth are cold."

"Like what?"

"Lava and rocks," Liz says. "Lava's hot. Rocks are cold."

I think about walking barefoot on the stone wall of our garden and their warm tops after an afternoon of sun. I think about the cold dampness of stones when I turn them over to look for sow bugs. All the stones in the shade are cool.

I have a lot of time to think about things that are hot and things that are not. Liz sleeps and a drop of drool dangles on her bottom lip. After a while, it falls off and makes a perfect circle on her purple blouse. I watch it dry. Liz will not believe me when I tell her she drools.

The plane rumbles and vibrates under our seats. I tighten my seat belt and shake Liz awake.

"Listen!" I whisper, squeezing her arm.

"It's OK, Rinnie. That's the noise the wheels make when they lower for landing."

"Are you sure?"

"Uh huh. I've heard it before." They are so big it makes the plane wobble.

A frightened breath untangles from my chest.

Maybe Liz is right about the clouds. She is very smart.

BUBBLEGUM

"Lizzie! Welcome back!"

"Lou!"

Lou swishes curved bangs out of her eyes. Her ponytail fans her neck and a strand of hair catches on her "counselor" badge.

"We have a new theater counselor," Lou says and unsnags her hair. "And she loves musicals." Liz loves musicals, too. "How about that, songbird?" Lou says.

A list of names stamped with a big red tree falls from the pocket of Lou's shorts. She stoops to pick it up and is freckle to freckle with me. Her breath goes in my nose. Bubblegum.

"Lou, this is my sister, Rinnie." Liz pats me like our dog. Lou pops a bubble.

"Here's your name on my list, Rinnie. It's nice to meet you. You're going to have a lot of fun this summer."

"I know! Lizzie told me," I say.

She hands me a bandana the color of pine needles with the words "Redwood Camp, 1962, Cold Spring, New York" sewn in white.

"Every new camper gets one of these," Lou says.

The three of us climb into the bus that waits to take us to Camp Redwood. It's filled with flashes of arms and legs, dashing across aisles, giggling, shouting—comic books and candy, popping through the air.

"Hi everyone," Liz joins the talkers. "This is my sister, Rinnie."

I smile a big tooth smile and give a little wave. We find a seat next to Lou, and she offers us some gum. Liz takes two and gives one to me. She is looking after me.

Lou counts heads and we roll down the bumpy road, singing. I think camp might be OK.

FIRST IMPRESSIONS

The entrance to camp is edged by two trees that hold a banner with the words, *Welcome Campers. Redwood Waits with Adventure.*

"One more song!" Liz shouts. I plaster my hands over my ears. I barely hear voices, and this new no-sound is soothing.

The bus lurches forward. Boom! I clutch the seat in front of me and swallow my gum. The bus is stuck between the two trees that hold the banner.

"Everyone out. We'll hike it from here," Lou says. Our first Redwood adventure begins. "Someone will get our gear later."

My shorts are stuck to my legs with sweat. I lick the salty corners of my mouth and think of the fizz from the cold Coke I drank on the plane.

"Where are the red trees?" I ask Lou. She laughs and says there are no red trees at Camp Redwood. It's just a made-up name.

No red trees? I wonder what else is made-up at Camp Redwood. I march into camp behind Liz.

LAND and WATER SPORTS

"Girls, today we pick up balls that have flown over the fence into the trees," Julian, the tennis teacher, says.

This is the third time my cabin is scheduled to play tennis. The first two times it rained. Eight girls hold new rackets. We have never stepped on the red and green courts that are divided by a dirty white net. I wonder what the nets are for. Julian sits by the fence and plucks at the strings of his racket. I gather tennis balls with my bunkmates and balance as many as I can on my racket. Julian waits for us to bring the balls to him. I'm glad we don't have to walk inside the fence. I don't want to be locked inside a cage, in the woods, so far from my sister.

A bell rings and Julian says it is time to go back to the bunk. On the way, we pass a building called The Ark. Inside, campers are practicing for a play. Liz is onstage dressed in a man's suit.

"Hi Liz!"

"I can't talk now, Rinnie."

"Will you come to my bunk before supper?"

"I can't, I have dance rehearsal."

"Can I come back and watch you?"

"No, the play's a surprise."

"How about after rehearsal?"

"Sorry, Rin. My bunk's having a scavenger hunt."

"But I want to show you something, a big bruise." I yell in a whisper, "I miss you."

"Can't hear you, sorry."

I catch up to my bunkmates and half hurry to put on my swimsuit that has real bows all over the front. It's time for sailing.

The Sunfish boats are slippery, narrow, and easy to fall off. Last time my sailing partner was a camper who thought I knew how to sail.

"Jibe!" she shouted. "Pull the sheet."

"I don't see any sheets," I said.

"The line, the white rope," she yelled, pointing with her head.

I snatched the line to my chest. Round and round the Sunfish spun. I felt like water—swirling, swirling—into the hole at the bottom of a toilet bowl. The Sunfish toppled into the cold water and waves made it hard to hold on.

"Please, God, don't let the flesh-eating fish get me, please make the lake-snakes swim to the other side," I prayed aloud. I whipped my legs through the water. If nothing could catch me, nothing could eat me.

My partner pulled the Sunfish upright and helped me onto its deck. Some of the bows on my swimsuit were untied and tangled together.

"There are no water snakes in this state," she said. "And the fish are too small to bite you."

I believe her, but just in case she's wrong today, I still pray while I make sure my ribbons are tied real tight.

WATERSKIING

The sides of the sun-bleached dock are rough and splintery. I'm careful not to rub against them while I wait for waterskiing to begin. A whistle blows and we line up on the dock.

"Waterskiing is safe as long as you follow the rules," Greg, the instructor, says. He's tan, and his arms have big muscles. Greg talks into a megaphone to make sure everyone hears him.

"Wear a life preserver and follow the hand signals you have learned. If you fall, stay put. The boat will come back and get you."

Mommy says to try everything. I take a deep breath. Standing on water looks fun but tricky. One by one, someone helps each girl put skis on. One by one, each girl jumps in the water. One by one, a boat jerks each girl away.

The safety instructions are posted on the door to the supply closet. I read them one more time before getting my skis. Next to the rules is a poster. It says, "Never get in the way of the motor on the boat." There is a picture of a boy lying on his tummy. He got in the way of the motor. His back is ripped open and his red, wavy insides are showing. Could Greg and his big muscles have pulled him away from the motor? That boy didn't have fun.

JUSTICE

"Stop pushing me."

"First give me the bag of pistachios." Sally, the bunk bully, is picking on Kira again.

"Stop snatching! I'm telling the counselor," Kira whines, her bottom lip sticking out like a swollen slug.

"If you tell, I'll break your head," Sally says, shoving a fistful of nuts in her mouth.

"Give me my pistachios," Kira says.

"Crybaby," Sally says, throwing the open bag of nuts on the floor.

Kira bursts into tears.

"Hey, clean it up," I say.

"Oh yeah, I'm really going to listen to another shrimp," Sally says.

"Clean it up, Sally," I say again.

"Follow me, bozo," she says, slamming the door.

We walk to the weed patch on the side of the bunk. Sally lunges, grabs my hair, and pulls really hard. She's heavy, but I'm quick. I plow into her stomach headfirst. Sally's grip on my hair opens, and she buckles to the ground. I'm on her stomach and punch, one, two, three, four, five times, until she pants, "I give!" and promises if I stop, she won't bother Kira again.

"Not good enough," I pant.

"I won't tease anyone," she huffs.

I press my elbow into her armpit and get close to her face. Four-ish blurred watery eyes look up at me.

"Owww! I'll tell Kira I'm sorry. Please, let me go."

I crawl off Sally. A hand tugs on my arm. It's my counselor.

"What's going on here? Are you girls OK?"

Sally lowers her look and coughs out, "We're fine, just wrestling." She gets up and rakes her fingers through her short hair to pick out weeds.

"Next time find a softer patch of ground to wrestle on. You could get hurt here," the counselor says. "And remember, you're girls."

When the counselor leaves, Sally hurries inside. I follow and watch Sally sniffle and use her arm to wipe her nose. Then she says, "I'm sorry, Kira," before hiding her head under her pillow.

TOP BUNK

Even though it is much too early to get up, I hear footsteps through the screened window next to my bed. A boy counselor and a girl counselor move between the scratchy brown tree trunks, their feet snapping twigs.

Rinnie, don't move a muscle, don't make a sound, I tell myself. Look! They're *holding hands*! He's *kissing* her—on the mouth! My shoulders hunch around my neck to quiet a snort. Haha! Their secret is my secret, too. It's harder to make my bed on the top bunk, but the view is perfect.

GOING HOME

Dear Mommy and Daddy,

Tomorrow I will be home. Here's what I will miss at Camp Redwood. I will miss swimming and looking out the window from my bunk bed. I will miss sitting on the hill after supper and reading comic books. Next year, maybe I can go to a different camp with no sailing, waterskiing, or tennis.

Love, Rinnie

P.S. Say hi to Verna, Emmy, Evan, and Croquette and tell them I'll be home soon.

BEDTIME

Mommy is downstairs knitting, and Daddy is kissing Evan goodnight.

"Be quiet, or Daddy won't tell us a story when he comes in," I tell my stuffed animals. I pull the blanket over our heads, but I hear Daddy's slippers slide over the carpet and stop by my night table.

"Rinnie, why are you lying on the edge of the bed? You're going to fall off."

"I can't move. My animals need room," I say.

Daddy looks for a place to sit down so he isn't squishing anyone and reaches for my hand. We thumb wrestle once, and he begins, "Once upon a time, there lived a beautiful princess who loved to climb trees. Her name was Princess Rinnie. The princess had a brother and a sister, but Rinnie was the only one strong and agile enough to climb the tangle of trees in the enchanted forest. *High ho high ho, up the knotty old trunk I go,*" Daddy sings, in a girl voice.

"Princess Rinnie knew a magical bird lived imprisoned on the highest branch of the highest tree, and no person had been able to free the beautiful bird. 'What a sad life to be able to see everything in the world for miles, yet no way to be a part of it,' Princess Rinnie said. 'It must be lonely.'

"It was then she decided to use her strength, balance, and bravery to rescue the bird. One afternoon, Rinnie slipped into the forest of jumbled trees and grasped branch after branch, pulling herself up over gnarled trunks, until she could see everything in sight for miles and miles. Princess Rinnie had found the tallest tree."

"Huh?" I say. I can't keep my ears open anymore. I feel Daddy's good-night kiss on my cheek, and his hand leaves mine.

"What happennn?" My lips won't move to make room for the words.

"I guess you'll have to find out tomorrow night, sleepyhead," Daddy says. He walks away, but before he closes my door he sings, "Princess Rinnie climbed my tree. Princess Rinnie rescued me. And to her I sing my praise. She'll live happily all her days."

DRESS UP

Layers of satin splash over my shoulders like a waterfall. The cold material gives me goose bumps. The bottom of my dress kisses the floor. In the mirror, I look like a purple flower, a fairy flower, tied in the middle with a fairy bow—almost as good as the ones Mommy ties.

I pat the lumps of hair on the top of my head that stick up from my Alice-in-Wonderland hairdo and hide as many bumps as I can with barrettes. Then I slip my baby-powdered feet into the glittery, silver, plastic high heels that grow pink feathers on their stretchy bands. My fairy shoes, my magic shoes, they take me everywhere I want to go.

I am on my way to a Princess Ball—far, far away. So far away, I can't hear doors slam or Mommy and Daddy fight.

All night long, I dance until it's time to turn into a pumpkin. Then I go home where everyone is asleep. The house is quiet. No doors slam, no parents scream. Mommy doesn't say "You son of a bitch." It's OK to take off my magic shoes.

THIRD GRADE

Mrs. Burrell greets me in the hallway of Endicott Elementary with a huge happy hello. She is glad to have me in her third grade class. We turn our desks toward the chalkboard and begin a new lesson.

Mrs. Burrell teaches us about poetry and how Mother Earth makes changes when winter melts into spring. She decides the best way for us to learn about poetry and the seasons is to write a song about squirrels, birds, and spring weather. We have to make the last word of each line in the song rhyme. For me, this is like searching for treasure. I hunt inside my head for the prize—golden words. When my name is called, words tumble out. The class shouts ideas until the blackboard is a garden of yellow-chalk words. I love Mrs. Burrell. She's the best teacher.

Next, Mrs. Burrell says, "I want you to write poems about the four seasons." She says we will collect the poems into a book called an anthology, and everyone will get a copy. Nothing can top this. The rest of the day I pop, pop, pop, up from my seat to show her all my poems, more than anyone else writes.

"Each one of you will decorate a cover for your anthology," Mrs. Burrell says, holding up colored paper.

My hands are so excited I have to hold them still. I take crayons out of my desk. The wax smells good. Soon, hungry birds on bird feeders chirp on the cover of my anthology. Time goes by too quickly, and we have to put our art away.

The bell rings. It's time to go home. Outside, I stop and take an extra look at the trees, the sky, and the apple-green grass. The world looks different today. I wish Mrs. Burrell were my mom, but she already has a child. On my way home, I decide to ring her bell sometime anyway.

MONEY TREES

Christmas is over, the New Year is four days old, and my sister, brother, and I help Verna and Emmy pack Christmas ornaments in a box for storage. This year's tree is the fifth one I remember and the biggest of all. Emmy came early today because our new ovens were delivered from Daddy and Pop Pop's business. Emmy has to make sure she knows how to use them before she cooks dinner. She said working the appliances is a snap. Now she gets to help us help Verna.

"Next year for Christmas, I want Santa to bring me a holiday," Verna says. "I won't be cleaning after dried-up Christmas trees. How come Jewish folk are celebrating Christmas, anyway?"

"Because we always do," I say. "Mommy says Christmas is beautiful. She says it'd be a shame not to decorate the house with winter smells, candles, and a Christmas tree with colored lights that twinkle."

"When your Daddy gets home from work, *he* can carry this tree to the screened porch. Tomorrow, the handyman will finally haul it away," Verna says.

"Thank—you—Lord!" Emmy says. "No more tinsel and pine needles dirtying up my afternoon carpets. I have to pick up every time someone tracks that mess through the house. Between Mrs. G's 'Can you do this for me,' and you kids, there's not a minute's rest."

"I'm sorry you're tired. Liz and I will wrap the ornaments and put them in the box. Emmy. You and Verna can sit and have a cup of cocoa," I say.

Verna wipes her forehead, and Emmy sandwiches her apron between her rough hands and laughs. "Out of the mouths of babes," she says. "Oh, honey, our job is to put up and take down, cook and clean."

"And to take care of us," Liz says with a smile.

"That's right, girl," Emmy says and climbs a ladder so she can reach the angel on the top of the tree.

"Hand me that frosty white snowman, Rinnie," Verna says. Her brown hands push bundled ornaments against the side of the box. "See if you can slip under the tree and catch that pointy gold star."

Liz and I scramble on our stomachs to reach it. Verna and Emmy talk softly and I hear them say, money grows on trees in our house, and Santa needs to bring them a tree like that.

After she carries the boxes of ornaments to the basement, Emmy says, "You kids stay clear of the kitchen. Company is coming for dinner, and I have a lot of work to do."

My sister, brother, and I inspect the empty tree.

"It's naked," Liz says. "All its clothes are packed away until next year."

Evan giggles and runs around the room. "The tree is naked, the tree is naked," he sings.

I stare at the empty branches. Without ornaments on the branches, it's easy to look for money.

"Where's the money?" I say, and shake a branch. Dry sharp needles fall on the carpet. "Where's the money?"

"What money?" Liz says.

"The money that grows on our trees."

"Money doesn't grow on trees." Liz turns her head, looking at me like I should know that.

"Verna says it grows on *our* trees, and she wants Santa to bring her a tree just like it."

"Maybe Verna needs more money," Liz says.

"Is that why she takes Mommy's old clothes home?" I ask.

"I don't know."

"If Verna had a money tree, she could pick money when she needed some and buy new clothes. She could play golf and tennis. She wouldn't have to get up and come here," I say.

"Verna is here because she loves us. Daddies go to work, mommies go to the beauty parlor, children go to school, and Verna takes care of us. She doesn't need a money tree," Liz says.

Just in case, I get my piggy bank and shake it until quarters, nickels, dimes, and pennies rattle out.

"Vernaaaa," I call. "Where are you?"

She is standing by the front door. The striped scarf Gaga gave her for Christmas is tucked around her neck. She pulls on matching mittens. "Okie dokie, artichokie. Time for me to catch my bus," she says. I give her a hug.

"Here," I say, handing her the coins. "They fell from our money tree."

Verna hugs me back and tells me to plant the money so another tree will grow.

I wave to her from the door. She bends against the wind, wrapped in her old furry coat and new scarf. She looks like a fuzzy brown caterpillar with striped antennae. I hope she's warm.

"See you when the sun comes up," I shout through the glass.

FOLLOW the LEADER

It's the first company we've had since Christmas. We all wait for our dinner guest, Rabbi Josh. Especially me. He is tall and handsome like Prince Charming. His eyes are so dark, it looks as if God stuck black olives in his head. His hair and eyebrows are a perfect match. Rabbi Josh, Daddy, and Mommy have been extra-special friends ever since Daddy was president of the Temple. Daddy likes to repeat what the rabbi said at the big meeting when Daddy stopped being president.

"Charles, excuse me, Chuck Gardener continued the work of his father-in-law, Simon. He did a superior job of streamlining Temple operations and was responsible for our three major fund-raisers that benefited Temple Chai more than any other in our history. Chuck was also the first Temple president to invite me to dinner when it wasn't Shabbat."

Then Daddy always tells us, "It's important to help those who help you."

I think of Verna. She took the last box of Christmas ornaments to the basement today. There is only one more piece of Christmas left in the house.

"Good-bye shiny balls, good-bye tinsel, good-bye candles," I say to myself.

Emmy won't let us in the kitchen because she's cooking a special dinner.

"Let's play library while we wait for the rabbi," Liz says.

Evan ignores her and bangs on his new kiddie piano.

The library is in Liz's bedroom, and Liz is always the librarian. There is one bookcase with three shelves. To me, the best thing about the bookcase is that it's lavender and matches the bedspreads. Liz has arranged all the books in groups. Mysteries, books Mommy wants her to read, and ghost stories are on the top shelf. Books about famous people and our Sunday school books live on the middle shelf. A dictionary shares the bottom shelf with a book of maps of every place in the world, along with Liz's collection of fake turtles.

"Can I check out this book?" I say, handing her a book with a picture of three men holding three swords that meet in the air.

"Not yet, Rinnie!" Liz says. "You have to enter the library first and remember to whisper."

I place the book back on the shelf, go into the hall, shut the bedroom door, open the door to the "library," and walk in.

"Good morning, young lady, are you looking for something special?" Miss Liz says, in her cheeriest librarian voice.

"Yes, I would like a book on dogs."

"I'm sorry, all of our dog books are checked out."

"Do you have any books on monkeys?" I ask.

"We have one, but someone stuck gum in-between the pages, and we had to send it to be repaired."

"How about raccoons?"

"Rinnie! Play right," Liz says.

"Excuse me," I say. "Do you have any books about famous people or detectives?"

"Why yes, we do. Let me show you where they are," Liz says, turning from her desk to the bookshelf. "You may browse as long as you like. Bring your book to me when you're ready, and I'll check it out."

"Eeny meeny miney mo catch a tiger by the toe. . . ." I say to myself, finger hopping from one book to the next. "Eeny meeny miney mo! This one looks good," I say handing the book with the three men and their swords to the librarian.

Liz writes *T-H-E T-H-R-E-E M-U-S-K-A-T-E-E-R-S* in her best cursive across the top of a note card. Beneath this, she pencils in Rinnie Gardener, January 4.

"You may keep the book for one week. If it's late, you'll be fined ten cents a day."

"What if I'm late because of a snowstorm?" I ask.

"Do the best you can," Liz says with a bob of her head to the left, then the right.

I write my name on the card and hand it back to Liz before leaving the library. "Come again soon. It was a pleasure to help you," Liz calls.

The smell of sugar and chocolate fills the house. Mommy leans out her bedroom door and tells us to wash our faces and change our clothes. The rabbi will be here soon. She doesn't have makeup on, and she ducks back into her room to put on her face. I can almost taste Daddy's spicy aftershave as it floats out the door. It mixes with the smell of candied carrots, roasted meat, and chocolate.

"Emmy's frosting the cake. Let's ask her if we can lick the bowl," I say, running down the stairs.

"I have to dust the books," Liz shouts.

Before I put one foot in the kitchen Emmy says, "Don't mess the pillows on the sofa. I just fluffed them." She puts a smoked salmon cheesecake topped with black fish eggs next to a plate of crackers on the mirrored table. "And don't take the first slice. That's for the rabbi." She narrow-eyes me and turns toward the kitchen.

The doorbell rings. Rabbi Josh is here! He squats down and claps my hand. I look into his black eyes. They shine like wet olives. His dark whiskers draw a line around his smooth white skin. There are no pits in his nose like Pop Pop's or brown spots on his thick hands. But mostly, his face is soft sort of like he's never said "No."

"Shalom, Rinnie. Have you had a fun winter vacation?"

"Rabbi, Rabbi!" I tug his coat sleeve, pulling him down the hall to the back porch. I fling back the curtain to show the rabbi the last best bit of my vacation. "Look!" I say. "We took our Christmas tree down today."

GOOD ADVICE

Daddy says it is always better to ask a question and know what you're doing before you do it. Today, I folded five sheets of notepad paper in half and taped the loose pages together. On the cover I wrote, A LITTLE BOOK OF QUESTIONS. On the inside flap is a big pink question mark. Across from the mark it says:

Why can't people sleep with their eyes open?

How does a pebble in your shoe cause so much hurt?

Why doesn't soap get dirty?

I'm off to a good start.

CRIME and PUNISHMENT

At home, Evan and I sit next to each other at the dinner table. We play games with our feet like "Got You Last."

"Sit up straight, stop wiggling, and eat your corn," Mommy says. "Rinnie, your example lacks decorum. Emmy worked hard on this dinner. Eat it."

What the heck is decorum? Under the table, I lift Evan's napkin from his lap and drop it on the floor. Evan swipes a buttery hand across his mouth to wipe off kernels of corn. Yellow bits stick to the sleeve of his wool sweater.

"Evan, please use your napkin," Mommy says with a tilt of her head and shoulders.

He can't find it.

"There it is on the floor," I point.

Evan ducks under the tabletop and puts the napkin back on his lap, kicking me.

Slowly, gently, I lift the napkin off Evan's lap and drop it on the floor again. It is so hard not to giggle until five fat fingers twist a handful of my leg.

"OUCH!" I jump and my hand knocks over the glass of milk in front of my knife. Slowly, then fast, the tablecloth turns into a soggy clump of milk.

"Dammit, Rinnie, that's the second time this week." Daddy points to the straight-backed chair in the living room, the Bad Chair. "Go. Now!" he says. "And no Croquette."

Evan snickers. Liz gives me a "Not again, Rinnie" look. She knows what I did.

I am not allowed to talk to anyone, and no one can talk to me. I've spent so much time sitting in the Bad Chair and looking at the planter next to it, I've named each plant. The two yellow speckled ones are Liz and Evan. Mom and Dad are the tall spiky ones. I am the one with the leaves that fold under and look like miniature umbrellas.

While everyone else finishes dinner, I tell stories to my plant family. When Emmy clears the dishes, I sneak a peek at the table. I don't like being separated from my real family. I miss my turn to share about school. And I miss dessert. It's too hard to have good manners when I sit by Evan.

SCARED

It's Sunday, and Verna isn't here. Bad words and screaming float up like ghosts from under my parent's bedroom door. I know to be quiet. Liz taps Evan and me on our shoulders and waves for us to follow her. We tippy-toe to the basement to hide from the scariness upstairs. On the way, Liz closes the open windows downstairs.

"This is private," she says. The good smell of new grass and the bad smell of fertilizer is shut out.

When the noise stops, I push myself up the steps to see what's happening. I hear Daddy stomp across the floor in his bedroom. Mommy is wrapped in a towel in the bathroom I share with my brother and sister.

"What's wrong?" I ask.

Mommy sits on the edge of the tub and lets out a sound like a clock that's running down.

"My heart is sad," she says, giving herself a tight hug. "I'm tired, and my heart is sad."

Water runs into the tub. "You have rabbit eyes, Mommy. They're pink! A bath will make you feel all better."

"Oh Rinnie, go away. Life is falling apart in here." One hand rises to her forehead and pulls the skin first one direction then the other.

The "I'm the boss" part of her voice is missing. Mommy looks like one of my rag dolls. Her shoulders are falling over.

“Mommy do you want bubbles?” I give her my bottle of Fairy Castle bubble bath. “Look up. Mommy, look up.”

“No, Rinnie, I don’t . . . want . . . bubbles.” Her breath chugs like a train. “I want . . . I want . . . ”

Mommy grabs her heart.

“I want you to go someplace else.”

Her fingers flick the air, and she opens the door the rest of the way with her foot so I can leave.

I look around. The walls look OK and the floor and toilet haven’t changed. Water still runs into the tub. I am confused and want to stay close to someone big, but there is no one to go to. I walk to my room and sit in the closet and play with my Barbie, the most ordinary thing I can think of doing.

WEEKDAYS

Pebbles tap against the window above my bed. I climb on my pillows and look outside. It's Verna, signaling me in our secret code. Instead of ringing the doorbell in the morning, Verna throws little stones at my window.

"7:00 A.M. is too early to wake Mrs. G," she says.

I jump out of bed and rush to open the front door. I'm the first person she sees! I've been awake a long time waiting to greet Verna and breathe her in. She smells better than the tulip stuck in her buttonhole.

"Hi, Verna!" I say, as if she has been away on a long voyage.

"Hi, Pancake!" she says back and tosses the day's newspaper on the floor. We go down the basement stairs to the laundry room. Verna takes her sweater off and hangs it on a wire that stretches across the room like a tightrope. She puts on her uniform, ties an apron around her waist, and rubs cherry lotion into her hands and arms.

"May I have some?" I ask.

I get a squirt of the candy-sweet-smelling cream. My mouth waters. The smell makes me hungry for breakfast. We go upstairs to wake Liz and Evan, and then Verna comes into my room and helps me make my bed. I put on my favorite red-flower-print shorts. They're faded because they used to belong to Liz. The red roses are pink and the washings by Juanita, our laundress, has turned the fabric old-blankety soft.

"Wear this fuchsia tee-shirt, honey-pot," Verna says. "It'll jive those shorts right up." I pick an orange elastic, brush my hair, and put it into a ponytail just like Verna taught me a long time ago.

"Put this on your pony," she says, handing me a pink and green striped ribbon. "Now you're lookin' sharp, girl."

I grin and give her two thumbs up.

"Tell your sister to hurry up, or she'll be havin' cold eggs."

I follow Liz's voice to the bathroom.

"Verna says to hurry up if you want hot eggs."

"Drat these stupid curls!" Liz curses some more and ignores me. "Drat these stupid curls."

But the curses don't help. She stretches and tapes curls to her head with her wet hairbrush "Darn it, I hate my hair."

Since Mommy told her bread crust makes straight hair curl, Liz eats only the inside part of the bread. I always eat my crusts, and my hair is straight. I guess it only works if you don't want curly hair.

"You look just fine," Verna says as she heads for Evan's room. She stops long enough to help Evan find his show-and-tell project for school, something fourth graders don't do, but I wish we did.

"I need something that moves things," Evan says.

Verna answers with her favorite morning words. "There's nothing as good as preparation. At night, before you hop in bed, get yourself ready for tomorrow: Pick out your clothes, lay out your supplies—think ahead. Look in your toy box, boy."

"I'll take my bulldozer," Evan says, reaching under his bed.

While I wait for Liz and Evan to come to breakfast, I take Croquette for a walk. Liz and Evan are downstairs when I return. Verna spoons scrambled eggs and bacon on our plates, fills empty jam jars with orange juice, and goes to wash the pan. Croquette jumps on my lap.

"Good morning, Croquee. Who's the piddiest doggie in the whole wide world? Who, who, who?" I say.

"You sound like an owl," Liz says. "Croquee you don't want to be piddy do you? No, you just want to be patted."

Evan pretends his eggs are mountains and uses his bulldozer to push them toward the dog. Verna plops the newspaper on the table. Liz and I fight for the comics.

"You two don't have time for anything but eating," Verna says. "Ward will be here soon to drive you to school. He won't wait for you, he can't be late. . . ."

"For seminary school," we chime in.

Verna licks her hand and pats down Evan's hair. "Mrs. G. hired him to take you to school and that's what he's going to do. Now finish up. Evan, use your fork and hand me that bulldozer. Never seen such last-minute kids."

"Not me!" I say. "I'm ready." And I stand by the front porch.

Mommy likes Ward a lot. I don't know why. He doesn't say much except hello, sit still, and good-bye. In three years, he's never asked any of us about school. I guess that's fair. We don't ask him what a seminary is.

NINE

Tomorrow is Evan's sixth birthday. My birthday won't be here for two months. Mommy took us to pick out a cake and party favors for his cowboy party. Evan chooses a white cake with horses made from chocolate frosting and cowboys swinging black licorice lassos. Water pistols are the party favors. I pretend the cake is for me. At camp, birthday girls and their friends get cupcakes in paper holders, and there is no such thing as party favors.

PERSONALITY

I sit between Mommy's legs, on the queen-sized bed. She brushes my hair. Tangles snag the bristles, but Mommy works them smooth. I feel the soft skin of her hands on my neck as she lifts my hair and wraps it into a French knot. Mommy lets go and it tumbles down my back—heavy, hot.

"Try a bun, Mommy," I lean into her body.

"Your hair is the best thing you have," Mommy says. "Don't ever cut it. It's your personality."

LITTLE BOOK of QUESTIONS

Why can't people sleep with their eyes open?

How does a pebble in your shoe cause so much hurt?

Why doesn't soap get dirty?

Why does a kid in my class have one green eye and one blue eye?

Why is it "I before E except after C"?

Why are fire engines red?

What is a personality?

BROWNIES

It is very late, past my bedtime. Brownies meet tomorrow. I take the Brownie dress from my closet. I love my uniform. It is the color of a chocolate bar. I am excited to wear it to school. I look good in it. My uniform smells clean. I check the hem. Mommy promised to fix the side that fell down last week. The hem still hangs down. I take my uniform and show her.

"I'm too tired to start sewing. Wear something else tomorrow, Rinnie," she says.

"Please, Mommy. All the other Brownies will have on their uniforms. It's the rule. We have to. Please."

"Tst, OK, OK."

"Really?"

"I promise, Rinnie."

"And do a GOOD job. Verna told me it is important to be your best self in every way, especially when you meet new friends. The Brownies are sort of new friends," I say.

Mommy takes the dress and scoots me out the door with her hand.

The hemmed uniform is on my bed when I wake up. All day in school I think about Brownies. I will paint my macaroni-covered jewelry box with real gold paint at the Brownie meeting. I've worked hard to make sure every noodle is in the right place. Today, I finally get to bring it home. I've known all along it is a present for Mommy. This is my favorite project so far—better than making butter from cream or braiding plastic for bracelets. It's even better than the running, jumping, and climbing I do at recess.

Finally! The bell rings, and it's time for Brownies.

A girl from a different class points at me and whispers to her friend. "Go back to the prairie! Did you leave your bonnet at home?"

A little group forms and giggles with her. I dash to find the bathroom mirror.

"NO!" From the back, I look like a pioneer in a long chocolate-colored dress. I fold the hem and press it hard with my fingers to make it stay up, but it doesn't work. I wet the hem and try again and again. The hem stays down. Now the back of my brownie uniform is wet and long.

"Mommy, you promised to do a good job!" I scream to the mirror.

When we stand for the Brownie pledge, I try to hike up my dress and lean forward so the back of my dress seems shorter. As soon as the pledge ends, I sit and don't dare get up until it's time to go.

I am the last Brownie in the room.

On the way home, I decide to keep the gold jewelry box for myself.

BAD DREAM

I wake up. The smell of ashes burns in my nose. A fire burns in my head. My ears want to drench the promise that repeats itself:

If you ever, ever, ever
Try to sneak away,
I'll be waiting in the night.
I'll be waiting in the day.
You never will escape me.
You never will be free.
You're my forever, ever, ever
You're the lock that fits my key.

It's the monster. I don't understand. But *it is* the monster.

HORSES

"Get your bikes!" I yell. "Here comes the DDT truck." Evan and I ride into the spray of fog, our own cloud on Earth. "Whoopee! Don't breathe. Hurry! Hurry! The truck's getting away," I say.

The cloud of insecticide evaporates until it is nothing but haze.

"Keep going, let's go around the block," Evan says. We fly past the Myer's house, past the Behrs'. We zoom by Stephan and Virginia Silbern's house. It looks perfect from the outside, a red-brick rectangle with white pillars growing out of the green lawn. Something is not perfect inside. Virginia is retarded. She doesn't have many friends in the neighborhood. Occasionally, her nurse walks her to our house. Verna always welcomes them with a plate of jelly donuts. Virginia laughs and waves her hands when she gets to the jelly part. It's fun to eat jelly donuts with Virginia, and we invite her to come back. Nobody is in the Silbern's yard when we zoom past. It's just the pretty brick house with white pillars and green grass that's always cut short.

Around the block we go, fast, as fast as our legs will turn the pedals. When we reach our yard, we jump off our bikes and run them to a halt.

"We have to feed our horses," Liz says. "Turn your bikes upside down and spin the wheels to help them cool off."

My horse's name is Bike, and I push the front wheel hard so it will still be going in circles while the back one spins.

"Good Boy, Bike, good boy."

"Evan, you turn the tires. We'll get more food," Liz says.

Hunks of grass stain our palms when we yank them from the lawn. We toss the grass into the spinning wheels. "Down the hatch," Liz says.

We pull grass and throw it as fast as the horses spit it into the air.

"My hands are tired," Evan droops his fingers. "The lawn is getting bald."

"You're right," Liz says looking at the shorn places. "Let's take the horses to the stable." I'm careful to walk my horse around the oil stain on the garage floor. I push Bike against the wall between the garbage cans and the snow shovel.

"Be back later. Rest up," I say.

SHADY LANE

"Did you eat the sloppy joes at lunch today?" I ask Liz on our walk home from school.

"The buns smell like rose perfume."

My legs travel in the direction I talk.

"No, and stop bumping into me. Stay on your side of the sidewalk."

I try, but after a few squares of concrete, I drift back into her lane, so she bumps me back. We thump bump all the way to Shady Lane.

"Shady Lane is our own temple of beauty," Liz says, looking up at the canopy of trees. "We have to take a rest. Stop here."

We spread out on the little hill that butts up to a green-shuttered house on the corner. Alongside the house is the darkest dirt I have ever seen and growing in it are yellow daffodils. A cement squirrel about to eat a cement nut stands guard over the flowers. I press my body into the ground as if I'm a mound grown by Mother Nature.

"I'm growing, Liz. Look how long I am." My feet nearly touch the sidewalk; my head is an arm's length away from the flowers.

"Watch out for bees," she says, gazing toward the sky. Above our heads are three trees with leaves bunched up so tightly it looks like they are holding hands and praying.

"Magic is over our heads. Can you see it?"

I look hard and say, "Yes," but I'm thinking, how does Liz know so much about magic? *My* favorite place is around the corner. I gather my school supplies and smooth the lawn in reverse, the way Liz showed me last time, so the flattened grass stands up. She gets up too and waves her hands over the indented grass.

"We have to make it look good, so the owner won't mind," she says.

Crocker Thall's house is next door. *Crocker, Croc-ker, Cr-oc-ker, what kind of name is that?* Maybe it means boy with lips that curl into a snarl. He's mean. He ditches in the recess line, hogs the monkey bars, and puts his pencil shavings on the floor.

Around the corner, the sun shines on a driveway layered with stones. This is my "temple of beauty" as the rabbi says. "Ten minutes," I say.

"Five minutes, Rinnie. Verna will worry if we're not home soon."

I squat and pick over the stones. Flat stones, streaked stones, stones with flecks of mica that sparkle and look like a wizard's wand touched them. "This one is beautiful, look. Look! See how pink it is? It looks like a pink diamond. Don't you think so?"

"You're right," Liz says. "Put it in your pocket. Now, let's keep walking."

"You go. I'll catch up." I sit on the sharp rocks and turn over more stones, looking for the best ones to fill my pocket.

OOPS

"Lizz-ie! Lizz-ie! Let me in." I pound on her door with my fists.

"No! I need some private time. Go to your room."

"But I want to play. I want to play," I whine, beating the door.

"Stop pounding on the door. I can't read."

"Let me in! No one wants to play with me, and I don't have anything to do."

"You're too cranky to play with, and you're supposed to be taking a nap, Rinnie. We have our dance recital tonight."

"*You're* not napping," I say. "Nine-year-olds don't take naps either."

"I'm resting," Liz says.

"I'll rest with you. Let me in!"

"Go away."

I slide to the floor, my back scrubbing the door. "It's lonely out here. I want company! Open the door. Pleeease."

Liz ignores me, and I stand with the door as my brace. "Liz-zie, Oh Liz-zie," I say in my sweetest voice. No answer. "Liz-zie."

"Fine!" I cry. My foot swings forward and flies back. In a minute, Liz stands in the doorway speechless. At the bottom of the door is a splintered hole the exact size of the heel of my shoe.

Liz's lips scrunch toward one ear. She looks at me and kneels to touch the hole. "Uh-oh, you're in big trouble."

"It was an accident."

Liz looks at me and sighs.

"Sorry."

"Go take a nap, Rin." She closes her door.

When Mommy sees the accident, her eyes pop so wide I could fall inside them. When they get small like needles, my stomach trembles. She anchors one hand on my shoulder and holds on tight. The fingers on her other hand wag close to my head. If they were lit matches, they'd singe my hair.

"Do you know how much it costs to replace a door? What is wrong with you? If you *ever* do anything like this again. . . . Stay out of your sister's room." Her fingers clamp harder with each word. "Go to your room and stay there!"

"Forever?" I ask.

"Until I say!"

Her teeth grip each other so her jaw doesn't move. "Why can't you be good like Liz? Go to your room, NOW. Just wait until your father comes home."

She releases my shoulder and swats my bottom when I turn around. I want to cry, but I rub my shoulder instead. I know I am bad, but it was still an accident.

LITTLE BOOK of QUESTIONS

Why can't people sleep with their eyes open?

How does a pebble in your shoe cause so much hurt?

Why doesn't soap get dirty?

Why does a kid in my class have one green eye and one blue eye?

Why is it "I before E except after C"?

Why are fire engines red?

What is a personality?

Why are some ladybugs black?

Why are some freckles big and others are itty-bitty?

Why does Temple have Sunday school on Saturdays?

WEATHER

"The temperature's rising."

That's code between Liz and me. It means Mommy and Daddy are fighting again. I'm hot, my hands are sweaty. I want to watch TV, but I can't sit still.

"Let's go for a walk," Liz says to Evan and me.

She puts the leash on Croquette, and I help Evan buckle his jacket. There's no one here to ask us where we are headed. Verna and Emmy don't work on Sundays. The air is crisp and makes my nose run.

"Don't cry," Liz says. "It will be OK."

"How do you know?" I ask.

She shrugs her shoulders, "I just believe that it will be OK."

I put my head on her shoulder for a moment, and she strokes my hair.

Evan runs with Croquette ahead of us. Everything is quiet, the carless street, the cold air, the smell of bare branches, and me.

"Well," I pause, "I believe in you."

INTUITION

Evan is acting like his seven-year-old self, sitting on the stairs, refusing to put his coat on and get in the car.

"Come on!" The words snap from my mouth like a whip. "Don't you know Mommy and Daddy are getting a divorce?"

Evan doesn't know what divorce means, but from my command, he knows he'd better move. I don't know how I know with such certainty, but I do. The car ride is our last one as a family, and no one talks.

Part Two
The Next Six Years

MOVING OUT

"Dad, where are you going to live?"

"Downtown, in a hotel."

"Is it far away?"

"Not in a car. I'll miss you though."

He lifts a box marked "Records."

I don't want Dad to feel bad, so I don't tell him how much I will miss him. I squeeze his hairy hand and walk to the door with him.

"See you next week, on Saturday. Be ready when I pick you up."

We kiss good-bye. Evan and Liz are outside cleaning his car with water pistols and rags. The white Ohio license plates with scarlet writing are spotless and glow against the silver fenders.

"Come on, buggers," he says. "Someone open the car door." Evan gets there first.

"Can I come with you?" Evan asks and moves so Dad can't shut the car door.

I see Dad shake his head and pick Evan up out of the way. Liz watches on the other side of the car.

"See you Saturday, Dad," I whisper.

DEAR GOD

"Now I lay me down to sleep. Pray the Lord my soul to keep. Bless Mom, Dad, Liz, Evan, my entire family, all my friends, and me. Bless Verna, Emmy, Mimi, (even though she hasn't been here in a long time), and the bad guys because somewhere inside, they have good. Be sure to bless Croquette, my best friend next to Liz."

I tighten my grip on the velvet box Dad gave me when I first went away to camp and pull it in close to my chest. Safe inside are the good luck and love coins and my angel pin.

I open the box to peek at my treasures. The moonlight bounces off the gold satin lining. It's so beautiful and cold. It feels like water. I make a wish on the good luck coin. I hope it brings Dad home.

"Please bless Dad an extra lot and tell him to come back. I am scared without him."

My pillow is wet. I dream the wetness is a river. Dad, Mom, Liz, Evan, and I are pole fishing in the river. Our lines tangle together.

"Don't worry. We can fix this mess," Mom and Dad say.

Dad pokes each pole into the soft mud on the riverbank and balances them, so they stand strong and straight. Mom works the strings like knitting needles, over under and over under. Together they untangle the lines and put fresh bait on our hooks. I catch a sunfish, and Dad takes it off the hook and hands it to me. I toss it back into the river.

"It wants to be with its family," I say and watch the fish swim away.

When I wake up, my pillow is damp, but there is no river or fish—or family together. Just a stream of wetness on my cheeks.

THE SENECA

The building is tall and its bricks are the color of dried blood.

"Come on in, look around, I just want to put a few things away," Dad says as we enter his apartment. It smells like furniture polish and emptiness. I keep my hands in my pockets, close to me and far from the strangeness of the room.

Records sit on a shelf crowded with Dad's collection of little cars and paintings he made that are the size of the coasters they lean against. He said Grandma Samuels was an artist, and she gave him scraps of canvas to paint. He painted the houses on his block over and over because he wanted to be an architect when he finished high school.

Dad must have used a dinky brush to paint the rows of storefronts and houses with people dashing in front of them. In one painting, a brick movie theater has my name on it and a foot shaped sign above a shoe store says "Liz's Footwear." I don't think there was enough room for Dad to spell Lizzie. Evan's name is on a grocery store, whose windows are filled with bananas, lemons, and limes. In another painting, the buildings all have names that end with "Gardener." Most of them are skyscrapers or parking garages.

"Dad has a new TV," I whisper to Liz. "It's so small." Next to it are two photographs. One photograph is of Dad's parents, the other one of Evan, Liz, and me sledding at Miracle Park last year when I was ten and a half.

"How do you like this big mess?" Dad picks up a box labeled *Golf Balls, Tees, Gloves,* and puts it on a shelf in the coat closet.

Stuffed in the corner is the golf bag that lived in the trunk of Dad's car.

"I don't think he's coming home," I say.

"He's not," Liz whispers, wiping her eyes.

Evan's folding paper airplanes and crashing them into the tower of records. One after the other, they hit the records and then crash to the floor. I slump into a wooden chair close to the bent-nosed planes and try to kick them back into the air. Without someone to send them off, they are lifeless.

How can Dad live here? It's not at all like home. There's no one to send him off to work. No one to make his breakfast, no one to kiss him good night.

"Do you like it here?" I ask.

He shuts the closet door, carefully. His head nods. "Sure, it's a nice place."

I make the kind of smile where teeth don't show, cross my fingers behind my back and agree, "Very nice."

"Last chance to go to the bathroom before we leave," he says.

Dad puts his jacket on and makes a call while we wait turns for the bathroom.

Before we leave, I take one long look at the dull brown rug and empty walls and ugly furniture. My eyes stop at the paper planes bent and abandoned.

SIXTH GRADE

Mr. Bonatura is my sixth grade teacher. He's embarrassing me in front of the class again. Mental note for my list of unanswered questions: Why does everyone think Mr. Bonatura is such a good teacher?

"Do I need to give you a microphone, Rinnie? Speak up," he says. "You're as quiet as a flea. Maybe Emmy should feed you extra vitamins."

Last year, when Mr. Bonatura taught Liz, Mom and Dad liked his jokes so much that they invited him to dinner—often. As far as I was concerned, he ate at our home too often. My parents liked him so much they requested him as my teacher. He knows our cook, Emmy, and where we keep the extra toilet paper in the bathroom. I know he likes lamb chops, medium rare, and crème de cacao in his coffee. You'd think he wouldn't want to advertise that he's been socializing with a student's family, but not Mr. Bonatura.

On a sheet of paper, I make a list to add to my book: Four Things To Never Ask A Teacher:

To come to dinner

To come to breakfast

To come to lunch

To ever visit your house

"Rinnie, you may get your project from the closet, and while you're there, bring me the paintbrushes." Mr. Bonatura's directions end my list.

I set my papier-maché horse on my desk and spread out the paints and a cottage cheese container filled with water.

"Do you want some candy?" Patricia Castillo, the girl who sits in front of me, whispers. She opens her desktop so I can peek inside. Scattered in the same place I keep pencils in my desk are rolls of Life Savers.

"No," I shake my head. What I don't need is more trouble.

Patricia whirls around and sticks out her tongue.

"Look how thin I can suck them," she says, whirling back around.

On her return trip, her elbow hits my cottage cheese container. Water drenches the floor by my desk.

"What happened, Miss Gardener? You better clean that mess up. There's no Emmy here," Mr. Bonatura says.

I give Patricia the evil eye and dry the floor. *Why are some teachers so awful?* I can't wait until seventh grade.

LITTLE BOOK of QUESTIONS

Why can't people sleep with their eyes open?

How does a pebble in your shoe cause so much hurt?

Why doesn't soap get dirty?

Why does a kid in my class have one green eye and one blue eye?

Why is it "I before E except after C"?

Why are fire engines red?

What is a personality?

Why are some ladybugs black?

Why are some freckles big and others are itty-bitty?

Why does Temple have Sunday school on Saturdays?

Why does everyone think Mr. Bonatura is such a good teacher?

Does Dad miss me?

What does bad look like?

CREEPY CRAWLERS

"Rinnn, you're using too much goo!" Evan watches the stream of red liquid fill the metal mold I've picked to make my creepy crawler.

"Well, I didn't use much green. I need to fill the mold with something," I answer. "Cockroaches have big bodies, you know."

"Just because you're gonna be in seventh grade doesn't mean you know everything. You're using too much!" Evan almost chokes on a mouthful of M&Ms.

"I'm using the same amount as you," I grumble. He snatches the squeeze bottle from my hand.

"Hey," I say, making snake eyes in his direction. His collection of bruise-colored creepy crawlers blends into the purple-blue countertop.

"Look how much stuff you used to make all of those," I say. "Please let me make one more. I'll make something small. A mosquito."

"You can make one tomorrow," Evan says. He takes aim and tosses the crumpled M&M package at a basketball hoop on the wall.

"Missed, damn!"

"You're not supposed to swear, Evan," I say.

"Damn," he says again, and tries another shot with a paper cup. "Damn, I was better yesterday."

"You better not swear again, or I'll tell Mom," I say. We both know Mom won't punish him, not her baby, not the only boy.

"Why don't you frolic on over to your own workspace?" He opens the woodburning set he got for Christmas and takes out a piece of wood with a picture of a horse burned into it. He irons his nose with the picture, and takes a deep breath.

"Ahhhh, it smells like a campfire," he says. I sniff the air.

"Better," I say. "It's like being inside a roasted marshmallow. May I burn a design in the wood?"

"Tomorrow," he says, biting into a Snickers bar. "It's still too new."

"It's spring," I say. "Christmas was months ago."

Evan ignores me and presses the hot tool into the horse's tail. A thin golden groove brands the wood.

"Make it darker," I whisper, standing on my toes, so I can see over his shoulder.

Evan glides the tool along the groove, toasting the tail until it's black. "The wood melts, like ice in a frying pan."

"Please. Can I try it?" I say.

"Tomorrow!" He keeps his head lowered and focuses on making the grooved horse stand out farther from the background. He takes another bite of candy and smears his lips with chocolate.

"You're going to lose our bet and eat all your Halloween candy before next year. You eat too much at one time."

"So do you." His mouth overflows with candy bar, and he's drooling.

I slide from my stool and shuffle past Liz's art area to my own, at the end of the counter. My supply cabinet is neat. In one glance, I can see exactly what's inside. A box of oil paints fastened with a gold latch, my tabletop easel, empty jars for turpentine, linseed oil, water, a box of used ribbons and swatches of cloth, glitter, a sketchbook, glue, colored pencils, an eraser, paper, canvases, and a list of collage supplies to scrounge for around the house. Thanks to Verna, I always have old sponges, rags, and the leftover stubs of soap to use for cleaning up.

I set up my painting equipment and sketch my own horse, eating grass in a meadow, on my canvas.

"Please Evan, if you let me use your woodburning set, I'll teach you how to use a palette knife."

"Nope." he says. "I already know how. Liz showed me."

"I'll make you an origami fortune-teller and you can write whatever fortunes you want inside the folded-over sides."

"I can do that myself," he says.

"I'll be your slave for the rest of the afternoon."

Evan looks up and smiles. "Come over and pick a pattern to trace."

Instead of tracing a pattern onto the wood, I draw my own design, a fish jumping from the water. With the hot tool, I slowly follow the pencil line, until scales glow the color of burnt umber, fleshy fins are airborne, and a dark striped tail clears the wavy water lines.

"Thanks, Evan. You're the best brother. My fish looks so good!" Maybe Mom will hang it next to my landscape paintings.

Evan whirls his finger above the worktable, mimicking a tornado, and lands on the creepy crawlers. They're squished by the twister.

"Rin, get me a Three Musketeers, a Mounds bar, and three chocolate kisses. Oh, and a glass of milk."

"You know Mom only keeps her favorite candies in the house, fudge or chocolate-covered cherries," I say. "Besides if you eat all that you'll get sick."

"I'm collecting it, not eating it, and you have those candies—in your Halloween bag," Evan says. "Mine are gone."

"That's not fair!" I say. "My candy has to last seven more months, and there's only half a bag left."

"You're my slave, and you have to do what I say." Evan folds his arms across his chest and sticks his chin in the air where his nose used to be. "It was your idea."

"This isn't what I meant, and you know it," I say, stomping to get my candy bag out of hiding. "I hope you burn your fingers, and I take back what I said about being a great brother."

"Hey, Rinnie, make that two Mounds bars and twelve chocolate kisses."

SEVENTH GRADE

"I brought your coffee," I whisper, stepping into the darkness of Mom's bedroom.

It's Sunday morning. Heavy curtains hide the eleven o'clock sun. Last night was Jeremy Shoen's Bar Mitzvah party. Maybe the coffee will warm Mom up before I break my news.

"Did you add two *heaping* teaspoons of sugar?" Mom rolls over and flicks on a lamp.

"Sure did." *Please be excited for me, please be excited.* "And I brought cream and the newspaper. Here." I hand the cold cluster of pages to her.

Mom props herself against a row of pillows and uses the newspaper as a tray. "What time is it?"

She looks at the clock. Mom's fingers fan wide, cover her eyes, and massage her face. Her forehead ripples, rises, and relaxes. The sleepy face remains.

I hand her the pitcher of cream and let the glimmer of gold around my wrist catch her eye. *Please be excited for me. Don't be mad.* Hopefully, it is too early Mom-time for lots of energy and clear eyesight.

"What's that on your wrist?"

"It's an ID bracelet."

"Who gave it to you?" Mom asks, blinking hard and sitting up in bed.

"Jesse Golden," I say. His name is a parade, and it's marching all over me. "He asked me to go steady last night."

Silence, coffee, and dread press hard against the tick, tick, tick of Mom's clock.

"Leah and Dan's son?" Mom plumps her pillow and turns to face me. "Do Jesse's parents know he gave you his bracelet, Rinnie?"

"I think he told them," I say, holding my arm behind my back, so maybe Mom will forget about the bracelet and ask me more about the party.

"So what does 'going steady' mean exactly?"

"That I'm his girlfriend." The next thought clots in my throat. "He thinks I'm pretty, smart, and important." I don't say *we kissed.*

"You know," Mom's voice rises, "if you go steady with Jesse, that means no other boys will give you the time of day."

"Uh huh," I chirp.

"No one else will be interested in you."

She beckons me to her, so she can take a closer look.

"This is an expensive piece of jewelry," she says and looks at me. "Too expensive for you to take. I think you should give the bracelet back—today. You don't need to go steady in seventh grade."

"But I really like him and other girls go steady," I say.

She shakes her head again. "No. I think I'll call Leah and Dan and see if they know Jesse gave you his ID bracelet. It's valuable."

"Don't call yet," I plead. "I'll think about what you said."

I walk to my room and hug Jumper, my stuffed rabbit, who's so old he can't hold his head up anymore. We sit in my rocking chair and Croquette joins the sway.

Jesse is sooo cute, guys. He has dimples. And, he has braces like me, freckles like me, and is short like me. Best of all, he picked me, Me, ME to go steady with!

The rest of the weekend I leave the bracelet on my dresser, covered with a red heart I cut from construction paper. On the paper is a list of Jesse's favorites: Color—blue, Sport—baseball, School subject—math, Food—mint chocolate chip ice cream, Girl—ME!

At dinner, Mom says I can keep the bracelet. Jesse's parents don't mind if I wear his bracelet as long as I give it back when we break up.

When we break up? What? I can't believe I have something so special for my own. I love going steady.

I'LL VOLUNTEER!

"Does anyone want chopsticks other than me?"

It's Sunday, our new day to visit Dad. Tonight we eat in at Dad's apartment. That means Chinese for dinner. It's Liz's job to set the table. Evan picks the television program this week, another western, and I help Dad unload the food. The perfectly folded white boxes are treasure chests waiting to be pried open. Dad says next year when I'm twelve like Liz, we'll switch jobs, but I like opening the boxes.

"Did you get extra fortune cookies?" Evan collects the slips of paper and tapes them into the fortune-tellers we make out of folded paper. "It's too hard to write so tiny," he says.

Dad holds a small sack open for Evan to inspect.

"Eight. Two for each of us," Dad says. "That enough?"

Evan shakes his head, smiles, and jerks his right arm down in a motion of victory. He knows after reading our fortunes, Liz and I will give them to him.

"I'll put the food in bowls," I say. Liz leaves the kitchen, hands stretched around napkins, plates, and chopsticks. Dad and Evan follow with glasses and a carton of milk.

The minute I'm alone, my heart speeds up as if it heard the starting gun of a race. It is a race. How quickly can I put everything in bowls, steal shrimp from the lo mein, swallow a spoonful of gravy from the egg foo yung, count the wontons in the soup to see if there is more than one per person, and pluck the biggest wood ear from the vegetables before someone wants to know what's taking so long. A little pinch of roast duck skin, another shrimp.

"Hurry up, Rinnie," Dad yells. "I have to get you home by nine."

I rearrange the food, so it looks untouched.

"Hereeee's dinner," I say, carrying a tray from the kitchen to Dad's coffee table.

By the third commercial, plates are empty, napkins are tossed aside, and the sheriff has shot the bad guy.

"Does anyone want the last egg foo yung?" I ask. Evan burps. Dad frowns at him, and Liz holds her nose. I take the gooey pancake and scoop the last bit of gravy onto my plate.

"Where do you put that, Rinnie?" Dad asks. "You're such a little runt."

"I dunno."

My stomach is already stretched, but I'm not ready to stop eating. There's still room for more.

POWER

"Stop! Stand against the wall," I order.

Tricia's arms drop to her sides. The look on her face is how I feel when Mom barks my name. The afternoon sun is still high enough to create shadows, and mine is tall. And menacing.

Tricia inches toward the stucco wall of the garage. A lift-the-flap book falls from her hands and lands near her patent leather shoes. Lizards and dogs stare from under the open flaps. Tricia whimpers like the puppy in the book. For a moment, I think of her older sister, Becca, who is a year younger than I am. We swim together at the club and play shuffleboard. *Will Tricia tell Becca I made her cry?* I hope not—it's my turn to push someone around.

I move in close and stare down at Tricia's face. Her eyes are huge and her mouth quivers. *Good.*

"Why are you cutting across our driveway? Who said you could do that?"

Tricia's silent.

"Answer me!"

I stare at those huge eyes, but I see myself using the same short cut in reverse. I often cross through her yard on my way home from school. My shadow swallows Tricia's. *Power.* I've got what I want. Then it's gone.

Empty. I'm empty, and mean, and smaller than Tricia is. I want to run away . . . from me.

"Go home, Tricia," I murmur. "I'm sorry. I won't bother you anymore."

Tricia stoops to pick up her book. She searches the ground with her hands as if she were blind. Her eyes fix on mine like I might kick her. She finds the book and runs through the gap in the bushes into her yard.

Have I turned into an animal?

WHERE DOES HURT LIVE?

Today is Sunday, and Dad will be here soon. We wait on the front porch and squish the red berries that grow on the bushes nearby and threaten to wipe berry goo on each other.

Like a lit jack-o'-lantern, Evan's round face twinkles with satisfaction. He's just swatted a handful of berries across the driveway. If it weren't for his huge chocolate eyes with eyelashes that curl back to his lids, happy buck-toothed smile, and funniness, he'd just be another fat boy. Liz and I aren't allowed to call him chunk-o, big boy, or anything that might let him know he's fat. He's the biggest kid in his fourth grade class.

Mom says if we call him names, he can get a complex. I'm not sure what a complex is, but Mom is determined Evan isn't going to catch it from his sisters. Mom describes Evan as "husky."

It could be all the folded-over butter and sugar sandwiches he eats while watching television, or, maybe it has to do with the divorce. Evan wore normal-size clothes before Dad moved away.

Liz looks at her watch. I am not sure if she is counting how much time she will have with Dad or how much time must pass before she returns home. She doesn't visit Dad every Sunday like I do. Dad doesn't question her about it often, but when he does, Liz shrugs and says she has work to do. Liz doesn't tell him she is Mom-sitting. She doesn't tell Dad it was more fun when we played miniature golf and went bowling by ourselves, before he had a girlfriend. She doesn't tell him she misses the smell of Old Spice on the towels and his scrawled signature on her report card. I watch Liz step back from Dad. Am I supposed to tell Dad that Liz told me these things?

I do what I am supposed to do. I always visit Dad and follow the unspoken rules that come to me from inside. I don't act too excited to see him until we pull out of the driveway, and I don't act too happy when he brings me home. I am very careful. It makes life with Mom easier.

Mom is angry that we want to spend time with Dad. Dad is angry because Liz sometimes snubs him. Liz is angry because Dad doesn't insist she visit. Evan is angry because Dad is gone. I am angry because my parents are changing my world, and I can't do anything about anything.

FLUBBER

School is over. The water ripples blue in Gaga's pool. Evan, Liz, a few friends from school, and I take a break from swimming to play SLAM. We take turns hurling a ball against the cement deck to see who can make it bounce the highest. Between each attempt, Evan gets dibs on the ball.

Liz yells, "Flubberize it! Flubberize it!"

He is the only one with the power of flubber. He catches the ball and rolls it on his stomach. Around and around, the ball follows the folds of skin hiding Evan's red swimsuit. They are like layers on a sagging cake. His flab transfers its bounce to the ball, flubberizing it for the next slam. Mom hates this game, but Liz and I know Evan thinks it's cool. His smile and eyes blaze as bright as the summer sun as he looks up to catch the ball. I'm glad Evan feels important.

PACKING

"One, two, three, four, five, six. One, two, three, four, five, six. There are six pairs of shorts for camp. Check them off the list," Mom says, putting them in the trunk and counting one more time, "One, two, three, four, five, six."

Verna is in the laundry room ironing the last of the white T-shirts to be packed. Every afternoon after swim lessons, it's the same old thing: Come home, listen to Mom count, listen to Mom count again, find a place to put a new pile of stuff, and count one more time. It's been the same list since I changed camps when I was eight. How hard can packing be?

"I don't want to have to send you kids anything this summer," she says.

"Mrs. G., those clothes aren't changing. Why do you keep counting them?" Verna says, shaking her head, hands on her hips.

"Rinnie is thirteen now. She may need something she didn't need last year."

I think she means in case I get my period, but we don't talk about it.

Verna bends over my shoulder and says, "Your mama is something else. She's going to drive me to crazy packing you kids' trunks. Croquette, get your paws off those clothes. I just ironed them." Verna shoos Croquie away with the towel that's tucked into her apron pocket.

I roll my eyes and pull my lips back into my cheeks. "You're not the only one."

"SHHHHH! I'm counting," Mom says, with a pencil between her teeth.

Camp Redwood is an erased memory. I pick up my tennis racket and strum "K-K-K-Katawauk, K-K-K-Katawauk, You're the only C-C-C-Camp that we adore, and the reason, every season, finds you better than you ever were before."

I can almost smell the pine trees and stables. I can see the sun's glint on Lake Katawauk, and I rock as though I am paddling a canoe, solo on the calm lake water. I take a deep breath and cough out the smoke of Mom's cigarette.

Mounds of blankets, toiletries, swimsuits, and campfire clothes hide the floor. Towels skirt the silk chairs. The sofa is covered with cotton panties folded in neat rows, balls of white socks, and striped pajamas. My riding helmet, jodhpurs, and boots are next to a flannel nightie.

"Seven pairs of high socks, seven pairs of tennis socks, right?" Mom says. "Rinnie, count them again."

"Seven pair high socks, seven pair tennis socks," I say. "Can I get a snack?"

This is the most boring job in the world. My mom is crazy about having exactly what's on the list provided by the camp.

Last week was the same routine, but with Liz, lucky her, she escaped on her bike to the summer recreation program at school. Three times a week any kid can bring lunch and play supervised games on the playground. It's a lot of fun.

Next week, Evan's stuff will be packed—only he gets off easy because he's Evan.

I'll probably have to help while he goofs off, like now. He's watching TV in the den and eating folded over butter and sugar sandwiches.

Verna hates the annual routine as much as Liz and me, but she *has* to help. She's getting paid. I hang around so I won't get in trouble later and because I feel sorry for Verna. I've heard misery loves company and if Verna has to be miserable, then I'll be the company.

"Check underwear off the list," says the voice of authority.

"You have the pencil," I say pulling it out of Mom's hair.

This is nuts.

I mean, how many times do you have to count the same things to be sure how many things there are? The living room looks like six families moved in and forgot to put their stuff away.

"Where are the T-shirts, the swimsuits, and the white shorts? You need two more pair of white shorts. Rinnie, try these on—see if they still fit." Mom hands me a pair of last year's shorts.

"I hate these shorts. They're too long. They're gross."

Last year, it was OK to wear any kind of shorts. I was in the third-to-youngest bunk. The most important thing to me then was making a present for every person in my family before camp ended.

"We're missing a pair of shorts. Did you move them?" Mom asks.

"One is enough," I say. "Remember what happens on Sunday?"

Sunday morning at camp is laundry day. Campers and counselors give their bags of dirty clothes to Susie, who is also the person who checks our hair with her rough hands to make sure it has been washed when we come out of the shower. Susie bellows all summer, "Clothes are supposed to have name tags so no one loses anything." The plan never works. My best friend, Terri, never got her beach robe back from the laundry and had to wear a bathing suit to and from the shower the entire summer.

I imagine sorting 200 piles of clothes: 150 for campers, 50 for counselors. The perfect job for my mother.

Monday is laundry day here at home. Juanita, the laundress, washes, dries, and presses clothes in the basement. I love to visit Juanita while she works. The smell of hot pressed clothes, steamy as a cup of soup, warms me, even in summer.

I picture the campers dressed in their Sunday whites, waiting in line to go to services. No one ever talks about God or Sunday school stuff. It's more about being grateful and loving nature or at least being aware of her beauty. They are the only services I can sit through without getting antsy. The older campers, the juniors or seniors, give the service and read poems, sing, and tell short stories. Each person holds a folded white piece of paper decorated with just-picked, soft, green ferns. If it weren't for the paper, the ferns would look like small wings ready for lift off—mini-wings that turn each paper-holding camper into a camper angel. One day, when I help give the service, I'll be a camper angel too with fresh-picked ferns for wings.

I'm dropped back into reality. "The shorts look great," Mom says. "I think you should have one more pair."

I agree about them looking OK. I must have grown. This summer I have a reason to look good. I have a chance to make inter-camp sports teams. I almost made the archery team last year, but one of the other girls distracted me. She had her own arm and finger guards, which were polished and smooth—not the cracked and scuffed guards the camp passed out.

I couldn't stop thinking what a good archer she must be to have her own equipment. When we were given the signal to shoot, I was still thinking about the fancy guards, and I hit the blue instead of the goal. I lost by three points because of how someone looked.

This year, I plan to be prepared. Being prepared is something I've been concentrating on.

"Here are the other shorts," Mom says. "They were under a blanket."

"Why do I have to try them on?" They look exactly like the pair of shorts I just took off. Mom gives me the don't-push-your-luck look.

"Try them just in case the laundry shrunk them."

I put them on. "Perfect," I say. "Am I finished yet?"

Verna carries in the T-shirts and Mom counts.

"Eight, nine, ten, eleven, twelve." Mom wants to make sure I have plenty of T-shirts in case I sweat and want to change into a fresh one. "Good. Now how many of them are sleeveless?"

I like the sleeveless tops because, as Verna says, "The sun can kiss my shoulders and leave freckles," which I like.

I have lots of freckles—the only one of us three kids, and the freckles are all tiny and cute. They are mostly on my arms, legs, and face. Mom says the sun is attracted to me because I have red hair. I am irresistible to the sun's affection. My friend Julie's freckles are so huge they hug each other. The sun must have licked her.

Verna counts the T-shirts again. Twelve. She puts them next to the socks: fourteen. Mom counts again—just to be sure. It's 4:00 P.M., time for Verna to leave so she can catch her bus. I finally get a snack. Mom stands knee-deep in her glory and counts how much more is left to count. She calls, "Rinnie!"

"Grrrrr." I hug Verna good-bye. She pats my back and brushes hair out of my eyes. Her hands smell like cherry lotion. I take a deep sniff. I won't smell anything so sweet until tomorrow.

"See you around like a donut," she says.

"See you later, alligator," I say back.

"Thanks, Verna," Mom says. Then we start counting bathing suits.

SISTERS

"You may be the pretty one, but Liz is the one with the personality," my mother's friend says.

"She had a head start," I answer. It's not the first time an adult has commented on my older sister's bubbly nature. Liz in action still astonishes me. Her words sail in the air as easily as a bird. Watching them fly quiets me.

CONGRATULATIONS

"Rinnie, is that you?"

"Dad? Are you home?" I grin so wide he *has* to hear it over the telephone. "Will I get to see you before I leave for camp?"

Liz hears me, twisting the phone so she can hear Dad.

"Allyson and I got back last night. The wedding went off without a hitch. Alana, Amy, and Jake gave their mom away. Allyson's parents did a fabulous job on their yard. Wildflowers bloomed everywhere, even on the canopy."

Dad says having a big family will be fun. Maybe for Alana, Amy, and Jake, but not for us.

"When does camp start?" he asks.

"In two weeks. I told you a month ago."

"Gosh, I'd love to see you, Buzzer, but I'll be in Europe—the honeymoon, remember? Allyson and I will catch up with you on visiting weekend at camp. I'll bring you coins from the countries we visit."

I hear a wiggle in his voice—the kind of wiggle that worms its way into a conversation and fills the space where something else belongs.

"OK," I mumble.

"Allyson and I wanted you kids at the wedding, Rinnie. But with your camp schedules, the timing was bad. Allyson's parents had enough to do without planning for three more kids."

"Tell Allyson I, I . . . " I don't know what to say. "Tell her I'm glad you married her." I bite my lips so the words can't jump back into my mouth. This isn't what I want to say. I want to stamp my feet and yell, "Allyson's kids were there. Your real kids should've been there, too."

Instead, I pass the phone to Liz, who, with an upward flick of her hand, wipes a smile onto her face. "Congratulations to you, congratulations to you . . . " she sings.

I give her snake eyes, crossing my arms over my chest to ward off injustice.

"Don't you feel left out?" I stage whisper.

Liz looks at me with surrender. She flips the phone to Evan who stuffs the last bite of a bread, butter, and sugar sandwich in his mouth.

"What else can we do?" she shrugs.

"Ha, whoa. Dad?" Evan says, swallowing.

Evan's eyes shine like polished ebony. He's happy to have a brother.

Dad must have asked if Evan was eating healthy stuff because Evan said he eats vegetables and fruit every day.

Yeah, I think. Only it's in the form of potato chips and jelly. Before Evan says good-bye, I signal for him to hand me the phone.

"See you in six weeks," I say. "Don't forget."

I hang the phone up and wonder what I am supposed to call Allyson.

COINCIDENCE

Mom isn't a great letter writer. She writes four letters during the eight weeks I'm at camp. You'd think by now I wouldn't be excited to get a letter from home, but I am. This one is a real eye-opener. Last weekend, Mom and Barry Segal got married. Two weddings in one summer. My parents are couples again. Only with other people.

"You can see the wedding photos when you get home," writes Mom.

Like I want to. My reason to see the pictures would be to make a match between my ears and my eyes.

"I wore a white lace suit with blue trim and carried pale yellow flowers that matched my hair. Everything was gorgeous—the weather, the sky, the flowers. It was perfect."

No kids perfect. Barry doesn't look like a peanut, but that was his nickname in college—when he and Mom were sweethearts. She said he had hair then. Now he has a fallen halo of hair. Barry's taller than my Dad, and his voice is softer. I used to call Barry, Mr. Segal. Maybe I'll call him Barry. If he's around a lot, maybe I'll call him Dad.

At least he's nice and treats us like real people, a much better choice than Tom Waistman, who talked to us like we were some kind of circus poodles. "Come here, Rinnie. What a good girl you are, Rinnie. Rinnie, your mother says you made choir, sing a few bars, Rinnie. . . . Evan, run for the ball when I throw it. . . . Lizzie, my little Lizzie. . . . " Better than Paul Blennon, too. He crooned "Fly Me to the Moon" when he came to pick Mom up for a date. When he blew his nose, the windows rattled. Barry may have a big nose, but he's never rattled the windows, or us.

FAMILY

We're headed northeast on Interstate 71. Then, between pit stops on Interstate 76, we zoom past fields stamped with cows, sheep, and metal silos. Liz, Evan, and I are home from camp. Our new and improved family is on the way to Dad Barry's hometown to meet his family. Leafy trees remind me of giant stalks of broccoli, and the evergreens could be upside-down ice cream cones. What's familiar becomes strange. The landscape mirrors my family, no longer familiar to me. I have extra siblings, parents, and grandparents. It could be Fantasyland or *The Twilight Zone.*

Barry tells us about his life growing up. Burton, his father, who was a magician, owned a chain of toy stores. His magic wand was passed to Barry and his brother, Marvin.

"Marvin and I used to put on magic shows for our friends. There was only one person who didn't pay admission, Elaine Elliott. Marvin fell in love with her in the fourth grade and married her on his twenty-fifth birthday," Barry says. He goes on, "I didn't want to be in the toy business like my father and brother. I preferred to work with numbers."

"That's how I won your mom the first time. I was good with figures." Dad Barry chuckles at his joke. We flick each other on the legs and make smirky smiles.

Billboards line the road like giant goalposts:

Take a hike—The Mountain State

Wheeling, West Virginia, Statehood 1863

Need a car? Visit the Auto Warehouse, next exit

Best Breakfast East of the Mississippi. Bacon and Beans Café, three miles ahead

Like the billboards, Dad Barry draws us a verbal map of his relatives so we know where we're headed.

"Grandma Sher had four sisters, one so smart she went to law school long before it was common for women to go to work. Grandma Sher was the youngest sister and helped her mother in the kitchen. That's why she's such a good cook," Barry says.

"What does she cook?" Liz asks.

"Everything," Barry says. "Latkes, tzimmes, blintzes."

"What about our new cousins?" Evan says. "Tell us about them."

Barry uses the last few miles to give us the lowdown on his nephews. Cousin Danny is the same age as Liz, and his brother Dennis is the same age as Evan.

Barry taught the brothers how to play chess, and they taught him how to do flips off the diving board. Dennis likes lunch and gym. Danny, gym and history. Blah de da dada. The only thing Liz and I care about is if they're cute.

We stop in front of a stucco house the color of oatmeal. A stocky boy with chipmunk teeth, egg-shaped eyes, and a stomach that jiggles under his T-shirt runs toward us.

"Hi, Unca Barry! Are these my new cousins? I'm Dennis."

"The menace," says a serious voice behind him. "I'm Dan, not Danny. Uncle Barry, Dad wants to know if you need help with anything." Dan licks his thin lips and takes off his sunglasses. Wow! His eyes are small but blue as a jay's feathers. He is slimmer and fairer skinned than Dennis.

"Meet my nephews," Dad Barry says, helping each of us out of the car. "Nephews, meet Aunt Rose, the prettiest flower in the garden. And your new cousins, Liz, Rinnie, and Evan."

Both of Mom's hands clutch her purse. No hand shaking here. "Hello, nice to meet you," she says.

"What do you think?" I whisper to Liz.

She doesn't hear me. She's busy giving Dan the once-over.

Dennis hands a baseball mitt to Evan and tosses him a ball. "Come on. Let's play catch in the yard."

Evan slips the mitt on his right hand.

"I'm ready," he yells. "Wow! That was a laser!" He winds up his arm and lobs the ball back to Dennis.

Barry's mother, my new Grandma, waves from the porch. Her thick glasses slip down her nose, so she has to lean her head back to see us. She reminds me of a sumo wrestler, big body, big belly, small head.

"Come in. Come in. I'm so glad you're here. You kids are just like Barry described you, cute, cute, and cute! Rose, you look as pretty as on your wedding day." Her voice is high-pitched and almost plinky, as if the highest keys on a piano were tapped.

Mom receives an unfamiliar hug that sends her hat sliding to her shoulders.

Grandma hugs me so tightly I almost suffocate in the folds of her apron. Her nose and Dad Barry's nose curve out at the same place. Forehead to forehead, their silhouettes make the shape of a sharp-angled hourglass.

Smells of vanilla and sugar escape through the screen.

"We're hungry, Grandma," Dennis shouts from inside. "Evan and I washed already. Hurry up."

Inside, an abundance of blintzes and relatives wait for us. I'm glad I wore my hair down today. Braids are cooler on a hot day, but down is more grown-up.

"Would you like more sour cream or maple syrup for your blintzes, Rose?" Grandma passes a bowl with a cow painted on it and a warm pitcher of syrup. The cousins short stop the toppings before they reach Mom. "Thanks, but no," Mom says, pats her stomach, and passes the sticky plate down the table.

Eating takes a long time because we have to be polite and put our forks down between bites and answer questions about school, hobbies, and camp. Finally, the grown-ups tell stories of Dad Barry when he was our ages. We devour Grandma's blintzes.

"How about we visit the store," Uncle Marvin suggests, when the dishes are washed.

Dad Barry is eager for us to see where he worked as a boy. Mom and Aunt Elaine vote for a change of scenery by walking to the porch. We follow.

"Your hair is so adorable," I hear Aunt Elaine say. "I love the layered look. It's perfect for your angled face."

"How nice of you to notice, thank you," Mom answers.

She had it styled yesterday, and I can tell by the sugar in her voice that she's glad someone noticed.

At the store, Uncle Marvin snakes us down aisles of pink for girls, blue for boys, and purple for both. Who decides whether something is pink or blue?

"Ah ha," Uncle Marvin says. "Hold your breath, here's the secret part. Hardly anyone gets to enter this room."

He opens a door that says STOCK ROOM, EMPLOYEES ONLY. It's a maze of unopened boxes with labels like *Board Games, Costumes, Batteries, Tea Sets—Porcelain, Tea Sets—Plastic, Tea Sets—Broken, Helmets—Construction, Helmets—Fireman, Helmets—Football.* Along the walls are shelves crammed with stuffed animals, balls, push toys, and little-kid art supplies. It looks as if a giant piñata exploded.

When we are ready to leave, he lets Liz, Evan, and me pick out something to take home. We have been taught to never take the biggest item as a gift from anyone. Liz chooses Travel Bingo. I take a drawing pad and the smallest box of markers on the shelf, and Evan picks a battery-operated plane. I guess, as Mom has said to Liz and me before, that Evan forgot his manners.

We make a parade as we noodle a path to the car. Grandma promises she'll visit and make blintzes. She smothers everyone with a squeeze, except for Mom who reaches out and grabs Grandma's arms before they flatten her. Dan smiles as we get in the car. Dad Barry turns on the ignition. Dennis stretches across the hood.

"Unca Barry, Unca Barry, stay until tomorrow," he says. Dad Barry pries Dennis off the car. Dennis hops in the driver's seat. "Take me with you."

Mom lowers her window and Uncle Marvin leans across her chest. In his hand is a squirt gun aimed at Dennis.

"Do it. I don't care." Dennis laughs. "You'll get Aunt Rose's hair wet."

Mom shoots Dennis with a look.

Bull's-eye.

"OK. See you later, Aunt Rosie." Dennis scoots out of the driver's seat.

Dad Barry pulls out of the driveway, waving out the window.

I knock Liz on her leg and mouth the words. "Do you think Dan is cute?"

"Do you?" she mouths back.

I raise my eyebrows and grin a toothless smile.

"Kiddos, you hit a home run with Grandma. She thinks I couldn't have done better!" Dad Barry says. "Everyone buckled up?"

The car bumps across a train track. Dad Barry hums to himself. I see him put Mom's hand inside his on top of the console.

"Oh my God," Mom says. "Stop squeezing my hand. It's like being with your mother all over again."

"What?"

"I'm tired of being constricted like some snake's dinner. One more helping of sour cream and syrup, and we'd suffer heart attacks." Mom pounds her chest.

"Come on. That's not fair." Dad Barry reaches for her hand again. "How would you welcome new family? Be happy. Did you have fun, kids?"

"Yeah! When can we go back?" Evan says.

"Grandma's a great cook," Liz and I say.

"Everyone needs a bear hug now and then," Dad Barry says.

Mom is stone still.

"Her blintzes with sour cream and syrup may not be health food," Barry admits, "but they're a good reason to visit!"

Mom mumbles something about Dennis and the squirt gun, then stops and clears her throat. I see her twist her wedding band. "I'll call and say thank you tomorrow." She sighs, her fingers busy with the gold band.

Dad Barry turns, winks at us, and starts humming. Liz, Evan, and I play Travel Bingo, and we drive off into the sunset. Mom stares past the billboards, soundless.

POP POP

Pop Pop leans over and gives me a moist kiss on the forehead, scraping my skin with the stubble on his face. His stomach, a personal retaining wall, keeps the rest of him from spilling into my space.

The trademark long day at the office odor that belongs to Pop Pop is a potpourri of rumpled clothes, deteriorating starch, hand soap, and bourbon, his before-dinner drink. Liz hears my stomach grumble, nudges me with her elbow, and whispers, "I'm starving. Let's go into the kitchen and check on dinner. Maybe Beulah has carved the roast beef." The words are code for if the maid has carved the meat, we can sneak the roast tomatoes and onions that have fallen off the slices.

"Oh yeah, Good idea."

Beulah is at the sink, and steam from the pot she drains closes in on her like fog. Liz and I steal the vegetables and shove them in our mouths before Beulah turns around. The intense flavor of seasoned fat, sweetness, and salt makes my stomach growl louder.

"Get away from that meat. Go tell your folks dinner is ready," Beulah gruffs.

Evan doesn't eat with us on Monday nights because he's at swim practice.

After we sit in our chairs at the table, Gaga steps on the buzzer under the rug. It rings in the kitchen to signal that we're waiting for dinner to be served. Beulah answers, hands balancing the heavy platter of meat, followed by silver dishes mounded with buttered noodles and candied carrots. It's the same meal she's made every Monday night for as long as I can remember. It's the one night of the week Gaga and Pop Pop don't have commitments.

"Can I have another piece of meat, please?" I ask.

Pop Pop carves a slice so thin, I don't feel anything when he puts it on my plate.

Liz reads the disappointed look on my face and buries a giggle.

"I'm going to want thirds," I say.

Pop Pop grunts. He thinks children should be seen and not heard, so the conversation rotates between adults.

"The stock market did well today."

If it did well, then why don't you cut the meat a little thicker, I think.

"Eva, the YWCA is expanding, and I've been offered a seat on the board.... Mom says you got your new sofa today, Rose. I suppose you'll need more money.... Eva, she spends money like a drunken sailor. . . . Mayor Carlson called, he wants us to host a party. . . ."

Liz and I break in to Pop Pop's monologue a couple of times.

"What kind of party are you having? Can we come?"

"Eva, tell those girls to be quiet," Pop Pop whines.

"Oh, Dear. They're trying to learn. Go on girls, ask your questions." Gaga is our champion.

"When is it, Dad?" Mom asks.

"Why? Do you have to go out and buy a new dress?" Pop Pop asks.

"What if I do? It's my money."

Mom's chin slices the air as sharply as Pop Pop's knife carves the roast beef.

"Your money, but it comes from me." Pop Pop bites like a viper. "Your trust is revocable."

"Simon!" Gaga's hands hug the table palm down. "Rose's fashion sense is a gift. Appearance is important to her, and she wants to make you proud. She should do what makes her happy."

Gaga's disapproval is the only thing that brings Pop Pop to his knees.

"OK, OK, Eva, if you think it's important. . . ." Pop Pop gets up and cha-chas to Gaga, arms outstretched, his napkin tucked in his shirt between the middle buttons. He holds her face in both brown spotted hands and kisses her cheek. His lips remind me of a triggerfish. Gaga is statue still.

"Thank you, Simon," Gaga says. "Now go sit down."

"That's my angel," Pop Pop says smiling and makes a rolling shuffle to his chair at the head of the table. He picks up the carving knife.

"Rose, how about another piece of meat?" He measures a thick slice.

After dinner, Liz and I do our homework until 8:30, when it is time to leave. Before we put our coats on, Pop Pop gives us a fish-lip kiss and hands us each a dollar bill.

"Don't spend it all in one place," he says, grinning to two astonished faces.

LITTLE BOOK of QUESTIONS

Why can't people sleep with their eyes open?

How does a pebble in your shoe cause so much hurt?

Why doesn't soap get dirty?

Why does a kid in my class have one green eye and one blue eye?

Why is it "I before E except after C"?

Why are fire engines red?

What is a personality?

Why are some ladybugs black?

Why are some freckles big and others are itty-bitty?

Why does Temple have Sunday school on Saturdays?

Why does everyone think Mr. Bonatura is such a good teacher?

Does Dad miss me?

What does bad look like?

Does Pop Pop know his smell is of rumpled clothes, cleaning supplies, and bourbon?

Does he know he and Humpty-Dumpty have the same shaped body?

LITTLE BOOK of QUESTIONS

Why can't people sleep with their eyes open?

How does a pebble in your shoe cause so much hurt?

Why doesn't soap get dirty?

Why does a kid in my class have one green eye and one blue eye?

Why is it "I before E except after C"?

Why are fire engines red?

What is a personality?

Why are some ladybugs black?

Why are some freckles big and others are itty-bitty?

Why does Temple have Sunday school on Saturdays?

Why does everyone think Mr. Bonatura is such a good teacher?

Does Dad miss me?

What does bad look like?

Does Pop Pop know his smell is of rumpled clothes, cleaning supplies, and bourbon?

Does he know he and Humpty-Dumpty have the same shaped body?

What is perfect? Really, what is perfect?

REALLY?

I'm at Katawauk and Mom wrote a letter! I think it's the twenty-second letter in seven years of camp.

Dear Rinnie,

I heard from Evan. He is swimming, running around, playing baseball, and having a good time. He says he needs new shorts and T-shirts the next size down. I am so proud of him. Dr. Edison was right in prescribing the thyroid pills.

Hope you are having fun. Play hard and beat those girls on the tennis team.

Love, Mom

LETTER TWENTY-THREE

Dear Rinnie,

Evan will take a camp shuttle from his camp to the airport, and you should pick him up at the United Airlines gate. He'll wait for you if he gets to the gate before you. From there, the two of you will fly home together.

Don't forget.

Love, Mom

EVAN, WHERE DID YOU GO?

As the Katawauk camp bus drops girls off at the correct airlines, the weather inside the bus changes. The warm feelings of chatter and laughter take a turn toward drizzle.

"Bye, everyone," says a sobbing girl I don't recognize. She blows kisses, and sniffles break out row by row inside the bus.

"See you next year."

"Don't forget to write, or better yet call me!"

"Remember sisters on the court, on the water, and on the stage," another girl says.

A hug fest erupts. Minnie, the bus driver, yells at us to sit down.

No one from my cabin is on the bus, but I know most everyone. My eyes are dry. All my "good-byes" were said at camp. I get to see Verna and Croquette in four hours, and tonight we'll go out for dinner like we always do the first night someone gets home from camp. Yay! Liz will be home in two days. She took a detour to her best camp-friend's house. Mom says it's her last fling before starting private school. I wonder what my last fling will be.

It's 7:30 A.M. when I get to the departure gate and hardly anyone is there. By the time the plane is ready to board, the only other passengers are four men dressed in business suits and a military guy who has been reading a worn-out book about Marilyn Monroe. Sitting next to him on a bench is a handsome, lanky boy with dark hair and a baggy white shirt that camouflages his loose jeans. It looks like a rope is holding his pants up.

Where is my doofus brother? He's supposed to be here, and he's not. The plane is about to board. Where is he? Damn, I'm hot, and I want to take off my sweater. But my hands are filled with the three-pound bag of pistachio nuts Mom sent to camp, a handful of comic books, my purse, and see-you-next-summer letters to read on the plane. I walk by the handsome guy. He's watching me. There is something familiar in his face. Is it his eyes, the color of brown M&M's? I walk past him again and stop to tie my shoe, taking in his angled face and candy eyes.

"Hi," I say, standing in front of him. "Going to Cincinnati?"

"Well, it's about time," rebounds the voice. "What took you so long?"

"Evan, EVAN? Is that you?"

"Duh. I wondered when you'd notice."

"Oh m-my God," I can't get the words out.

"Look!" I say to the serviceman. "Look at my brother! He's gorgeous! Don't you think he's gorgeous? He's so skinny! Isn't he cute?"

Evan jumps up, grabs the dusty duffle bag by his feet, and then my arm. His pants drag on the ground.

"Come on Rinnie, we gotta board."

My feet trip on themselves as I move forward. "He's lost tons of pounds!" I shout. "He's my brother. Doesn't he look great?"

"Shut up. You're such a weirdo."

I follow Evan to our seats. He reaches in my bag for the comic books, and I let him.

"You look great! How much weight did you lose? How did you do it?"

"I dunno. I took the thyroid pills Dr. Edison gave me, and the counselors made me do everything: swim every day, play baseball, volleyball, go mountain climbing, waterskiing, horseback riding. . . . They wouldn't let me eat sugar, butter, and white bread sandwiches—or desserts."

"Did you care about no desserts? No s'mores?"

"Nu-uh. I was too busy. The more weight I lost, the more fun stuff I wanted to do. Look."

Evan uncrumples a piece of paper with a chart on it. It has his weight on it for every week of camp and a line that moves nearly straight down.

"I lost forty-three pounds."

"That's almost half of me!" Evan was a tubbo, but I don't rub it in.

"You were cute in a round sort of way before camp. But now, you're going to need a little black book and new sneakers."

"What for?" Evan says, looking at his dirt-splattered shoes.

"The girls are going to chase you. Good thing you can run now."

"Girls! I'm only eleven!" he boy snorts. "When I run, it'll be playing baseball!"

FIRST DATE

Mom, Dad Barry, Evan, and I are at the top of the stairs looking at family photographs on the walls and waiting for Emmy's call to dinner. Instead, the phone rings, and Emmy calls for Liz. A boy named Donny Glover wants to speak with her.

Red-haired Donny Glover, tall junior high school basket-ball star and not-so-secret crush is on the phone for Liz. When Liz hangs up the phone, she glows red. Donny Glover wants to take her to a movie. It is her first date.

"Wahooey!" Dad Barry shouts, and he slides down the stairs on his stomach.

Croquette scrams out of his way.

"Wahooey. Liz is going on her first date!"

GOT YOU LAST

I look up and the first thing I see is Evan's face. He hangs his tongue out the side of his mouth, grips it between his teeth and winks one eye. The game is on. I have to catch him looking at me, wink, stick my tongue out at him, and then look away before he can do it back to me. But I'm too slow.

"Got you last!" Evan's hand skims my fingertips.

Oh, a doubleheader! He made the face and touched me. Evan hides behind Mom, knocking her umbrella from her hand. The stairs to the National Archives are slippery from the drizzle and make a getaway difficult. Mom is the perfect shelter. Evan knows there's no way I'll bee-buzz around her and risk our game, or the day's calm. This is our first vacation with Dad Barry. His arm is around Mom's shoulders. I can't get to Evan. He's perfectly guarded. We've played this game for years.

Liz stops to read from a brochure. "The National Archives building in Washington, D.C., was built in 1934. Its records date back to 1774 and include the Declaration of Independence, the United States Constitution, and the Bill of Rights."

"That's about 194 years older than you," Dad Barry says. "Keep walking. Let's get out of the gloom."

Two giant vases stand at the top of the stairs.

"Rinnie, these Oriental urns are as tall as you," Dad Barry says, stopping to measure us both as I skim past.

"They're stunning," Mom says, stooping to take a closer look.

A man in a blue uniform and a brimmed hat with gold trim approaches us. "We're proud of these," he says. "They are very old. Ancient, actually. It's remarkable we have a matched set."

"Come on, I want to see the Declaration." I rush to the entrance. When Evan passes me, I poke his leg with my foot. "Got you last," I whisper, and walk inside.

The ceiling towers above me and I wonder what kind of ladder the painter used to reach it. Bronze and glass cases hold documents with fancy pointed letters. A sign says the cases are filled with helium and can be lowered into a fireproof and shockproof safe in case of danger. *That is so cool.*

"Liz, look at the signatures!" I say, hunting for one I recognize—Benjamin Franklin! I can see his hand dipping a quill pen into a pot of ink. I hear the feather scratch on paper, and my eyes zigzag along the looped lines that follow Ben Franklin's signature.

"John Adams, Samuel Adams, John Hancock—pretty impressive," Liz says.

The five of us gawk at maps and hundreds of official papers. The paintings of famous people and of battles stoke our imaginations for most of the afternoon.

Once outside the building, Evan's on my trail again. I face him and step backward; my arms extend like spokes. Closer and closer, Evan slinks toward me, ready to pounce. I shift my weight and my slip-on shoes give way under the wet marble. Something jams hard into my back. My body flails and my arms push against it, sending it crashing down the stairs. The echo explodes like thunder. It's the urn—the very old, ancient actually, porcelain urn.

"Hurry, hurry! We have to get out of here," I yell. I dart to Mom and pull her arm.

Her hands cover her mouth. She's frozen. Dad Barry is still inside.

"Come on!" I yell.

Too late. The man in the blue uniform and gold-trimmed hat hovers over Mom. She flutters her arms in the air. Maybe she wants to fly away. The deep voice of the guard is low, but I hear him ask, "S-H-E-R, correct? Where are you staying?" For a minute, I'm glad my last name is Gardener. Then I look at the wreckage. Can I dig myself out? Dad Barry comes and takes my hand. The guard escorts Mom toward us with a brisk motion.

"We've been told to leave and not return," Mom says. She hustles us to the taxi stand at the bottom of the stairs and lights a cigarette.

"I'm sorry, I didn't see it," I say.

"Enough is enough! You and that stupid game! You're so immature!" she snaps, and looks at me hard. "You almost sent us to jail. It's always something with you. What is your problem?"

"What about Evan?" I say.

"You're older, you should know better," Mom says. She's almost purple. "I'm absolutely mortified."

The only calmness about her is the long draws on her cigarette. I'm glad Dad Barry is here, even if he doesn't talk.

"When we return home, you will write a letter of apology to every member of the board of directors. You'll have plenty of time to do it because you're grounded young lady," Mom says through gritted teeth. "You're supposed to be a mature example for your brother."

I am, just not one you like.

Liz flashes an "I'm glad I'm not you" look and whispers, "How could you not see the urn? It was almost as big as you."

I shrug and whisper back, "I didn't see it, OK?"

NOTE to MYSELF

Dad Barry helps us with homework and talks to us about what's going on in our lives. He doesn't try to be interested. He really is.

GRANDMA SHER II

Grandma Sher is making good on her promise. She stands at our stove filling blintz skins and browning them in butter. A dish towel hangs at her waist, smeared with jam and cheese. There must be a zillion calories on her towel. My mouth weeps at the smell.

"Are they ready, Grandma? Did you make a lot? Will you show me how to roll a blintz?"

"Slowly does it," she says, spreading a spoonful of sweet cheese across an empty shell. We don't want to tear the wrappers." Grandma shows me how to use two forks to fold each side in, sort of like making a bed. Carefully, Grandma puts the pale-filled pancake into the sizzling butter and lifts out a speckled golden one.

The kitchen counters are dredged with flour, sugar, dirty bowls, and melted butter. Verna isn't here to clean the mess. Mom paces around Grandma, confining her to the stove. The olive-green kitchen carpet is powdered white with flour and footprints. We're the only family I know with carpet in the kitchen, and I bet Mom is sorry about that now. When Grandma talks, Mom lights up a cigarette and pretends she doesn't hear. Dad Barry whispers in Mom's ear, and they move toward the door. His voice is soft, but his look is serious. Mom's eyes get squinty. Her hands are on her hips, and her lips move fast.

"Brunch is ready," Grandma says, waiting for everyone to sit down before she abandons her post. Dad Barry and Grandma talk, but we kids eat the blintzes while they are hot. Mom sips coffee, cup after cup.

INGENUITY

It's my fourteenth summer. Evan's eleven, and for the past year there's been talk of him leaving home and going to live with our father. No one asks me what I think, but I have been extra nice (most of the time) to Evan so he will want to stay. Although Dad lives only a mile from us, we don't see him as much as I would like. Officially, we're supposed to be with him every weekend—on Sundays. Unofficially, we visit only if we finish the chores Mom assigns that morning, before Dad arrives to pick us up. Although the maids come almost every day, we still have to clean the house: vacuum, empty ashtrays, dust, straighten the rooms, and be sure Mom's had her two cups of coffee, with cream and sugar, in bed before we're permitted to leave. Dad Barry misses chores. He works at Temple, in the office, on Sunday mornings.

"Should we wake Mom?" I venture, knowing that could be disastrous.

"Well if she sleeps in, we miss Dad," Liz says. "I wish he'd come back later."

"He can't. He has his tennis game. I have an idea—a really good one!"

Fifteen minutes later, I place a carafe of steaming hot coffee and a small container of cream and one of sugar on Mom's nightstand. "This way she can pour it herself," I say, patting myself on the back, but not for long. The aroma of coffee stirs Mom to life. She leans forward on her elbows, glances at the nightstand and collapses onto her back.

"What's that?" Mom says.

"Look, Mom, now you can have your coffee whenever you're ready. You don't have to wait for us to get it. There's sugar and cream and a little napkin, too," I say.

"OK, smarty-pants."

Here we go.

This isn't going to work. Mom's voice follows the back-and-forth rock of her head.

"I'm not ready for my coffee. I've only been up ten seconds. And by the time I get ready, the coffee will be cold. I want one of you girls to bring the coffee when I ask and check back fifteen minutes later. If the cup is empty, then it's time for the second cup. What's so hard about bringing me hot coffee? Two cups please."

A BRIEF MISTAKE

It's February. The cold outside seeps inside, too. Dad Barry has helped warm up the house by smothering frustration with laughter. Things loosen up after he marries Mom. It's good and then it's bad. It takes nineteen months, and then the pretty ribbon that wraps us together unravels. Mom prefers Carl, the house painter. Carl with the twinkly-blue eyes, tan skin, blond hair, easygoing hello, and smile with an open slot for a missing tooth. Carl has something Dad Barry doesn't. Mom says Dad Barry isn't man enough for her. I'm not sure what that means.

Evan wants to move to Dad's house. He can't stand the sadness and dishonesty. He hasn't learned how to forge a wall of steel between himself and other people yet. He doesn't know how much strength five hundred calories a day gives you. But I do. Every calorie I don't eat is a deposit in the "Bank of Being Me." It makes me stronger. I haven't saved enough yet. Mom says she needs a getaway, and she wants me to be in the getaway car with her. I don't get a vote about divorcing Dad Barry, and I don't get a vote about keeping Mom company in Colorado.

TICKET to PARADISE

Liz is at Gaga and Pop Pop's while Mom and I are in Colorado.

It's odd being alone with Mom. My grandparents are the ones who take me on trips. I use the time to explain to Mom why she can't see Carl.

"The lawyer says it's the surest and fastest way to lose Evan. You won't have a chance to keep Evan if you have a relationship with Carl." What judge would give custody to a mother who runs around with a boozer, while she's still married to someone else? I don't say this last sentence.

Mom promises me everything will be OK. Mom says she wants to take me to a special restaurant for lunch—to celebrate our trip. I feel happy. The host leads us to our table. Waiting for us is Carl. I'm not a travel companion at all. I'm an excuse to travel.

MORE CARL

Mom smiles at Carl and tilts her head enough that I notice she's doing what I do when I'm flirting. Carl pulls out her chair, winks, and gives me a big grin and an extended hand. It's oddly clean, no paint under his nails, or in the creases of his palm.

Carl orders a milkshake, extra thick. "Hey," he says, "What did the teacher say to the kids who were slow learners?"

I pause.

"Ketchup," he says before I can even figure out why he's asking. "What school do you go to, to learn to greet people?" This time he waits.

"Hi-school?" I say.

"They're teachin' you good at that school," he smiles. "Still liking the flowers I painted on the doors of your bedroom closet? They came out pretty darn good for a first try," he says. "It's a big change from painting walls."

"They're very pretty," I say.

Mom changes the subject and tells Carl how happy she is to see him. Carl tells us about his cowboy adventure on horseback yesterday. Mom rotates the conversation from herself to Carl and back again while we eat until the waitress brings the check.

I guess Carl's not so bad. He's easygoing, a jokester, nice to me. On the other hand, he isn't as well educated as my family. He smells like whiskey, and he has a wife and kids in Kentucky. Carl has a feel for people, though, and keeps Mom off my back. When she's with him, I may as well be on Mars.

This time is no different. After lunch, we take the Pike's Peak Cog Railway to the top of the mountain.

Carl pulls a cigarette from his shirt pocket and pokes it between his lips and says, as well as he can, "Why don't you run to that boulder over there?"

"OK," I say and wonder why he wants me to do that. I take off. By the time I reach the boulder, I have to hang my head between my legs.

"The air is so thin up here it grabs the air right outta ya, eh peaches," Carl says.

"Yeah," I gasp. When I look up, a guy in uniform stands above me smiling.

"You must be a flatlander," he says. "Me, too. I'm stationed at Fort Carson now." I don't know what he's talking about and he can tell. "Fort Carson, the army base," he says, his voice rising, "But I'm an Okie through and through."

He shows me a wavy blue rectangle on his arm. Centered on it is a brown circular shape and arrows and a branch with leaves.

"This little beauty is a tattoo of the Oklahoma state flag. Yes ma'am. I'm an Okie through and through. And a gentleman," he adds. "Do you need a hand up?"

"I've got it," I say. His outstretched hand is smooth, but calloused and doesn't look like it belongs to such a boyish face.

Carl must think I need a playmate and invites the Okie along for the day. When he accepts, I'm surprised Mom allows an older guy, and a stranger, to be my companion, but I don't say anything. Instead, I run my fingers comb-like through my hair to make it look better and thank myself for shaving my legs that morning and putting on makeup. We tour a cave, drive through the Garden of the Gods, and climb among Indian ruins. All the while, I'm ma'amed and complimented. Before dinner, we stop at the two-bedroom, out-of-the-way cottage Mom says she's paid for. Mom and Carl go into one room, and the Okie and I are left to talk in the other.

He wants to do other things. In half a giggle, he's on top of me. I struggle to stop him from undressing me. His belt buckle presses into the space between my pelvic bones.

"Help!" My voice shakes. "Help!"

Carl darts from the other room, wrestles the Okie off me, and pushes him toward the door. The soldier looks like a little boy: huge eyes, dropped jaw, bewildered. He tugs up his pants, jabs the air with his middle finger, snatches his jacket off the floor, and stumbles into the driveway yelling. He's not ma'aming me now.

"Let's go to dinner," Carl says, with an "Ahem." Mom picks up her purse and jean jacket, glances at me, gives Carl the car keys, and they are out the door.

I rearrange myself, tuck my flannel shirt into my jeans, finger brush my hair, and leave the cottage. There is no conversation about the Okie.

The next day, Mom and I move to a regular hotel with a lobby for talking. Our room has twin beds and light green walls. It's pretty. There is a desk and a cow-skin covered chair across from my bed. Along another wall is a window with curtains that match the bedspread. The window is open to the Colorado sky. Today, we ate breakfast at a historic hotel and drove to the Royal Gorge in Canon City. The second-highest suspension bridge in the world crosses the gorge. I looked down and spit. Now it's night and constellations fill our window. There's a crescent moon. Its curve is perfect to hang a wish on. It has been a good day, just Mom and me. Now it is time to get a good rest.

I wake to squeaks and movement from Mom's bed. It's dark and impossible to see, but I can feel. Something isn't right. Someone is in bed with Mom. I hear groaning. The blanket moves up and down rhythmically. They are doing something I don't want to know about. I grab a robe from the end of my bed and steal out of the room. My stomach's queasy. The elevator takes me to the lobby. There, I use an empty armchair for a bed. I fold my legs up to my chin and rest my head on my knees. It's quiet.

In the morning, Mom shakes me awake. She doesn't ask why I left the room. She doesn't say a thing.

I hate them. I want to be another person in any other place.

"You're losing Evan, you know."

Mom tells me to be quiet. "There was no reason for you to leave the room last night."

She's angry and doesn't care that I hate her not caring. Carl's disappeared. He left after our "night together." Two days pass. We haven't seen Carl. When she isn't on the phone, or at the hotel, Mom drives around and drags me in and out of bars looking for him. One bar is like another, dim and smelly. Sunlight turns to moonlight.

A car with bright lights pulls into the parking lot of the bar behind us. A man and woman are in the car. Carl wobbles out. He's drunk, and he smells. Mom runs to him. She yells and begs him to stay with her. I call to her but she doesn't answer. She grabs for Carl. He hits Mom, knocking her to the ground. I am scared and run to help.

"Mom, are you OK, are you OK?" I cry, stroking her forehead.

She bats her arm at me.

"Go away," she says. "Leave me alone. Go away."

Where am I to go?

NOTE to MYSELF

Dinner was a disaster. Mom is out again. I ate standing over the sink: Three grapes, five nibbles of salmon (one ounce?), five artichoke leaves, bowl of lettuce with sliced cucumber and green pepper, four green olives, one quarter slice corned beef, two teaspoons jam—from the jar, big gulp milk, one sugar-free frozen yogurt bar, two bites spinach casserole (egg whites, spinach, salt, parmesan cheese), two salted almonds, and two raisins. I'm glad it's time to go to sleep. No more food. I swear I'll do better tomorrow.

BIG SHOES

"If Carl calls, remember, don't tell your grandfather," Mom says. "It's very important you don't tell Pop Pop. Rinnie, do you hear me?"

"Yes," I drawl, not looking up. I go back to reading about the fall of the Roman Empire in my world history book.

The phone rings. "Hello? This is Rinnie."

"It's Michael Seiden. Is your mother there?"

It's Mom's lawyer, again. Does Mom tell Michael that Carl calls her? I want to tell him Carl calls, but this is legal stuff—big stuff—and I'm not supposed to get involved. I hand the phone to Mom.

"Yes. No. I haven't talked to anyone," she says.

Her fingers move up and down dusting the air. She wants me to leave and close the door to the den.

There's nothing I want to hear. I already know too much. Carl has moved into my mom's life, and Dad Barry has moved out.

It's strange not having Dad Barry here, to ask if I need help in math, to lose to in gin rummy, and to run interference between Mom and me. I miss his big grin and droopy nose. I miss the face that echoes Grandma Sher.

It's strange not hearing Dad Barry and Pop Pop talk business on Monday nights when we eat at my grandparent's house. Dad Barry never liked working for Pop Pop. He's an accountant at heart, not a distributor of restaurant and kitchen equipment. My father left big shoes to fill when he stopped working for Pop Pop. And Pop Pop begged him to stay.

"It's difficult to find a vice president with your father's work ethic, intelligence, charisma, and foresight," Pop Pop told us after the divorce.

Poor Barry.

The tinkle of crystal beads drifts from the dining room. Someone must be moving the candleholders. The tinkling sounds like the swing of charms on my mother's gold bracelet. The prettiest charm is the circle of flowers dotted with a ruby, an emerald, a sapphire, and a diamond. Dad Barry gave it to Mom on their first wedding anniversary. Tiny letters engraved on the back of the charm say, "For Rose, the loveliest bloom of all." I remember Dad Barry's face, all shiny, eyes crinkly, when he gave her the gift box.

Now he's moved away. I was just getting to know him. I just started calling him Dad.

INTEGRITY

"Rinnie, I have to go see Michael. I'll be back by six. Tell Evan no television until his homework is finished," Mom says. She's in such a rush she forgets her purse and has to come back inside. "If anyone calls—anyone, tell them I'll be back by six."

I nod and continue to read. Final exams are in a week. The phone rings.

"Is your mother there?'

"Carl?"

Silence. "How you doing, peaches?"

"I'm fine. Mom's not here."

"When will she be back?

"I'm not sure, maybe six."

"Tell her I called."

I stare at my book, but my mind reviews Pop Pop's orders. "Tell me if Carl calls." I pick up the phone then place the receiver down and squeeze my head to stop the swirling inside.

I'm the rope in tug-of-war. I don't want to lie, and I don't want Mom to punish me.

Pop Pop says, "Each time your mother sees or talks to Carl, she makes her situation worse. She's complicating her divorce and hurting your grandmother. If I don't know about the calls, I can't do anything to help."

Mom warns me, "If you tell your grandfather Carl called, he will be furious with me, and you'll upset your grandmother. It will be your fault I'm in trouble."

I want to do the right thing. The rope strangles me. What is the right thing?

Do I call Pop Pop? Do I relay Carl's message to Mom? If I don't and she finds out—I'll be grounded again, or lose the phone in my room, or not get my allowance. I want to keep my plans with Jack for Saturday night. I'll tell her. I'll tell her after I call Pop Pop.

LEGALITIES

Everyone warns Mom: Gaga, Pop Pop, her lawyer, Liz, and me. But something didn't click. Carl stays. Evan goes. The judge doesn't have to rule about Liz and me. Dad thinks we should stay together. He says three more kids are too many to take. Allyson already has to drive Alana, Amy, and Jake around.

NOTE to MYSELF

Doubleheader could describe this week. Two major events were finalized: ninth grade final exams (Latin exam was awful) and saying good-bye to Evan.

Not sure which was harder. Actually I am sure, but I don't want to think about it.

REPLACEABLE

We stand outside Dad's house. I'm finally alone with him.

"Why didn't you ask Liz and me to live with you?" I ask Dad. "You're so busy. We never get to talk anymore." It's been nearly four months since Liz and I have been Mom's only housemates. I miss Evan.

"Allyson and the kids need me. You have your Pop Pop to take care of you," Dad says. "You and Liz need to stick together and be with your mom."

I need you. I want to say. *It's so easy for you to rearrange your life and so hard for me to be pushed aside.*

But I know there isn't enough room between the garage and the bushy philodendron that grows on the sill of the kitchen window or any place on the planet for this conversation. If I upset Dad, he will want to spend even less time with me. Things grow here. I want to be a part of this.

Though it's late autumn, unusually warm, and we wear shorts, I'm chilled when he speaks. My arms and legs prickle with goose bumps.

"It's good for Evan to live with me. A son needs a father. Unfortunately, there is space for only one bedroom in the attic."

Through the kitchen window, I see Allyson water the robust philodendron. Her white teeth glisten against her tan skin, intensifying the darkness of her eyes. Mahogany-streaked hair spills from the opening in the back of her baseball cap. No wonder Dad wants her. She's beautiful, and Alana's her physical clone. Dad traded Liz and me for Allyson and her kids.

"Excuse me." I dash to the bathroom. I hate that my eyes blur and sting. I hate that Dad should see this.

When the bathroom door closes, the full-length mirror on the back of the door reflects the muted pink walls that blend into the muted pearl-colored floor. I feel as if I'm inside a giant shell. The mirror's gold-dusted frame embraces me in its perfect rectangular world. The pastel colors join in a silent lullaby to calm me. I am protected. A miniature gold crown and a tarnished silver hand mirror rest on a plaid upholstered table. The crown belonged to Grandpa Gardener's mother, and it's covered with rhinestones. I place it on my head and stare into the mirror.

"The Queen is not amused," I say. "Today, the Queen has a proclamation. I proclaim that stepchildren of the same age may not try out against each other for school teams. They are not permitted to be in the same class at school. They may not even enroll in the same school."

What were Dad and Allyson thinking when they transferred Alana to my school? Did they think I wouldn't notice? Did they think of me at all?

Every day of the school year, I carry more than books in my backpack. I lug extra assignments, one from Mom and one from myself. Mom's was specific, "Be better than Alana. Dress better, look prettier, study harder, be smarter, act funnier, have more friends." The assignment I assign myself is harder to achieve. Be perfect. Dad and Mom might want me then.

I dislodge the crown from my hair and place it back on the table next to the hand mirror. Can happily ever after happen?

EVAN

Right from the start, I knew my baby brother and I would be buddies. Everything about him was likable: His chubby cheeks, his curly black hair that formed the letter C on his forehead, his pink gums wet with drool, and his two tiny white teeth. I especially liked his sparkly eyes that reminded me of shiny pennies. I always wanted to take him to preschool for show and tell.

I looked out for Evan. When he fell and skinned his knee, I was the one who held his hand and washed away the blood. "Call me Nurse Rinnie, and then pretend I'm the wind," I'd say, as I blew away the sting of soap and water.

I taught Evan to climb the maple tree by first holding onto the split branch. "Hold one limb in each hand and walk up the tree until you can grip a higher branch, then pull yourself up. I'll push from the bottom."

I taught him to ride his bike with no hands and the value of giving in when I sat on his back and slugged his shoulders.

He taught me to tie the knots he learned in Cub Scouts, to build model planes, and to give in peaceably if I didn't strike a bargain when he tortured my friends with his stupid ideas.

We entertained each other with knock-knock jokes, pickle-eating contests, playing cards, and squishing gooey red berries on each other. We did homework together, shared a bathroom, and got sick at the same time. We told ghost stories in the dark, wrestled, and played basketball. Then one day, life changed. We used to be such good friends, Evan and me. Will we ever be again?

COOKING LESSON

"Theo's coming over for lunch, and I told him I'd make it myself."

"He's a really good boyfriend to take you up on your offer. What are you making?" I ask Liz. "It's a good day for something hot like chili."

"I'm making Theo's favorite, hotdogs and salad. But I need your help."

In the eight months Liz and Theo have dated, Liz has never cooked anything for him or anyone else. She's better at drying dishes. It takes three seconds to figure out what Liz wants: instructions.

"The key is getting the lettuce really clean—no grit. Wash the lettuce with soap and make sure it's absolutely clean because lettuce spiders bury their eggs in the leaves."

"How do you know?" Liz asks.

"Verna told me," I say, crossing my fingers behind my back.

Liz separates the lettuce leaves and searches for spider eggs as if she's performing an autopsy. She squirts a drop of detergent on each leaf and massages the thin membranes with the tips of her fingers, then rinses the leaves in warm water.

"Gently," I say. "Be gentle. Now, dry the leaves with a towel. Be sure to get all the wet spots."

Liz pats and dabs at the slips of green.

"How's this?" she says, handing me a leaf.

"Still a little wet," I say handing it back to her.

She dries it a second time.

"One more light mop around the middle," I say, handing the leaf back to her a third time. Liz presses the lettuce with her towel.

"Good. Now tear the lettuce into a bowl and toss in some raw vegetables. Time for the hot dogs." I reach under the stove, grab a pot, and fill it with water. "Put the hot dogs in the water and boil them for thirty-six minutes. The important thing is to turn them without stopping, or they will cook too long on one side."

Liz sets a timer and her attention to the bubbling hot dogs, turning them slowly, evenly, continually. The scent of hot dogs saturates the house. Croquette whines for a taste.

"You're doing great, even Croquie approves."

The doorbell rings.

"Keep stirring. I'll get it." I sprint to the door.

"Hi, Rin. Smells good . . . like hot dogs," Theo says, dropping his coat over the banister.

"It is hot dogs. Liz is in the kitchen. She's been turning them in boiling water for the past thirty-one minutes," I tell him. Theo crinkles his forehead and knuckles my head.

"Hi Theo. Lunch will be ready in five minutes," Liz yells.

"I hope she's making something else," he says.

"She is," I reply. "History."

DR. DIDIER

The station wagon glides over the blacktopped road. The ride is smooth, like the unbroken ice that lines the side of the road.

"There is someone I want you to meet," my mother says. My daydream of cantering over the treeless hills, breathing in the smells of grass and horses stumbles over her voice, and then comes to a halt. One more year and *I'll* be behind the driver's wheel, steering my life.

"What?" I say.

"A friend of mine wants to meet you. I've told her all about you."

"Why can't you tell me why we're here? I could be washing my hair for Lesley's party tonight."

Should I straighten my hair or let it frizz? Mom pulls into a driveway and jingles the keys out of the ignition.

"This is it," she says.

I follow my mother up a slight slope and into the overly bright foyer of a one-story building.

"In here." Mom gestures, opening the door to a room the size of her walk-in closet. A hook by the door holds keys. One dangles from pink beads that spell out *bathroom.* On the opposite wall is a picture of a lake with a lone person in a canoe. It reminds me of last summer at Camp Katawauk. Three of us stole a canoe and paddled to the far side of the lake to spy on the boys' camp. That night, we had a dance with their camp. I met a boy named Will, and we wrote letters to each other the rest of the summer.

He was a year older than I was and filled me in on what tenth grade would be like. "It's kind of the same as ninth grade, just more intense," he said. "You really have to think ahead to college and apply yourself." I thought he knew everything.

The place is silent as Mom and I sit on the bench, waiting for her friend. A woman opens the door. She smells sweet, like peach incense.

"Hello, Rose," she says beckoning Mom to follow her. "You must be Rinnie," she continued. "I am Dr. Didier."

"Wait here," she says pointing to the bench. There is no cushion on the bench, and "here" is uncomfortable.

Finally, the door opens again.

"Come in, Rinnie," the doctor says softly.

The décor is creamy. Two thick leather chairs, the color of buttermilk, rest next to a small table that looks like a footbridge between weathered rocks. Mom sits in one chair, the doctor in the other. I step past a coffee table covered with magazines to a nubby sofa. The room feels sanitized—in a well-done way. Everything matches—even the maple picture frames above the sofa hold documents the color of wheat. Their black letters jump at me, " . . . Dr. of Psychiatry . . . " A psychiatrist!

No one speaks. It is lushly uncomfortable.

Then Dr. Didier says, "Rinnie, I believe in being straightforward. I hope you can appreciate this."

"OK," I say.

"Rinnie, your mother says that you are incorrigible. She says you are, well, out of control. A real problem."

I tilt my head, ears up, to catch the falling words. All I hear is rappa-rappa-rappa. There's a machine gun. I'm paralyzed. I clutch my throat. I'm not paralyzed. Rappa-rappa-rappa. It's my heart! Can they hear it too?

"Rinnie, your mother says you make her life miserable."

Pause.

"Rinnie?"

"Mom?"

Mom's face is expressionless. It could be cardboard.

She crosses her legs and plants her purse like a shield. Her blue eyes dart like quicksilver. There's something spiteful in her silence. Something removed. As if she is a puppeteer, pulling the strings on a marionette.

The strings yank my neck and unlock my voice. I do not recognize the sound. The girl inside my changing body, who believes in fairness, is drowning. Her last words struggle to surface.

I rocket to my feet, while the world turns to a teary blur. "That's not true! That's not true! It isn't true!" This is a trick. Mothers don't set their children up. Mothers don't lie, not like this. "Mom?"

The tears run inside me, and I choke. Just tell the truth, Rin, just tell the truth. But if I do, I'll sound "belligerent." Who would believe me? The doctor? Mom's ally?

"It's a lie! It's a lie!"

"Your outburst is unwarranted and uncontrolled," the therapist says. "We've seen enough. Leave the room."

I glance at Mom. "How could you?" I clench my arms and leave my shadow in the line of fire.

On the way out, I hear Mom murmur, "I told you she was a monster."

The ride home over the black pavement is cold as ice. There is no horse cantering across the hills. I ache. Where is the nice mommy to stroke my head? Where is the nice mommy to sing away my pain and tell stories with happy endings?

There must have been a few times when Mom was proud of me. Was it at the country club when the mommies sat at the edge of the pool talking and laughing? I clung to Mom's legs, counting her freckles. She liked my watery hugs, and I liked riding her legs as they pushed back and forth through the clear water. Was it when she took Liz and me fancy-clothes shopping at Franchons?

"Ohhh, the fabrics are stunning. The attention to detail is simply incredible. Look at the satin roses on the cuffs of this lace dress," she'd gush. Liz and I played tea party under the clothes racks while Mom picked out things for us to try on. Mom liked to buy pretty things. Was she happy then?

The good memories with Mom feel warm. I wish I had more.

"Come into my parlor," said the spider to the fly, "'Tis the prettiest little parlor you ever did spy. . . ."

SOCIAL ACTION

Sometimes it's hard to tell who likes Theo more, Mom or Liz. Occasionally, Theo includes Mom in his and Liz's plans, which makes Mom swoon.

"She's always hanging around. It's hard not to invite her," he says. "Besides, I like her. And she likes that I like her."

Theo's right. Mom likes him more than any of our other male friends, and she wants him around, even if it breaks her rule: "No boys upstairs."

Mom once said, "If bad weather makes it too dangerous to drive home, your dates can spend the night." So far, my dates have always gone home. Not so for Theo.

Tonight, Mom invites Theo to spend the night. It's not pouring outside. There's no blizzard, no tornado warning, the roads aren't icy. But Theo will spend the night because Mom wants him to. Does Liz want him to stay? Maybe yes, maybe no. In the end, it's not up to her. I'm some kind of alien here—when I say I won't vacate my room, I become "the problem." Mom and Theo are a team. I have to sleep in Liz's single bed, and she and Theo will sleep in my double bed.

I want to scream, but who's listening?

NOTE to MYSELF

I form a circle with my two arms and step inside it. If I can slide my circled fingers to the middle of my thigh on both legs, and keep my fingertips within an inch and a half of one another, I'll eat real earth food. How much harm can a chocolate kiss be? Better than one that's unwanted.

ANOTHER NOTE to MYSELF

I clasp my thumb and my pointer finger around my wrist.
There is a window of light between my fingers and my wrist.
Wiggle room. I need it when someone gets under my skin.
Flesh doesn't stretch like latex.

LITTLE BOOK of QUESTIONS

Why can't people sleep with their eyes open?

How does a pebble in your shoe cause so much hurt?

Why doesn't soap get dirty?

Why does a kid in my class have one green eye and one blue eye?

Why is it "I before E except after C"?

Why are fire engines red?

What is a personality?

Why are some ladybugs black?

Why are some freckles big and others are itty-bitty?

Why does Temple have Sunday school on Saturdays?

Why does everyone think Mr. Bonatura is such a good teacher?

Does Dad miss me?

What does bad look like?

Does Pop Pop know his smell is of rumpled clothes, cleaning supplies, and bourbon?

Does he know he and Humpty-Dumpty have the same shaped body?

What is perfect? Really, what is perfect?

Why can't Katawauk go on forever?

Could I be a counselor at camp next year?

SUNDAYS

Dad's Jaguar rolls into the driveway, and he honks the horn. In a few weeks, I'll be able to do that with no supervised driver.

"My turn to sit next to Dad," I say, even though I know it isn't.

"You sat next to him last Sunday," Liz says, inching her way in front of me.

"It's Liz's turn," Dad interrupts. "She missed the last two weekends."

Three stop signs and two red lights later, we make a slow turn into the driveway at his house.

"OK, you guys," Dad says. "I've got some work to do. Alana and Amy have friends over and Jake's at baseball practice. Allyson made sandwiches for lunch. Help yourselves. We'll catch up later."

Alana and I are stepsisters, not buddies. Our friends aren't the same, and I don't want to hang out with them. Amy's four years younger than I am, and we have nothing in common. It's been this way for nearly three years. I'm only a couple of miles from my house, but I might as well be on another planet.

I try to find something wrong with the comfortable furniture; the mustard-colored carpet, and the artistic way Allyson has arranged the crystal and china trinkets in the living room. I search for bad lighting, cabinets with no snacks, or dirty piles of laundry. There must be something wrong. There must be something wrong because I never feel welcome here.

I am afraid to touch things: the gold and glass bowl on the iron table, the delicate porcelain flowers in the Chinese vase, the silver filigree frames that look ancient. Nothing says we want you here. Photographs of Allyson's family line the walls. There is only one of Liz, Evan, and me. It's on Dad's desk in his office. I need permission here—can we bake brownies? Is it OK to drink the juice? Can I go upstairs to Alana's and Amy's rooms? Upstairs belongs to the children that live here.

We watch TV and wait for later when Dad has time to talk, and then we talk about school.

"Are you doing your best?" Dad asks.

Before it's time to go home, we eat dinner. Allyson makes Rice-A-Roni and roast chicken every time we visit. It must be her specialty. Alana, Amy, and Jake talk about friends from the neighborhood and funny times when Grandma Gardener visited them. I'm quiet. At eight o'clock, it's time to go home. The Jaguar flies out of Dad Land and lands in my universe.

"Hi, Mom. We're back."

UNBELIEVABLE

Pop Pop wrote a letter. Stamped on the front of the envelope is a picture of a bald eagle on a six-cent stamp. In the corner are the words:

"Miss Rinnie Gardener

Senior Bunk

Camp Katawauk

Denmark, Maine"

Gaga and Pop Pop NEVER write—ever! I do and don't want to open the letter. The envelope feels thin. It can't be more than a page. What if Croquette died? What if something else bad happened? Then I remember. Pop Pop took Liz to New York for a long weekend after school ended. We were eating dinner at his house when he broke the news.

"Number One," he gruffed. "How would you like to go to New York and see Times Square and the play *Sleuth*?"

"Yes, Yes, Yes!" Liz cried. "I definitely want to go to New York."

"Simon, you can't take Liz without Rinnie. It's not nice and Rinnie worked as hard in school as Lizzie," Gaga said.

"I'm not taking Liz because she worked hard in school. I'm taking her because I think she'll have fun. She loves theater."

"Theater or not, don't you think the girls would have more fun together?"

"My mind is made up. Rinnie, maybe we'll go to New York next year."

Gaga didn't press and Pop Pop didn't budge. I think he feels guilty.

I am shocked and have to reread his letter:

Dear Rinnie,

I hope camp is fun and keeping you on your toes. Do every activity you can. It costs a lot of money for me to send you there. I'm sure you are one of the top tennis players in camp and will win a Blue ribbon in the annual horse show. Remember to wear your riding helmet and wash your hands as soon as you're done horsing around. When you get home, I'll tell you about my coup in the stock market this week. Maybe we can go to dinner at your favorite restaurant when you get home.

Love, Pop Pop

I'm glad he did well in the market this week. It means he'll be nicer to Mom.

I CAN DO IT

Dear Mom,

I wish Camp Katawauk lasted all year. It's worth counting all my clothes seven times. Here's a list of the good things so far. (Some of this you already know.)

I'm second doubles on the tennis team.

Our next swim meet is tomorrow, and it's against Camp Pine Meadow. Remember, we sunk them last year? Thanks for the advanced stroke lessons over the winter.

Marie (the riding instructor) says I'm definitely going on the four-day riding trip and can ride Little Guy, my favorite pony. YEAH!

My oil painting is finished! It's my all-time best. I have an artist's tattoo—oil paint under my fingernails.

Life is like a sundae with all the toppings.

We played matches in tennis to see who would make the team. I was tied a set apiece, 6–3, 4–6, with my opponent. In the first game of the third set, I double-faulted twice in a row and flubbed a return. I was so mad at myself—after all my hours practicing, sweating, and shriveling in the muggy Maine heat.

The tennis instructors beat us (little joke) with the phrase, "Your serve is the only stroke you have total control over. Make it count."

I slowed down and won the last set, 7–5. Yay! They don't call me "Ace" for nothing.

I was like the girl in the book you gave me, Champions Don't Cry. *I didn't give up.*

Riding is the best though. Marie calls me her Little Flower and lets me help around the stables. I shovel muck, curry the horses, and make sure each horse's halter and saddle is hung in the right place. My friend Kris and I are the only campers who get to do this. Marie teases me about wearing a bra. She says I don't need one. That's because she doesn't wear one. It's mortifying when she says this in front of the stable boys. Next weekend, her husband, Kirk (remember him—he was here last year), will join her at camp. He calls me "Marie's Little Flower."

My campfire clothes are perfect! It's a vacation not to wear green or white shorts. I've gotten tons of compliments on my Hawaiian shirt and hot pink pants. Thanks for sending my bulky striped turtleneck sweater. Better four weeks late than never.

Now you can see why camp is so wonderful. It's like the other side of the world. I used to think air currents held birds in the sky. But now I think it's the freedom to fly that keeps them overhead.

Can't wait to hear from you.

Love, Rinnie

P.S. This is what I have used up or replaced. Toothpaste, soap, hair elastics (I lost them), stamps, and batteries for my flashlight.

DO YOU MISS ME?

Dear Mom,

Please write to me. My mailbox is collecting spiders and dead flies.

Love, Rinnie.

P.S. I've read all my comic books and am saving them for Evan to read.

DO I MISS YOU?

Yes, I miss everything about you, Katawauk: the smell of pine trees after the rain, walking on soft brown pine needles, the lake shimmering in the sunset, canoeing, sailing, and even diving into your way-too-cold water. I miss sitting on the big rock next to the canoe house—my pew—my place to listen to the waves pull themselves from the lake onto my feet, sponging my ankles, and the owls that hoot at night while the bats dart overhead.

Yes, I miss you. The friendships you offer, the teamwork you insist on, and your opportunities to learn, practice, and become skilled at things like archery, tennis, and riding. And you gave me the chance to discover a different life. I really miss you.

RITUAL

In the dark of night, under the covers, I lie back on the mattress. My pillows are above my head. I put my hands on my diaphragm and touch my ribs. "One, two, three. . . ."

I count as I feel each one. My hands follow the curve of my torso, which slants downward like a sledding hill. My hands stop when they reach the flatlands—the sunken valley between my pelvic bones. The bones rise from my abdomen like high, steep hills. I turn on my right side and place my right arm under my head. My left hand finds the circumference of my upper right arm. The measurement is unchanged. My hand still wraps around the top of my arm with ease. It's time to close my eyes. It's time for good dreams.

NOTE to MYSELF

Today, Verna saw me wrapped in a bath towel. She came to my room to put my clean clothes away. She looked at my shoulders and legs and exclaimed, "Where's your cushioning girl? Your face is looking like it needs some blowing up! If you're plannin' to Chanukah shop with your sister, you're gonna need long underwear to warm those skinny legs."

I took it as a compliment. I'm smiling.

SOAPSUDS

Now that Dad Barry is gone, Mom says, "There's no reason to keep Emmy here at night when you girls can cook dinner and clean up afterward. You can stay up later to complete your homework."

Mom has no idea how much work the teachers pour on in the beginning of the year. They must think students don't need sleep. I think it's a law at Cincinnati Girls' School (CGS), the private school we attend, that girls have at least five hours of homework a night, which means by the time we grab a snack after school, prepare dinner, eat, and clean up, we'll get to bed by midnight.

Liz and I make an efficiency plan. I cook. Liz sets the table, fills the water glasses, and lends me a hand. We both clear the dishes, wash, dry, and put them away, wipe down the counters, throw the napkins down the chute, shake out the tablecloth, and sweep the floor. Mom can't figure out what takes us so long, and we don't tell her. We take our time with the dishwashing part.

Our time may be hijacked but not our partnership.

Liz is the dishwashing lady in the TV commercial that says, "The plate's so clean, I can see myself." She holds the plate like a mirror and angles it to catch the light.

I do the rinsing. My hands plunge into the water, slosh it around, and clutch a clean plate. "My hands are so soft . . . they could be mistaken for a baby's behind," I trill.

Mom makes this a job. Liz and I make it our half hour of fame.

JACK

The first time I hear Jack's voice, I want to strangle him.

"Go, shorty, man on your tail . . . pass, pass . . . move those legs!"

His voice chases me up and down Cincinnati Girls' School's hockey field, and I bolt. I'm left wing because I'm fast, but not faster than the speed of sound. Who is that? Why is he picking on me?

"Go shorty, GO!" prods his voice.

Guys from Cincinnati Prep Academy for Boys often come by after school to watch our intramural games. After that game, Jack shows up every time we play. One day after a game, he sticks a gold star on my forehead.

"You deserve this," he says. "You shine." I bite my lip and smile.

It's not hockey season anymore. Now I play basketball in gym. But Jack still gives me stars, and now he shines for me.

NOTE to MYSELF

I left lunch on the counter at home. School served cheese-burgers with baked beans . . . again! Potato chips, cinnamon applesauce—the kind made by adding Red Hots candy. Beans and cinnamon applesauce on the DO NOT EAT LIST I made as a guide. This must be a Halloween meal—food disguised as good for you—too many carbohydrates, too many calories. I took the cheeseburger out of the bun and squeezed it between two napkins to get rid of grease—gross but effective.

I'M HERE TOO

The screaming wakes me.

Please, please let Liz be in bed. Make it so it isn't happening again. Let her sleep. The ranting grows louder.

"You damn kids! I can't think straight, between you and your grandfather."

I walk the hall to Liz's room. The bed sheets are flung back, signaling a hasty exit.

Why doesn't Mom wake me? I knock on Mom's door, blocking out the muffled tirade about life's hardships. "Please let me come in. What's wrong?"

"Go back to bed," Mom snaps.

"Liz is in there. She's always there, but you never wake me."

I put my ear to the door and hear, "Damn lawyer . . . Pop Pop calls him, the lawyer calls me, and I have to call them both. It's driving me crazy. You kids don't cooperate. . . ."

Big sobs. I rattle the knob, more sobs. Mom is crying, and Liz's voice is slow. "It's late. I'm tired Mom."

"Let me in. *I* can help," I plead.

"Shut up! Go to bed! It's 3:00 A.M."

"The noise woke me, let me in."

Liz opens the door, slack-bodied. "I can't take anymore. It's been hours. I'm going to bed."

"Nobody cares," Mom says. "If I weren't here, you girls wouldn't notice. It doesn't matter if I'm alive or dead."

"Good night, Mom! I have school tomorrow," Liz goes to her room. I help her remake her bed.

"Damn it. All you think about is yourselves," Mom barks.

"Mom always wakes you. She never wants me."

"You're lucky," Liz says. "I wish she'd let me sleep. Go to bed." She rolls over and pulls the sheets around her head. I cross back to Mom's room.

"Mom? Mom? Goodnight, Mom."

"Nobody cares," she cries, shutting the door.

November isn't a month to be thankful for.

TWO POEMS

POEM NUMBER ONE

If
Mom
is right,
the best thing about me
is
my hair.
I'm
lacking
charm.
Painted instead
with strokes of
selfishness, stupidity, troublemaking.
What to do?
Hide
the flaw.
Decorate
the surface.
Streak hair, reduce waist, sculpt limbs.
Looking good.
I'm
dressed to flirt,
to tease,
to please.
Mannequin,
me.

POEM NUMBER TWO

Every day,
Every night,
I go to war.
Against myself.
Eat, Whack!
Binge, Stab!
Starve, Thump!
Ambushed by thought.
"Let me alone,
I've suffered enough,"
I cry to my master.
My regiment of Rules
rush in,
Double-edged swords in hand.
"Follow us. We'll protect you."
And when I don't,
rules cut me down.
"Liar. Slacker. Weakling!" they yell.
I crawl back,
wounded.
And beg to start again.
I am Rule's prisoner.

There's an algebra exam tomorrow, and I have to review with Mrs. Patrick, my math teacher.

"I'll hurry," I promise Liz.

This shouldn't take longer than finding x to the 9th exponential.

"Follow? Follow?" I say mimicking Mrs. Patrick. Each time Mrs. Patrick writes an algebraic equation on the board and gives an example of how it works, "Follow? Follow?" follows. She's her own multiplication table. Liz had Mrs. Patrick last year, and we both had her the year before. That's a lot of following, but I'm still lost.

"OK. I'll wait for you in the library and do homework."

By the time we walk home from school, Verna's gone.

"Rinnie, it's your turn to go upstairs first," Liz says.

"Come with me. I'll look first, but come with me." The house is quiet. Emmy hasn't worked here for months. "Maybe she's sleeping." I cross my fingers. Liz stands behind me, one hand over her mouth.

I try not to think. Instead, I pray, turn the knob, open the door, sweating. We do this every day. It's a noose that never loosens.

No blood, no pills, no body. "Mom's not here," I say, letting go a deep breath.

"Good," Liz says. "We're good until tomorrow."

ONE MORE POEM

Eighth, ninth, or tenth grade,
Marbles move beneath my feet
I try to balance,
Imperfectly.

MONDAY MORNING

"If we had to decide what to wear every morning, you'd never get to school on time," I tell Liz.

"Then I guess it's a good thing we have to wear tunics," she says, pulling on the blue potato sack dress our headmaster calls a uniform. Liz fools around with the sash, tying a bow with equal openings for each loop.

Why does she care how her bow looks? There aren't any boys to look good for.

"I'll bet you can wrap your sash around you twice," says Liz.

I ignore her, though it might be true.

My backpack hunches my shoulders when I sling it on my back. I have homework and books in every subject to lug to school.

"We'd better walk to school fast. It looks like it's going to rain," I answer.

"Our backpacks will get soaked," Liz says. "Take a big umbrella."

"I weighed my backpack last night. There are thirty pounds of books inside," I say, grunting at the thought of having to carry one more thing.

Mom's voice trails from the stairway, "I have to go out this morning. Get in the car. I'll drop you off."

"Wow! Really? Thanks," I say.

Verna hands us umbrellas and whispers, "Don't know what makes this day so special."

I get to the car first and sit next to Mom.

"Just in time, it's starting to precipitate," Liz says.

I like the preciseness of the word pre-cip-i-tate. Mental note—good word to use.

The mile-and-a-half drive to school takes only a few minutes—but it's long enough to know Mom is in a bad mood.

"Don't expect this tomorrow. Walking to school is good for you. It helps your brain think better," she says, her face as stern as her voice. "I swear, someone might think you'd melt in the rain. OK, girls, we're here. Out!"

Liz, drags her backpack out of the car, slings it over her shoulder, and opens her umbrella.

"Hurry up, Rinnie," Mom says, as if she has to go to the bathroom. I turn to say good-bye when Mom hurls her fist into my stomach. My chest lurches toward my legs and severs the space for air or words. I stumble out of the car, and Mom steps on the gas and heads off.

"Ooh, oohh," I moan, gasping for breath.

"What happened?" Liz asks.

I shrug and struggle to keep the muscles in my face still so the tears won't leave my eyes.

Liz balances her backpack, the umbrella, and me, and the two of us stagger up the path. Liz's body trembles next to mine.

"What did you do?" she says again.

I might come apart and wrap my arms around my body like packing tape. "N-N-Nothing. Why did Mom punch me?"

"I don't know, Ace," my sister says. "Are you OK?"

"It hurts . . . hard to breathe . . . walk in front of me, just in case I cry." This is a secret I want to keep to myself.

FAMILY SECRET

At night, when it is dark, I pray.

"Mrs. Kane, please call the police. Mom won't stop screaming at me. You must be able to hear it." I will myself into my neighbor's life. "Look in our window, see Mom act crazy." I don't know the words that describe Mom's craziness. It's bad enough to ask the neighbor to help me in my prayers. To name what Mom does would be complete betrayal. And that is unforgivable.

"Please call the police. Please get help," I cry.

Hidden inside lives my fantasy. Mrs. Kane invites me to dinner in her cluttered, just-baked-bread-smelling house. Her kids and I do our homework together, and I fall asleep on the sofa. She doesn't make me go home. I stay all night and dream of good things—kite flying, a trip to the zoo, blowing bubbles. The glare of my overhead light and Mom's swearing and raving can't wake me up. The night with Mrs. Kane is homey, happy, and safe.

But Mrs. Kane doesn't look in our windows, or call the police, or invite me to dinner. I listen to Mom complain about me. Liz is away at a month-long program in London to study literature and theater arts. She got lucky.

The polish on Mom's nails doesn't shield their sharpness. Ten pits form where Mom clutches my arms. Her head is so close to mine, the whites of her eyes are wiped out by blue.

Jackhammer jaws spew cuss after cuss at me. Am I supposed to split apart?

My ears hurt; so do my arms. Her grip is too tight to break without deepening the pits. I blink my right eye and then the left, right eye, left eye, right eye, left eye, slowly like the signal of an oncoming train; one blink after another.

"Stop that!" she says.

"Stop what?"

"You know what!"

I tilt my head as if I don't know what she means. Her hands squeeze tighter around my arms. And I blink one eye and then the other. Blink. Blink. Blink. I hope this will distract her, make her go away.

"Goddammit, STOP IT!"

Mom loosens her grip and drops my arms.

"To hell with you," she says, storming off.

The blinking worked, though her temper ignited fire in her fingers and branded me, black and blue. It is our colorful secret.

Once I told Gaga and Pop Pop about Mom. I told them she slaps my ears and makes them ring. "I'm afraid of losing my hearing," I said. I told them that she twists my arms behind me and yanks my shoulders, and once hit me with a belt. Pop Pop looked at Gaga.

"Rose wouldn't do such a thing," Gaga says, turning away. "I'm sure you're exaggerating, and I'm disappointed you would say such a thing."

Courage has left me, and I'm mute. My family doesn't believe me. There is no one I can tell. Betrayal is unforgivable. What would family friends like the governor and the mayor think? It's our little secret.

BEAUTY

Like spring, I'm emerging. I have cheekbones. Liz says my head is so thin it looks like it's shrinking, but I see cheekbones. I like the way my face feels when I stroke downward from my forehead to my jaw. The gentle glide of my hand hitting moguls of bone and hollows of skin is smooth. My fingers drip like syrup off the ridges.

The V made by the bones at the bottom of my neck makes a perfect nook for my chin. When I press my head into the nook, there is no double chin—no extra roll of skin.

I like the way my arms cut into my shoulders and bulge at the bone. I like that my lower arm and upper arm are nearly the same size. Nothing to hide. I'd be a bad magician.

"Nothing to hide up my sleeve," I'd say.

It feels good to press my leg into my torso when I raise my leg to shave in the shower. There is no squishy stomach to get in the way, just a smooth highway of skin against my leg.

But when I look at the top of my legs, I see tree trunks—thick stumpy tree trunks. My pants say petite, but it isn't true. I hate my legs. I hate my tree trunk legs. I hate the muscular way they look from tennis and riding. Why couldn't I have the kind of muscles that don't stick out, like Alana and Liz? I'll go for another jog. No more dark meat chicken. It's fattening.

ELEVENTH GRADE

"You wanted to see me?" I say to Mr. Heuland, my English teacher.

He sits on the edge of his desk and ruffles his hand through his hair. His mouth opens to speak, but instead he clears his throat and cleans his eyeglasses on his nubby sweater. The open window blows autumn into his office.

"Your essay on *The Scarlet Letter* was excellent," he says. "The examination of hypocrisy and alienation far surpassed our class discussion. You wrote as though you became both Hester and Dimmesdale. This is fine writing, Rinnie." He taps the scroll of paper that is my essay in his outstretched palm.

"I liked the story. It shows the cost of breaking rules, even unwritten ones—like loyalty. I, I mean, Hester's life might have been different if she had told who Pearl's father was. At least she wouldn't have been alone."

"Loyalty can be a tricky thing," Mr. Heuland says. "Especially when it is compounded with love, or duty. Hester became a cripple by her choice."

"I suppose." Images of Mom, Carl, Pop Pop, and Dad Barry hover like flies. I gather my hair off my neck and wish I had an elastic to make a pony. It's getting hot.

"I wish today's discussion on courage was as stimulating for you," Mr. Heuland says. "May I see your doodles?"

Mr. Heuland caught me drawing. "I was listening. I really was. I just didn't feel like talking."

"Four days in a row and not a peep? A failing grade on a pop quiz? Spacing out in class? Not laughing at my jokes? That's not the Rinnie I knew last year. Everything OK?"

"Fine. I'm tired. Too much homework." I force a yawn.

Mr. Heuland makes that little hum of agreement grown-ups make when they want you to think they believe you, but have something else in mind.

"OK, go home. Rest. But first, finish *Their Eyes Were Watching God.* Here's a heads up on tomorrow. Come to class prepared to discuss the concept of being true to yourself. I expect big things from you, Rinnie. You have something special." Mr. Heuland hands me my essay. "Don't let the Sandman cripple you." He chuckles.

"Thanks," I say. "I'll try not to disappoint you."

"Hey," Mr. Heuland stops me as I step across the threshold. "If there's a problem, I can mention you to Mr. Algrin. He's a good counselor. The school wouldn't hire him if he wasn't."

"I'm just tired." I yawn again and head for the back stairwell.

"It would be confidential," Mr. Heuland's words chase me across the hall.

It doesn't pay to have the same teacher as your older sister. By the time you have the teacher, he thinks he knows everything about you. But he doesn't.

NO MORE POP POP

"Please, God, please. If you save him and make him well, I promise to quit smoking."

Mom's body presses against the closed door to Pop Pop's bedroom. The skin on her face droops like her tear-filled eyes. Big deal, she'll give up smoking. Pathetic. Gaga and the doctor are on the other side of the door talking in muted voices. You can't bargain with God, especially when you've contributed to the problem. Maybe she should have thought of that sooner. I'm incidental like a thirteenth place setting. I don't know where Liz is, maybe in the pink room crying, or in the backyard in the withered garden. That's where I'd be if I weren't here. Things live, and they die. I need to see it.

It's biology and math. Diabetes, plus clogged arteries, plus overweight, plus ice cream every night, and raisins every day, and no exercise equals heart attack. The doctor told Pop Pop to stop eating that stuff. Pop Pop lived the life he wanted. I'm sure I'm sad; I love Pop Pop, but with science as a backbone, it's hard to cry.

LITTLE BOOK of QUESTIONS

Newest Entries:

Why do I feel so ambivalent about Pop Pop?

Where are my tears?

Will I turn into her?

THAT'S HOW IT IS

"Watch your step when you get out," Uncle Matt says. Though he looks like Gaga, his thick hands and rolling walk remind me of Pop Pop. He knows I'm not used to wearing high heels and a long formal gown. My velvet dress slides like a feather duster across the leather car seat. The damp November air sends a chill under my jacket of bunny fur. I hope it doesn't shed on my dress.

"I'm fine, thanks," I say. "Could you hold the umbrella a little lower? The mist will frizz my hair."

Liz scoots to the edge of the back seat, hikes her dress around her knees, and steps over the puddle that separates the car from the curb. Tucked under umbrellas, we smooth our black dresses into glossy folds of velvet and satin, tug our white rabbit furs so they rest just below our shoulders, and give Uncle Matt the OK to start walking.

He escorts us through the reception hall to the dining area of the private club reserved for the annual Cincinnati Girls' School Father-Daughter Dinner Dance. This is the first time I'm invited; the event is for juniors and seniors only. Attendance is mandatory. Mr. Harper, the headmaster, thinks this ritual strengthens school spirit and that will help make us the premier private school in Ohio.

"Let's look for a table near a corner," I say. "Someplace tucked away."

"Back there, to the right," Liz says.

"Good eye."

Uncle Matt follows. He's here to please us.

Narrow aisles squeeze between a maze of chairs. Crisp white linens, crystal glasses, and wreaths of ribbon and flowers decorate the tables. We pass table after table of people dressed in tuxedos and beautiful gowns in our search for a place to sit. I'm mesmerized by how good some of my classmates look.

Courtney should always wear her hair down! Pink is definitely Whitney's color. I tried on that velvet dress Lisa's wearing! It looks better on her. It needs someone tall. Wow, Diana looks just like her dad.

"Hi, Rin."

I look around and see a table crowded with classmates, their faces flushed with laughter. A husky field hockey star named Sara and a man with the same curly hair and skin color block the faces of a girl whose long nails match the deep pink of her dress and that of a man next to her wearing a scarlet cummerbund.

"Rinnie," the voice says again. "It's Alana." She moves her chair to the side so I can see her.

"H—hi," I say, caught off guard.

"You look really pretty tonight," Liz says.

"Hi, geezers," Dad says. He straightens his scarlet cummerbund. "You girls look pretty good, too."

"Hi, Matt" he says to my uncle. "I'd invite you to sit with us, but—"

"That's OK," I spit out. "There isn't enough room and besides we have a table near the back."

"Oh, Suzanne is here," Liz says, looking off into the distance. "I'm going to say hello."

Liz brushes Dad off with an upward wave of her hand and walks toward the corner table, Uncle Matt at her side.

My heart stopped moments ago, and now I feel my brain shrivel. I can't think of anything else to say.

"Well, I'll see you later. Have a good dinner." I make sure my lips smile when I turn to walk away.

I won't cry, I won't cry, I tell myself. *I won't cry!* I'm here with my uncle, and my father is here with my stepsister, and that's how it is.

When I reach the table near the corner, it's empty, except for Liz's beaded purse and three 7-Ups with twists of lime on the rims that Uncle Matt ordered.

Liz and Matt swirl across the dance floor, fox-trotting, dipping, and cha cha cha-ing. Liz loves to dance and so does Uncle Matt.

I sit at the table and pretend I'm somewhere else, a long way off. And mostly, I don't cry.

IS POP POP FOREVER?

It's been two months. Impressions of Pop Pop are everywhere. Gaga has taken the reins of their far-reaching philanthropic lives and has replaced acquiescence with resilience. She's lighter without losing weight—at least her own. I actually think Gaga's enjoying her life more without Pop Pop's physical presence. Mom only answers to herself, spending more time with Gaga and more money on decorating the house and clothes. Not that much has changed for Liz and me. It's strange that way. We don't talk much about our grandfather. There's no need. He still guides me with his critical voice.

LITTLE BOOK of QUESTIONS

Newest Entry:

Is there a difference between a father and a dad?

ALWAYS

I can't feel the firmness of the carpeted kitchen floor, or my body sitting on it. All my feelings are poured into Croquette's warm body, spooled against itself, ignorant of all things other than this spot and her worn pillow. She holds on to each breath and lets it go, her lungs making the shallowest of ripples across her chest.

"Deeper, breathe deeper, Croquie," I plead. "I know it hurts. You don't have to."

It's 2:00 A.M., then three, then four, and we lie next to each other. I pinch a nibble of dog food from her untouched bowl and place it in her mouth.

"Dr. Morton operated on your tummy, and your job is to get better. Eat, you have to," I whisper.

Croquette takes the morsel, and it dissolves in her mouth. She doesn't swallow so I swab her mouth with my finger so she won't choke.

I stroke her gray hair, feeling every rib. You're so thin, I think. How can you get better if you won't eat? Maybe you'll feel better in my lap. The whimper that echoes through my ears bludgeons my senses, and I relax her limp body onto the tired pillow.

"I will never leave you, Croquie. I promise. You are the best dog in the world. Go to sleep, baby dog." I hum music

I've never heard before and shutter the rest of the world away.

I wake up in my bed and rush downstairs to the kitchen before Liz and Mom wake up.

Verna is red eyed. "Croquette passed. She went to heaven."

Verna pulls me to her, and we both cry.

NOTE to MYSELF

Baked beans again for lunch today. Gooey, brown, sugary. Smelled fattening.

Whitney announced, "No dessert for me, I'm on a diet." A chorus of "Me too!" harmonized around the table. It must be the bulldozer-shovel-it-in diet. Shelly, Lisa, Leah, Courtney, they all ate hot dogs (with the bun), chips, and beans.

The only food left was the platter of brownies.

Some diet. Half a hot dog, no bun, no beans, no chips. A cup of skim milk. That's a diet. But I shouldn't have eaten the hot dog. Had to cut the hot dog in two, and bury half with salt, so I wouldn't eat it all.

It's hard to eat when other people are around. I can't focus on my food.

Have to add hot dogs to forbidden food list. It was way too good.

CHIP on a SHOULDER

"Are you going to use Pink Pearl or Berry Blush?" Liz calls. "I'm organizing the nail polishes by color and want to put them away."

"I want the one that dries the fastest. Can you come in and check my outfit?" I ask, hurrying to wrap a strand of hair around my curling iron. "Ouch, that's hot." I wince and suck the burned finger.

Chip will be here in twenty minutes. We have a double date to go to the movies. Mascara and blush are a pleasant change from the no makeup rule at school. Chip will be surprised. A spray of perfume, and the starched smell of soap and hair gel is veiled by Lilies of the Valley. Ten minutes and counting.

I slip into my black jeans and nubby blue sweater, modeling in the mirror on the back of my door.

"I like the look," Liz says. "Unfussy and classic. You look very nice, very thin, but very nice. Wish I could lose weight like you."

"Clean, fresh, and ready to . . . "

The door careens open like an out-of-control race car and crashes into me. Lizzie slips out.

Mom stands between me and the excited girl in the mirror. "Where do you think you're going?"

"I have a date with Chip, remember?"

"Not tonight. You're not going anywhere!"

"Mom, I asked you four days ago, and you said it was OK. Chip will be here any minute."

"I canceled your date."

"You called him? You told him not to come? You, you can't do that . . . it's taken me over an hour to get ready. I just straightened my hair. Why did you do that? What did I do?"

She dumps the purse I just filled on the bed. "You're not going because I said you're not going." Mom's voice is as even and hard as an iron rod. "Clean up the mess on the bed and put the purse away."

"You can't just call and cancel for no reason and not tell me."

"You're grounded, young lady, and will be until you learn to stop talking back."

Mom leaves my room. My internal compass points nowhere. It's broken and lost. *Where is terra firma? This house is quicksand, and I'm sinking.* Liz sneaks into my room.

"Do you know what Mom did?" I blurt.

"I heard. She's crazy, Rinnie. Don't let her get to you."

"What about Chip? He'll think I'm so rude! I really like him."

I start to cry and feel crazy, too. If only I had been smart enough, pretty, funny, witty enough, a star athlete, then things would be different. For one, Dad would have taken me, too.

BEING THERE

OW! My face stings, and the handprint blooms red in the mirror. That one hurt. The force of Mom's hand punctures my hearing. For a moment, all sound turns off, except a mute voice that drones. *Don't cry. Don't let her see you cry.*

I use my hands as a helmet to shield my head from the hail of blows that rain down.

"Who do you think you are, you little snot? I'll tell you. You are a kid, a kid, hear me?" The screaming sears my ears, and they want to burst.

"It's your fault Emmy said it's too stressful to work here, and it's your fault Evan's gone. You've got me so crazy, I backed into a car at the grocery store. Shape up! SHAPE UP!" she yells, shaking me by the shoulders again.

Her fingers dig into my arms. "You don't care if I live or die. You don't care about anything but yourself. You're nothing but a fat ass, a whore."

My shoulders mold to Mom's hands as if her fingers are made of steel. She shakes backward, forward, backward, forward. My head and shoulders joggle in rhythm. I imagine the half-severed head of a chicken flapping side to side.

What will happen to my brain? Don't cry, don't cry. She's crazy.

"Mom, if you hit me again, I'll hit back. MOM! If you hit me again, I'm going to hit back! Do you hear me?" I don't want to hit her. I want to diffuse the bomb inside her. A well-developed bicep launches her palm to my neck. Smack!

I smack back. Mom's breath comes in short, shallow gasps. The tightness in her jaw slackens. My inside scorches like the frenzy of a million ants scuffling for the same crumb. I warned her, "If you hit me again, I'll hit back."

What have I done? Sinned.

Mom snorts in air and snorts out disgust.

"You can trust what I say." I look into her eyes.

"You're a monster! Monster! What child hits her mother?" she sizzles, glares, drops her arms, and exits.

Victory and guilt compete for my attention. Did I really hit Mom? Now I've really done something bad. Or maybe, it was something good.

THE PUZZLE

Verna left half an hour ago. Liz works on her homework upstairs. Kenny Kreiger and I are the only other people at home. The Saturday afternoon sun streams into the family room windows onto the jigsaw puzzle Kenny and I have almost finished. Only a few more pieces and the picture of polar bear cubs on an ice floe will be ready to be glued together and placed beside the other finished puzzles in the art area.

"If I get the last piece," I say, "I get to pick the movie we see tonight."

"If I get the last piece I get to pick the movie, and you have to buy popcorn," he answers.

No problem. The sun is so bright, it's easy to see the tiniest differences in color. I'll find the last piece. I've done the puzzle before.

Kenny and his twin sister, Kelsey, have been in Sunday school with Liz forever. He has a crush on me. I can tell, because he likes to put his hand on my neck and massage it lightly. He doesn't do that to Liz. It feels good.

"Everyone knows it's good luck to put the last piece of a puzzle in," I say. "And I have it in my hand—as soon as you put your piece in I'll pick the movie."

"No way. You don't have the last piece without me."

I grab the piece from his hand and wave it in front of his face, inching closer to tempt him.

In a second, Kenny pins my arms over my head. His body straddles mine, in a canopy of blue and white stripes and denim.

"Gimme. Let it drop," he says, putting his knees on top of my legs to keep me from kicking.

I warm inside and wiggle my hips causing Kenny to put more weight on my thighs.

I shake my head. Hair falls across my forehead. Laughter swallows my words.

"We'll do this democratically." Kenny's fingers skim the hair from my face, and he sits back on his legs. "You have a choice. Release the puzzle piece or be prepared to die laughing. And stop looking so foxy."

I stop squirming and look up as if he had spoken Zulu.

"Too slow," Kenny snickers. He bends low, and attacks my sides with his fingers. "I need to come up for air," I pant.

Kenny's strong hands pull me up by the shoulders. Behind him looms my mother. Her arms cross over her chest, and she stands as if she's just been over starched. It's clear, by her squinty eyes and lip licking, Mom thinks Kenny and I have been doing things. She glares and huffs out.

"Wait here," I say to Kenny.

"Mom? Mom?"

She bloodies me with a look. I list backward.

"I leave you alone in the house with your sister and a boy and look what I come back to."

"Mom, you've got it wrong. We were . . . "

"Don't back talk me, Rinnie. I saw you. It isn't enough to give you tennis lessons, riding lessons, buy you beautiful clothes, and send you to the best school. You thank me by acting like a slut."

"But, Mom, we were wrestling!"

"I saw him on top of you. Don't lie to me. Go to your room."

"What about Kenny?"

"He's out of here."

"You can't do that! We weren't doing anything."

"Don't tell me what I can and can't do."

Her hand stings my jaw. "You think you run this house. You think you know it all. You think you're the mother. Well you're not and at the rate you're going, you never will be."

I don't know what she's talking about.

"You're crazy," I say. My cheek burns with pain from another slap. "You're crazy, and I'm going to Gaga's."

I shoot down the stairs. "Kenny, take me to Gaga's!"

Mom stands at the top of the stairs and screeches, "You spoiled little brat. Do you think your grandmother will want to take care of you once she finds out what you do when I'm away? I'm the mother. You listen to me. Get up to your room and stay there."

I wrench a jacket from the hall closet.

"Don't you dare step out of this house."

"Come on!"

I pull Kenny's striped shirtsleeve. His face is contorted, and it frightens me. Will he ever want to see me again? Would I ever want to have him here again?

"If you take her, you're just as bad as she is," my mother screams.

She's on the landing stabbing the air with her finger.

"If you really like that girl, you'll tell her to stay home where she belongs."

Kenny grabs his jacket. "Come on," he says.

PAVING the ROAD

"Come in."

The voice is more mature than I expected. I've seen Mr. Algrin in the halls, but this is my first visit to his office.

"Take a seat," he says, like we've been friends for a long time.

He moves a box of tissues from his desk and puts his feet in its place.

"Hope you don't mind. It's been a long day, and I could never get away with this at home."

I know what he means. Shoes on the furniture is akin to assassinating Emily Post, Mom's authority on etiquette.

"Rinnie. That's an unusual name."

"It's like the dog, Rin Tin Tin." I wish I felt as brave and smart as that dog.

"OK, Rinnie like the dog. You made this appointment, so what brings you here?"

I wander through my thoughts, as though exploring an enormous cave. Everything feels so bewildering—so unreachable. The speech I practiced vaporizes.

I slump into the chair, head down, arms crossed. There is so much to climb over in the cave. One false step, and I could fall.

"Is this confidential?" I ask, lifting my chin so the words won't sound garbled.

"Absolutely." Mr. Algrin smiles. "Unless you intend to harm yourself or someone else, or if information about physical or sexual abuse comes my way." His smile wanes. "I'm a mandated reporter. That means I am required by law to report any abuse I think might be taking place."

"Who do you report to?"

"The Department of Family Services."

He leans in, his hands cupped between his long legs. "Is this your first time talking to a counselor or psychologist?"

"Once I talked to someone with my mother, but it didn't last long."

"How long did it last? A month, two?"

"About fifteen minutes."

"Short," he says.

"But not sweet," I answer.

"Well, I hope we can talk about that later if we need to." Mr. Algrin is a lot calmer than Mom's shrink, Dr. Didier. His crumpled socks, worn belt, and the cowlick it looks like he surrendered to even before waking up, spell "laid back."

If I were Rin Tin Tin, Dr. Didier would be a pit bull, and Mr. Algrin would be a Labrador. He looks soft.

"Mr. Heuland mentioned you might stop by." He leans in again, the way people do when they really want to hear what you have to say. "So what's up?"

I'm in the cave. It's cool, and in spite of its size, the cave is crammed with obstacles—formations too hard to reach.

"I don't know."

"How can I help?" Mr. Algrin looks through my eyes as if there are directions inside my brain.

"Don't know." My chest hurts from the breath I hold back.

“I think you might know,” he says in a voice as sure and steady as the ticking clock that hangs above his desk. Ten minutes until class.

I shrug. The passageways in the cave narrow. It’s difficult to inch through them without touching the wet walls. The walls pocked and hardened by time are unwelcoming. I want to turn around. I want to be in the sun—twirling, arms wide. I want to dive into the warm air that carries the songs of birds and the scent of flowers. I want to disappear.

“Sometimes I feel invisible,” I whisper. “Like being on a remote island, alone.”

“Invisible, huh. Size-wise, there’s not much to you. Do you eat?”

I stare him in the face and pinch the skin covering my ribs. “Of course I eat. I’m the cook in the house.”

“That doesn’t mean you eat,” he responds.

“I promise. I eat.”

Mr. Algrin shakes his head in agreement, as if to say, “OK, I believe you,” and moves on.

I’m glad he doesn’t ask what I eat. What would I say? *Only things with three ingredients or less. No sugar, no carbohydrates. No oil.*

“You have a sister in school, don’t you?”

“She’s a senior.”

“Are you friends?”

“Best.”

“Any brothers?”

“One.”

“Is he younger or older?”

“Younger. He lives with my father.”

“Do you see him often?”

"Who?"

"Both of them."

This is like a game of Ping-Pong, ping for me, pong for Mr. Algrin. The ball is back to me. Ping.

"No. I see my dad more than Evan, because Evan does stuff with his friends. I see my dad once a week, sometimes."

Mr. Algrin clears his throat and stands up. He pours himself a cup of water and offers one to me.

"Rinnie, here's how this works. I rely on the information you give me to understand the obstacles in your life. The only way I can know this is if you share with more than one-word answers. It takes a long time to build a road using pebbles."

"You're right, it does," I say.

But inside, I'm confused. The road is dark, and I don't know the way.

NOTE to MYSELF

Today, Thursday, was ONE BIG PIG-OUT! Mr. Heuland stopped me after English class to talk. He's concerned about me. After school, I changed from my baggy tunic to something even baggier, my overalls. Too afraid to try on my jeans.

Tonight, I got in bed and felt the valley between my pelvic bones. There's a hill there now. Maybe it's the diet Cokes I drank this afternoon. If I keep eating like today, nothing will fit. I can feel my thighs spreading. The more I think about it, the more I eat. Here's what I ate:

Breakfast: Four fat carrots, two raisins, the longest celery stick in the package, three cups warm water.

Snack: Starving by 10:15, *eight* dried tomatoes halves!!!, two teaspoons of peanut butter, two more raisins.

Snack: 11:00, hard-boiled egg without the yolk, two more carrots, a saltine.

Lunch: Lettuce with tomato, cucumber, and two radishes cut into small chunks, a medjool date, big apple, bite of Jamie Silverman's lox, bagel, and cream cheese sandwich without the bagel.

Snack: 4:00 P.M., another medjool date—too delicious, none tomorrow. Diet soda.

Dinner: Half a chicken breast, lettuce with vinegar, ten green beans. Verna made the chicken, didn't want to hurt her feelings, two raisins, one strawberry, a few capers.

Snack: 8:02 P.M., one huge helping of strawberry jam out of the jar on my finger.

Can't think this hard without getting a headache.

FRIDAY RULES—NO PIGGING OUT!

Write down everything I eat.

Breakfast: Three medium carrots, a bite of a saltine (I spit it out).

Lunch: Bowl of lettuce tossed, chunk of chopped cabbage, one-half dill pickle, cup of cooked cauliflower, peel of a small apple. When I opened the baggie filled with cauliflower, Jamie, the girl next to me, gagged and said my lunch smelled like I was eating a skunk. It sort of does, but it has fewer calories.

Dinner: Three bites chicken breast, one carrot, one stalk broccoli. Mom didn't eat much more than I did, though she did smoke two cigarettes with her coffee.

Jittery all day, couldn't stop thinking about what I ate, what I can't eat today, what I've eaten so far. Have to stay in control.

Thank you, thank you, thank you, for letting me get through the day without pigging out.

SATURDAY

Breakfast: Ran out of carrots, huge stalk celery, one dried tomato, and two raisins.

Lunch: Hard-boiled egg, white part only, three celery stalks, two raisins.

Dinner: Mom out on a date. Cheese from a slice of pizza. Spit half into my napkin, swallowed the rest, half-cup tomato juice, six peanuts, small bowl Jell-O, half a leftover fortune cookie—fortune said good things come in pairs—so I ate two more raisins, two teaspoons jam from jar. Remember, put carrots on grocery list.

I hate seeing everything I eat written down. It's gross. There's so much stuff. I don't like how disorganized it looks with my scratch outs. Have to stop changing my mind. Or spitting food out. Next time, I'm using a pencil.

THANK YOU

Beep. Beep. Beep. Jack's Chevy skids around the corner on the wet pavement.

"Hop in, you might melt," he says through the open window. Drops of rain splatter his face.

I hustle into the car as fast as I can, careful not to lose my balance. The books in my backpack reel side to side in rhythm with my steps.

"Thanks. My shoes are beginning to leak."

"I'm going to call you Charlotte Atlas." Jack takes my pack. "How does a skinny girl like you carry a load like this?"

"I'm not so skinny. These uniforms hide a lot," I say.

It's a good thing my legs are short, and the seat doesn't need to be pushed back. Crammed against the back of my seat are books, a baseball, a bat, and assorted pieces of clothing. Each time the car starts or stops, the baseball rolls into my feet.

This isn't the route Jack would take if he drove directly home from school. He came this way to get me.

"How'd you know I'd be walking home?" I ask.

"Lucky guess. It's raining, slippery from the leaves on the ground. . . . I know your mom," he says, shifting gears to neutral as we creep toward a red light. Jack, always money conscious, says it saves wear and tear on the engine to shift to neutral and glide, rather than to downshift to first and then up again.

"Where's Liz? I thought she'd be walking, too?"

"She's at Susan's. They're putting together a skit for Latin Club. You know, 'veni vidi vici.'"

"Hail Caesar," Jack extends a rigid hand. My bare legs, wet and cold, shiver back in response. Then I lean over and kiss his cheek.

"Thanks for coming to get me."

I DON'T WANT to SHARE

Every girl needs a Jack in her life. He's smart, captain of the football team, funny, popular, and he adores me. He's the only one I believe when he says how pretty I am because he's Catholic, and he'd never lie. Jack mostly abides by his religion, but frays the edges by staying out too late with me.

"You're like a windup toy with a jolt of enthusiasm," he tells me. "You're always ready for an adventure."

I have his letter jacket. In Mom's eyes, he can do no wrong. She even forgave him for parking in the driveway when she tore out of the house in a fit and smashed into his Volkswagen.

We date until I fall into deep like with Bruce. Jack and I break up but remain buddies.

Jeff, Chip, Tom, Bill, Vince, Gary, they all hang with Jack. And I date them all, one by one. Like a bowling ball knocking down pins, I rolled through the sophomore and junior boys at Cincinnati Prep, the brother school to CGS. Now, there's a senior I want to go out with. I ask Jack to drop a hint. Fait accompli. My entrée to the senior class is a success. I know some guys from the public school I used to attend and go out with them, too. Mom loves it when my dates make a point to ask how she is. I think it makes her feel pretty. I love knowing the guys think I'm cute enough or interesting enough to date—at least once. Weekend nights are something to look forward to.

The movies, parties, restaurants, all away from home, are like splashing in a pool on a scalding day.

I invite most guys to come inside for a soda after a date. The light in the family room is always on. Next to the light, thumbing through a magazine is Mom . . . waiting.

"Come in!" She says to my dates. "Would you like a Coke? We have plenty. Rinnie, get your date a drink. Would you like some cookies? Rinnie, bring cookies, too. What'd you think of the movie? Hi, whomever, it's good to see you again. Tell me about school."

Gross!

She sits on the sofa and tucks her legs under her like a schoolgirl. "That's so interesting. What else are you up to? Really? Tell me more . . . "

She acts like I bring the guys home for her.

More than once I've said, "Mom, tonight my date and I would like to visit with each other—alone. Please don't sit with us and talk."

My mother has become deaf.

Occasionally, I wonder why so many guys ask me out. Why I have so many repeat dates. What they want. I always come up with the same answer, and it isn't as Mom said, because my hair is my personality. Whatever they want, I give nothing away but conversation with Mom and soda.

CLUE

The hallway is empty. The only other kids at school this early are the ones who come in for extra help before classes begin. The door to Mr. Algrin's office is open. He's expecting me. Copies of *American School Counselor* fall across the cluttered desk like a landslide. A pile of small rocks lays half buried under the magazines. Mr. Algrin balances the phone receiver between his shoulder and neck, gathers the journals, and drops them in a box labeled "CATCH UP." I wish life were as easy to arrange. Mr. Algrin crooks his neck deeper into his collar. It looks uncomfortable. He cups the receiver. "I'll be with you in a minute," he mouths, turning his back to me.

I hear the words "love you too," before he hangs up. To me, the words are mysterious.

"Have a seat," he says, closing the door. I sit in the oversized armchair. Mr. Algrin offers me an oversized mug. White slips of paper rise from the top like albino French fries. Each crinkled paper has a fortune printed on it. I pull one from the bottom and read aloud.

"Look for answers where the eyes can't see."

"Where do you suppose that is?" Mr. Algrin asks.

"In the dark?" I say.

Mr. Algrin turns off the light. "Maybe," he says. But light from a small window keeps his office from being dark.

"How'd it go this week?" Mr. Algrin tries again.

"I got a good grade on a poem. I used *The Catcher in the Rye* for references."

"I'd like to hear it if you have it with you."

"OK," I say, feeling pride press through my line of defense. I sort through the graded papers in the back of my binder until I find the verse:

Standing near the edge, of the ledge,
On some crazy cliff . . .
I catch everybody—keep them whole.
No one calls my name,
I'm apart all alone,
On some crazy cliff . . .
Standing near the edge, of the ledge,
Roots barely taken hold.
Catching souls in my shoots,
Stemming punishment
I'm a weed overgrown
Apart all alone
On some crazy cliff.

Struggling to survive I contrive,
Order, truth, and fact
Trusting no one, even me
Taking heed of etiquette
Please and thank yous fly
Apart, on my own, all alone
On some crazy cliff.

I gaze at the paper in my hand. It's quiet. Maybe Mr. Algrin fell asleep.

"Wow. Thanks for sharing. I like it," comes his voice. "Can we talk about your poem?"

"OK." The chair's lost its coziness, and the temperature feels colder.

"You use a lot of words of estrangement. There's, hmm, there's a sense of over-responsibility."

I look at the hangnails I've chewed and try to fix them with my teeth.

"Well, I was thinking of Holden Caulfield, *The Catcher in the Rye*."

But I know the catcher didn't care about punishment or etiquette. I do. A tired list of things I want to be runs through my head: honest, open, brave, loved, skinny, perfect.

Mr. Algrin continues. "What do you mean by the phrase 'I catch everyone, keep them whole' or 'Stemming punishment'?"

He's the catcher, and I'm caught. I look right at him and say. "Things grow for different reasons. I don't want people to hurt. I don't want them to bleed pain. I can catch them and keep them safe."

IF ONLY

If only I was prettier,
Smarter, wittier, funnier, a better athlete, a boy?
Dad might have stayed.
Dad might have asked me
To live with him.

If only I weighed less,
Was lankier, cuter, bubbly, pert,
I'd be visible.
I'd be something
Special.

If only I knew which clothes would fit when
I dressed each morning,
If only the numbers on the scale didn't
Dictate how I feel,
And I didn't think about
What to eat, when to eat, or how much to eat,
All day long,
I'd be happy.
I'd be safe.

If only there was more to me
Than how I look,
Pretty dresses, matching shoes, mascara'd lashes
I might be
Enough.

RINNIE the LIONHEART

"Rinnie the Lionheart, come on in."

My feet almost glide across the threshold. There's something about Mr. Algrin's manner that's magnetic.

Rinnie the Lionheart, the words roar inside my head. My cheeks burn with warmth.

"You know, lions are bigger, stronger, and maybe even braver than Rin Tin Tin."

Mr. Algrin half smiles, almost challenging me.

"You're brave to come talk," he continues, "to share your poetry, and the vulnerable side you like to hide. You're brave to want to make things different."

His voice, like a soft rain, puddles in my eyes. The heat from my cheeks pools in my heart.

"It takes courage to trust," I manage to keep my voice level.

"You're right. And there are different kinds of courage, Rinnie—and different kinds of trust. It's huge that you trust me. It's even huger for you to trust yourself."

I chew a nail until the edge is ragged. The wall separating Rinnie at school and Rinnie at home is disintegrating. How much do I tell? How much do I keep tucked away?

Mr. Algrin reaches over a heap of magazines that remind me of condemned buildings to a row of books on his desk.

"Take a look at this, Rinnie." He hands me a book the size of a piece of toast.

Harold and the Purple Crayon.

"Hey, this is one of my favorite books!"

"Mine, too," Mr. Algrin says. "You and Harold have a lot in common."

"Oh yeah?"

"Harold's inventive like you." Mr. Algrin leans toward me, arms resting on his knees in the "I truly mean what I'm about to say" position. "When Harold creates his world, he always takes care of himself."

"It's easy with a crayon," I say. "You draw what you like."

"You have a box of crayons, Rinnie, with colors like discipline, loyalty, strength, courage . . . you get to draw what you like. It's your adventure."

The bell rings for first period. "I'll think about that," I say.

I'M HAROLD

Sixty-four rounded harlequin tips, arranged by shade, point up at me. I pinch a crayon, twist it in both directions, and pull the slender stick from the box. Little black letters spell "plum" on its side—a juicy color.

"This plum-colored crayon is very Harold-like," I say out loud. The fragrance of "new crayon" makes my skin tingle. I hold the crayon and feel a surge of possibility. It's stepping off a precipice into an unknown adventure.

I draw two parallel vertical lines followed by a horizontal line to connect the vertical posts at the bottom, then an inverted "V" to cap the shape. It's a house.

Tip, tap, tip, tap, tip, tap. The crayon between my fingers marks time on the tabletop. *Whose house is this? My house?*

I place the crayon on the table, chew on a hangnail, and stare at the purple shape. There are no windows, no door, no chimney. No doorbell to ring nor welcoming walkway. No one can get in. No one can get out. It's like prison. *Who lives here? I want to know. I want to know why.*

LITTLE BOOK of QUESTIONS

Newest Entries:

Who names the colors of crayons?

Who lives in the house?

Am I the house?

FRIDAY

Our session is almost over when Mr. Algrin takes a blank piece of paper from his desk. "It must be tough to have so little time with your father," he sums up the past fifty minutes with twelve words.

I shrug and give a nod that says, "Well, yeah, but I'm used to it."

He makes three columns on the paper. The first is labeled *Things I'd Like To Do This Week.* The second is *Things I'd Like To Do With My Dad.* The third column has no label.

"Homework," he says, handing me the paper. "Write down four things you'd like to do in the first column. Write down four things you'd like to do with your dad in the second column. Pick something from column two, write it in the third column, and ask your father to do it with you."

"The third column doesn't have a label," I say.

"It will. Think about what it could be."

I tuck the paper into a book and before I leave I say, "I can't believe you're giving me homework."

CAN'T YOU SEE ME

"Hi Dad, it's Rinnie."

"Hi Buzzer. What do you need?"

"I'd like to go to the tennis club this weekend and play a set of tennis . . . with you."

"I already have a game both mornings."

"That's what makes it so perfect. You'll already be there. I can hang out in the break room, do homework, and we can play after lunch."

"It's a possibility. Let me see if Alana wants to join us for doubles. We can find a fourth on Sunday."

Alana? No, no, not Alana! I squeeze my eyes tight and black out Dad's idea.

"What if just you and I play?"

"Alana will be at the club. She'll want to hit balls, too."

"Could you and I warm up for half an hour before we play doubles?"

"No can do, Rin. Maybe for five or ten minutes. My knees won't take it, and I want to make it through our foursome."

I wish we could just be us for a change. "Alright. See you inside Sunday. Look up. I'll wave to you from the window." I jiggle the receiver back on phone.

"I have to get out of here," I scream. I grab my peacoat and snatch my pizzazz hat. Some of the faux diamonds have fallen off—a lump in the oatmeal.

The breeze whisks my hair and stirs my thoughts into a lumpy stew. *I should be grateful Dad watches out for all of us. I wish there was no Alana. I'm selfish. I should be glad we all play tennis. I wish I was more important to Dad.* My hat blows off and cartwheels down the sidewalk.

"Crap! Crap! Double Crap!" I shriek and stomp the balls of my feet as if I were smashing grapes. A fire hydrant rescues my hat. I pull it over my ears like a helmet and sit on the curb. The muscles in my jaw surrender to the silence and my bum to the cold.

"I may not have gotten the response I wanted, but I accomplished the homework for Mr. Algrin," I tell myself. "That's worth something. Maybe an A for Anguish or a B for Bravery, or a C for Compliant." I walk home, my hand nailing my hat against my head. By the time I reach the front porch, I've figured out the label for column three. Things I've Survived.

NOTE to MYSELF

Mr. A. suggested taking a walk, making a phone call, or writing my thoughts down when I want to stuff myself with food. Great ideas, if only I could remember them.

RECIPE for SWEET DREAMS

At night before I fall asleep, I lie on my right side, my right arm crooked in a ninety-degree angle by my head. I wrap the fingers of my left hand around my right arm above my elbow and below my shoulder. I can nearly touch my fingers to my thumb. No saggy flesh here. Just lean muscle.

ANOTHER FRIDAY

It's Friday, study hall, 2:00 P.M. Time to see Mr. Algrin.

"Come on in, Rinnie," Mr. Algrin says when I tap the doorjamb. He cracked open the door so I don't have to juggle my books and wrestle the handle.

"Wow, your office is," I pause, "neat."

It's unusually clean in a tidy sort of way. Even the papers in the wastebasket look as if they'd been placed there with thought. The room smells like spring.

"A change, isn't it," Mr. Algrin says.

I search for the tumble of books and the scrambled piles of magazines. The "CATCH UP" box is empty. A clip has been added to the curtain so it now hangs straight.

"Yeah. Are you OK?" Funny *me* asking Mr. Algrin if *he's* OK. He isn't an "I'm the voice of authority" type of adult. He's more like a "Wanna get a soda? Tell me who you are kind of adult." I like it.

"I'm feeling good. Great as a matter of fact." He spreads his arms wide as if to hug the entire room and everything in it with his smile.

"I'm going to be a father." He nods his head agreeing with himself. "First time. Have to acquire some better habits."

"A father? That's great."

"Do you think so?" he asks.

"Sure."

"Well," he says, "it is a little intimidating. No one teaches you how to be a standout parent. Tell me, Rinnie, what's important to you in a father?"

My lips shift to the left. A low thinking sound eases out.

Mr. Algrin sits forward in his chair and cups his chin with his fingers, his thumb supporting his clean-shaven jaw. He looks like The Thinker from one of Mrs. O'Claire's art books on sculpture.

"A father has to be . . . " My head presses into the cushioned back of the armchair, and I gaze at the ceiling. *Maybe the answer is coded into the little holes on the ceiling tiles?* I'm quiet.

"Earth to Rinnie. Come in." He pauses. "What are you doing?"

"Connecting the dots," I say, still looking at the depressions in the tiles.

Mr. Algrin is relentless.

"Rinnie, what makes a good father?" His voice sounds like he really wants to know.

"Specifically?"

"That works."

I won't look at him. I don't want him to see that this is hard for me.

"Well, you could read stories to your baby even when she grows up and learns to read on her own. Teach her to ride a bike. Play word games. Build a volcano from gravel and glue with her for her science class. *I wish Dad had actually let me help him build.* And you can make green eggs and green milk on St. Patrick's Day." *I loved St. Patty's day.*

"All interesting ideas," says Mr. Algrin. "Did your father make green eggs and milk?"

"Yep. And we had ham, too, like in the book—every St. Patrick's Day, until he left."

"Must have been a big change when he left. No more green eggs and milk or games?"

"No more green eggs and milk." I think of Alana, Amy, and Jake with my dad. I've seen them at the country club playing together and been at their dinner table where they laugh and tell stories; I pretended to understand.

"No more games," I whisper, sitting up straight. I put my clenched hands to mouth. "I think . . . a good father spends time with his child even when he thinks she doesn't need it anymore. Even when," a breath ripples in my throat, "even when there are lots of kids, a good father finds time for each one." I hold tight to my hands and look him straight in the eyes. He doesn't need glasses to see me.

"Thank you, Rinnie. Thank you. That's well taken. You are not only smart, but courageous, and someone I'm glad to know. I can learn a lot from you."

He holds out the jar that contains the blank white slips of paper. "You get to write one this week," he says.

NOTE to MYSELF

Maybe if I didn't eat and disappeared, Dad would notice. He certainly doesn't see me now.

MEASURING

I place my hands on my waist with my index fingers touching my belly button. Then pivot my hands backward without lifting my thumbs. My top hand crosses the other. I can almost touch the wrist of my bottom hand. On the slip of paper I took from Mr. Algrin's Fortune Jar, I write: *It's going to be a good day.*

WHAT'S MY STORY?

Mr. Algrin has music playing when I enter his office.

"Do you like Gregorian chants?" he asks.

"Never heard one."

"You're hearing one now," he says.

I listen to the words but can't figure them out.

"Italian," Mr. Algrin says. "The language is Italian. The chants are named after Pope Gregory I. He was the bishop of Rome in the late 500s and early 600s."

"Sounds like men heaving a heavy cart uphill to me."

"How so?"

"Sounds slow, laborious, and monotonous."

"Or calming, peaceful, and harmonious." He opens his eyes wide as if he just discovered electricity and smiles. He pulls a small paper portfolio from under his desk.

"I borrowed these from Mrs. O'Claire," he says, pulling out two pictures.

"This one," he lifts his left hand, "is the *Mona Lisa*. You've seen it before. Some say the beauty of the work is Mona Lisa's mysterious face, the half-smile. Others hold that the face isn't beautiful at all. It's masculine. They say it's the use of light and dark that makes the painting beautiful." He places the picture on the table and holds up the second.

"I've seen this one before," I say, smiling broadly. "It is a Kandinsky."

"Right you are, Rinnie. What do you see when you look at it?"

I think about what Mrs. O'Claire said to consider about modern art. "It has a lot of diagonals, which create action, and the action is emphasized by the bold colors." I pause. "The colors unite the forms that represent real objects, but the objects appear as abstract. And it's happy. I like it."

"Until you said that, I would've said it looks like someone threw a pizza on the canvas then took black paint and made some random strokes."

"I get it. Beauty is in the eye of the beholder."

"And more," he says.

I wait for him to explain.

"Beauty is the story and the Beholder is the author."

"I'm lost."

"Not lost, just wandering, Rinnie the Lionheart. Check your compass. You're the mapmaker, the author."

"You're saying I can choose where to go?"

"And how to get there."

"If I'm the author, I write the story. I decide if it will be beautiful."

"Bingo!"

I quiver. Inside my head, I see a luminous haze of moving parts, yet there is clarity. For a moment. Like a shooting star, the image blazes and disappears. My brain's expanding at the speed of light. Mr. Algrin's voice nips my cerebral growth spurt.

"This is your adventure." He stands like an exclamation point punctuating his words. He smiles down on me.

My life. My adventure. I get to write it, I think. And, I do, on the slender slip of paper I pulled from Mr. Algrin's jar the week before.

WHY I HATE LIVER

Mom has been complaining for months of being bloated every time she eats eggs. But really, it's every time she eats anything greasy. From her angled lopsided walk, it's easy to tell she's in pain. I don't follow her too closely because she's been tooting, and it stinks.

Gaga told Mom to call Dr. Dryfus. Liz and I have told Mom to see Dr. Dryfus, but she won't make an appointment. Once Mom said she had "rectal bleeding." Even we knew this wasn't a good sign and insisted she call the doctor. We've given up. She doesn't listen to us.

Maybe because her stomach's gotten so round and because she can't zip any of her pants, she finally went to the doctor's office last week. The doctor said something about a shadow on the liver. Something is definitely not right, and Mom's going to the hospital tomorrow. A hospital with a specialty.

TIME

"Six weeks to six months to live, *if* she has chemo," the doctor says. The words are splinters, short, sharp, and deep. My mind skips to what I know of six months' time.

Mercury can rotate around the sun six times. A baby can learn to crawl. Spring buds can blossom into leafy branches, change colors, drop, and crunch. Branches become barren once more. A spider can lay more than one hundred thousand eggs. . . .

Six weeks in school lasts forever; six weeks now feels like seconds.

Six months ago was spring. I took the PSAT practice test for college. Liz shopped for an elegant satin belted formal in anticipation of the New Blossom Ball she was invited to. Evan still attended military school where the sun always shone. He didn't want to go to high school here. He wanted to fly planes. Gaga did endless charity work. Mom did normal things, too. She shopped, played cards, got her nails done, laughed, and lunched with her friends. She bathed herself, used a fork and spoon, and ate food—six months ago. Who'd have thought then that we'd be taking turns sitting at a medical facility that specialized in cancer care? Six months ago.

The doctor listens to Mom with his stethoscope.

"Her breathing is labored, worse than yesterday. I'm afraid she has pneumonia." He frowns. "We can't administer chemo until the pneumonia is gone."

Oxygen and drainage tubes and IVs are new body parts for Mom. Her hands are red from clenching the bed rail. *It takes energy to die.* For a moment, I want to run away.

The doctor sees me wince and takes Mom's hand. "Rose, you have a grip like a vise," he jokes.

"I'm practicing for my golf swing." She chokes on the words and lays slump backed, fragile, against a pile of pillows. Mom's hands drop from the rail, red palms flame against the white sheets.

Without moving, those hands telegraph a message, as electrifying as their power once was. *Mom holds the rail not for comfort, but for life! As long as her fingers encircle the rails, she knows she's alive!*

I'm on fire and shivering at the same time. The desperation in those red, irritated palms pricks me like a thousand needles. Desperation infects me! How do I make everything OK? I watch Mom clutch life as she's clutched everything—tighter and tighter until it disintegrates. My legs give way. I lurch and crumple into a chair and listen to the beep of monitors.

Names from childhood slip from Mom's lips. Her eyes are closed. She raises a hand in the air above her mouth, fingers V'ed as if a cigarette rested between them. In and out, in and out, Mom moves her hand above her lips.

Oh my God! She has an oxygen tube stuck in her nose, and she's puffing on an imaginary cigarette. Oh my God! Make her stop! I want to yell. This is sick. Of course it's sick. She's sick. That's why we're here.

"Lizzie, look," I say, imitating the smoking motion. "That's disgusting."

"It's spooky. She's somewhere else," Liz answers, stepping back, as if she might get cancer from the nonexistent smoke.

"Let's get out of here," I say. Liz and I link arms and blow kisses to Mom through the invisible smoke.

For a change, the waiting room is empty. Liz and I sit at a table with an unfinished puzzle of antique valentines. We've worked on it all week. Yesterday, we completed a lace heart that reads, *Affectionately Yours*. The heart is delicate.

"Do you think it's coincidental that the tables are covered with puzzles?" I ask Liz.

"I don't know. Why do you ask questions like that?"

Hidden in the scrambled cardboard chips lies a perfect picture. Each piece, part of the whole, yet dependent on the others. If one piece is lost, the entire picture changes. Does that make the picture incomplete or just different?

HOW DO YOU SPELL MONSTER?

"Your mother moves in and out of consciousness. The increase in medication we gave her reduces the pain, but it also fogs her mind. Yesterday she was lucid. Today is not so good," the oncologist reports.

"Can Mom hear us?" I hope she didn't hear the medical resident with curly hair ask me to meet him for a Coke.

I lean close to Mom's ear. "Mom, can you hear me?"

"Let her be, Rinnie," Evan says. He propels a paper airplane in front of the window. It soars past the clouds and glides to the airplane graveyard on the floor.

"Maybe she'll wake up later." Liz looks up from the newspaper and bites her painted fingernails. "Does anyone have a nail file?" She uncrosses her legs and removes her shoes.

"You aren't going to gnaw your toenails, are you?" Evan asks.

"I have an emery board in my purse, dear," Gaga says. She jostles through her plaid tote and unloads a wallet, glasses case, an address book, compact, and pen, all the color red, before she pulls the emery board from a gray plastic sleeve. Gaga hands it to Liz and rearranges the contents of her purse.

"Pop Pop brought the most luminous red roses to the hospital when your mother was born. Her skin was as velvety as the petals. That's why we named her Rose," Gaga muses.

"Mom, wake up," I say again. The words settle like dust, too faint to make an impression. "I love you, Mom. In spite of what you said, I love you." I hope she hears me. I think of yesterday when it was my turn to sit with Mom while the others went to lunch. . . .

"Can I get you anything Mom? Would you like some ice cream?"

"No. I'm not hungry."

"Mom, you have to eat. You have to eat to get stronger for the chemo."

"I'm not hungry."

"How about fudge? You love fudge."

"TV." Mom grunts, lifts a few fingers, and points to the dark screen. The effort it takes for her to raise her hand prompts me to move my own. The heels of my hands massage my temples and soothe my need to ask why I was treated differently from my sister and brother.

"Ask," I plead to myself. "Ask."

I'm scared to ask and scared to hear the answer.

I remember when Mom encouraged me to jump from the dock into the lake at camp. "It's only cold for a minute. Jump!" she wrote. "Don't be afraid."

I hated the cold. I hated the things that made the bottom rough, slimy, or squishy. I didn't want to touch those things.

I'm on the dock, and I have to jump.

"I have to ask you a question, Mom."

She turns toward me.

"Why did you treat me differently from Liz and Evan?"

"Because with you . . . I created a monster," Mom whispers. "You were the bad seed."

"What? I didn't hear you. I'm a monster?"

"Yes. You heard correctly, a monster."

She strains to shift her position. Her abdomen, distended and tight with fluid and tumor, insulates her from my interrogation. I don't want to be responsible for making her weaker. I don't want to be a burden. Besides, I'm not a monster . . . am I?

ONCE UPON a TIME . . .

It's shortly after two in the morning when the call comes. Our request not to resuscitate was followed. I tuck my nightie into a pair of pants and slip on a pair of bell bottoms, a flannel shirt, and a pair of cowboy boots. The air is heavy with the coming day's chill, but the hospital will be warm. The scuffle of Liz's fur slippers rakes the ground behind me.

By the time we get to Mom's hospital room, several nurses have gathered to assist the doctor. One nurse asks if we'd like to wait in the hall while the tubes in Mom's chest are removed.

"I'll wait downstairs for Evan and Gaga. He's picking her up. They'll be here soon." Liz pulls a tissue from the box on Mom's bedside table and blows her nose.

"I'm staying," I say.

True to the end, Rinnie. I hear myself think. *You have to find out the how and why of things. It drove Mom nuts. Now she's dead, and you're still at it.* I have to understand, I tell myself. I'm a salmon swimming upstream.

"What time did she die?" I ask.

"Her saturations dropped quickly. She expired at 1:57 A.M. We're sorry for your loss. Your mother was a fighter," the doctor says.

"Yes, she was," I say.

"Did you take the vitals?"

"They're recorded," a nurse says, as she clips a pen to her folder.

"What did you take?" I break in, worried a piece of Mom is gone without my approval.

"Vital signs—blood pressure, level of oxygen, pulse, respirations."

"Oh, OK." I pause. "May I touch her?"

The doctor nods. "If you like. She was a fighter," he says again. "She never gave up. I liked her."

Mom's arm is cold. When my finger presses where her pulse should be, there is little give. I rest my palm on her wrist. It's small, like mine. I outline the hilly ridges of her knuckles. The hilly ridges . . . cold, like the hills in Miracle Park in winter.

"Can we go sledding?" We beg our parents. It's the snowiest day of the year. "Miracle Park! Miracle Park! We want to go to Miracle Park!" we scream.

Mommy and Daddy drag our sleds up the hill again and again. Liz, Evan, and I swoosh down the hill. It's cold, but it's fun. The cold keeps the snow from melting. The cold makes our hot cocoa taste better. It doesn't hurt to be cold, Mommy.

Are you still inside your armor of flesh? Do you know your body has stopped working? I watched out for you, but you saw something else. You didn't see me.

Mom and I were two sides of the same story. It began the same for both of us.

Once upon a time, two baby girls were born. Like all babies, these babies wanted to be loved. Like all babies, these babies were lovable. Like all babies, these babies came without directions. Once upon a time.

The babies grew and so did their desires. One baby grew up in a fine house with parents who smiled fine smiles at the world. But as the baby became a young girl, a hole grew that bled into her heart—she couldn't please her father.

The other baby also grew up in a fine house, with parents who smiled fine smiles at the world. But, as this baby grew into a young girl, her parents argued every day and every night. One day, her parents went their own ways to live their own lives. This young girl had a hole that bled into her heart. Her parents, busy with their own lives, couldn't take care of her.

"It's time to remove her from life support," says the nurse who took the vitals.

"Will blood gush out?" I ask.

"No. Don't worry. She'll be OK."

"Be gentle."

"We'll be careful."

One nurse lifts Mom's shoulder while a second nurse gathers the tubes. They adjust the hospital gown Mom wears and pulls the sheet up under her arms. I brush her hair off her forehead with my hand.

Evan, Liz, and Gaga knock on the half-closed door.

JUST for ME

One by one, we exit the limousine, our heels dimpling the wet grass. The drizzle thickens and turns the sky to an ashen gloom. I can't imagine a better day for a funeral. It's a soggy cream puff sort of day.

Except for the gravestones, the cemetery—with its perfect slopes—could be the park where we used to sled. Several men offer to hold an umbrella over me as I work my way to a white canopy, but I've stopped worrying if the flip I worked so hard to style gets wet.

"No thank you," I say. "My grandmother is still in the car. Make sure she's under an umbrella, please." My face is wet, but there are no tears.

The slanted rain bastes my legs. I count sixteen raindrops. One drop for every year of my life.

"Rain is God crying," Mom used to say.

Two rows of chairs, four across, wait, empty. A man escorts my grandmother, my Gaga, to the seat closest to the rabbi. Gaga's sister, Aunt Millie, follows and is about to sit next to her, but I squirm in first. Liz and Evan follow. It's our mother being buried, and we want front-row seats. My aunt finds a chair beside my mother's brother, Uncle Matt. Mom would love this casket. It's . . . beautiful . . . shiny . . . dignified . . . the best of the best.

I glance behind me. Behind a collection of familiar faces, bundled against the cold, is Verna. Wrapped around her is one of Mom's old coats. A paisley hat with an upturned brim, another hand-me-down from Mom, shields her head. I recognize the unusually tall lean silhouette and sloped shoulders next to Verna from the one time Mom and Dad took us to her home to drop off a New Year's gift. It is her husband. The person who wanted her home at night.

"Please lower your heads for a moment of silence," the rabbi says.

I wonder if Mom's head is by his feet or at the opposite end. Her view would be best if her head was near the rabbi's feet.

"Death is a part of life," the rabbi says. "God controls the length of our days. But we are in control of what we pursue in life. We are in control of the pursuit of life. For fifty-six years, Rose Samuels Gardener pursued life—and happiness, wholeness, and mastery—all of her days."

My heart aches. She didn't find it.

"God is the Rock," the rabbi continues. "His work is perfect. Everything he does is just and fair."

I prickle. *Fair?*

Gaga dabs her eyes and gives my hand a gentle squeeze. I squeeze back and don't let go. At the funeral home last night, Mom didn't look like my mom. Her face was fuller, her hair a shade too dark. Visitors came and went. When Jack, Kenny, David, and other friends from school came by early, we retreated to the anteroom. It gave Liz, Evan, and me a chance to get some fresh air. Members of the Knitters Guild, Mom's bridge club and their husbands, the lady golfers from the club, Gaga's best friend Violet, a slew of people from Temple with whom Mom had grown up, and Mr. Bonatura, our sixth grade teacher, stayed a long time. Clerks from the stores we patronized came to pay respects, but when Mr. Algrin and Mr. Heuland walked in together, I could hardly believe my eyes. *They're here for me!* I reached for a tissue for the first time. I never expected teachers from school to come *here*.

"Rinnie," Liz nudges me. "Stand up." It's time to lower the casket into the ground.

A cemetery employee turns a lever and slowly the bronze casket, with my mother inside, disappears.

SUPPORT

The kitchen is overrunning with family and friends. People mingle in the living room, the den, and on the oriental carpet in the front hall. Coat racks fill the butler's pantry. I make a quick list in my head of familiar faces.

"I'm sorry about your mother, Rinnie."

It's not your fault, I think, but I smile and say, "Thank you. It means a great deal that you're here."

Violet, my grandmother's friend, is in the kitchen directing. "Desserts go on the dining room buffet. Flowers in the den—make sure they have water. The kugel goes in the microwave, put the extra one in the fridge. No, no, it's full, put it on top of the spinach casserole. They'll keep each other warm. The fruit platter goes on the table—the main table with the garden salad and the Jell-O molds. Keep the brisket hot. We'll bring it in when the family is seated."

I paint a landscape in my head—a deep valley buttresses a mountain range. Colors merge yet the forms are clear: a roast chicken hill, a flat field of brisket, a kugel pasture crowned with thistles of sepia.

Violet sees me squeeze through the butler's pantry.

"Rinnie, your mother was such a dear," she says holding my hands. "She went so fast. No one knew Rose was sick. Poor Eva, to lose her only daughter. Thank goodness she has you three grandchildren."

"How are you doing?" she says. "You know when Eva was in the hospital giving birth to Rose, I was in the next room giving birth to my daughter. I never saw two cuter babies. I'm so sorry."

"Thank you. It means a great deal that you're here," I say.

Violet continues. "Find a seat with your brother and sister at the dining table. Your grandma, uncle, and the rabbi will join you."

I count six chairs and nod. Mom would approve. The commotion and conversation is all about her.

"Come look at the sweets table," Mrs. Peck says, grabbing my arm. "Do I have enough of a selection? Maybe I should put out lemon bars and the apple strudel?"

One more dessert platter and the table will collapse, I think.

"This is a work of art," I say. For me, they may as well be garish cakes and pastries painted by a pop artist, something I won't eat. The desserts go against my rule: no sugar and no carbohydrates, nothing with more than three ingredients. It's too hard to keep track of what I eat if something has more than three ingredients. For more than two years, I've leaned on the rule. It's more than solid. It's immovable.

I look for Liz and Evan, so we can sit next to each other.

Aunt Millie is sitting at the dining table, smiling, greeting people like an usher at the theater.

"With Millie at the table there isn't room for the three of us," Liz says, looking at me.

"If there isn't room for all of us, there isn't room for any of us," Evan says.

"Why is Aunt Millie there anyway? We're the children, not her," I say. "Mom would be appalled."

"It's not right that on Mom's funeral day, we aren't sitting with Gaga, and Aunt Millie is," Liz says.

Evan cocks his head and says, "It figures."

I try to make sense of the arrangement in my head. Millie is Gaga's younger sister by sixteen years, and it might give Gaga comfort to have her nearby. On the other hand, Mom and Millie were like fire and ice. Gaga knows they competed for her attention like spoiled children. It's an insult to Mom for Millie to sit by Gaga. It's our time, *my* time, to be important in Mom's death, if not in her life, and Millie interferes. How does it happen that my time with Mom is always interrupted?

REMEMBERING

If Pop Pop were here, he'd be by his beloved Gaga, hand on her shoulder, a burly tree staked to its source of strength and reason. Gaga's slumped stance cries despair; her raised chin, courage.

The rabbi says a prayer, and food is passed in a flurry of hands as we watch. Liz, Evan, and I leave to sit in the breakfast room with our cousins. The painted figures on the walls of Chinese men pulling rickshaws and women dressed in robes, fluttering fans, close the space around the rectangular table. It's crowded in a nice way; we haven't gathered in a long time.

The morning's drizzle blisters into a thunderstorm. Raindrops pop against the windows. Green pine needles and charcoal-colored sky flow wet into wet, behind the rippled glass.

"Remember the day Mom drove us to the club? It rained like this . . . lightning split a tree." A movie rolls in my head of us bug-eyed kids, holding hands in the back seat of the car, terrified. My fingers drum the wooden table in answer to the rap, rap, rapping of the rain.

"I remember that!" Liz says. "Mom couldn't see the road and stopped under a tree. Scarrrry! Evan, you slept through the whole thing, as usual." Liz smiles big. "Mom turned the storm into a game. 'Who can guess what God's doing to make so much noise?' We sang wet weather songs."

Liz glances outside, humming, "Rain, rain, go away, come again another day."

The calendar rolls backward in my thoughts. That day, I decided God is playing crack the whip when I see lightning and hear thunder. My arm circles my head, snaps forward, and retracts. "Did you hear my thunder, Jef-fie?" I wring the name out and turn toward my same-age cousin Jeff.

"I wasn't scared in the car. I covered my head because I hated the song," he says.

"You peed in your bathing suit," his brother, Joey, adds.

"You weren't Captain Courageous, Joey. My hand looked albino after you crunched it," Jeff says.

"Mom was cool that day," Liz cuts them off. "She kept us calm. She kept us safe."

"Yea," I acknowledge. "She did." I loved Mom that day.

"Did Aunt Rose really chase your neighbor and wash his mouth out with soap?" Cousin Jodi's question breaks my reverie.

"Oh, you mean Eddie Kahn," Evan says. "Mom chased him through the house for saying *hell*. No swears allowed, unless they were hers." He zips his mouth with his thumb and forefinger.

"Hell," Joey says. "Washing his mouth out took chutzpah! Your mom. . . ." He shakes his head.

"She washed all our mouths out with soap, and all I did was call Evan stupid," I stick out my tongue at Evan.

"All I said was shut up," Liz says.

"She never caught me." Evan blows a kiss in my direction.

As the only boy, youngest child, and part-time resident of our house, Evan was immune to Mom's temper.

"Mom did some nutty things. Maybe to show she was in charge." Liz's remark stirs a dollop of bittersweet into the conversation.

We all know, from the day Mom and Dad divorced, Pop Pop controlled Mom's life with his tongue and his checkbook. Even after his death, she remained his puppet, his voice a part of her own.

"I need money," she'd say.

"You spend too much," Pop Pop would respond.

"I need money."

"I'm cutting off funds."

"Let me do it."

"You're irresponsible."

A blow to the ego. A left hook to the heart. They're down for the count. The untimely bell of silence.

"Pop Pop wouldn't let her grow up," I sigh.

A little whirlpool of pain spins behind my eyes. Pop Pop's voice is like distant thunder in my ear. *Why didn't you consult me before making a decision. . . . Hi, Mr. Blah-dee-dah. You remember Eva and my two morons, Liz and Rinnie. . . . Rose, stop with the beauty parlor. Do your hair yourself, like the morons. So you think you know as much as I do? Then why have you had two husbands?*

Evan leans away and balances his chair on their two back legs. "For all his smarts, financial ability, and philanthropy, he was a great businessman and a terrible parent and grandfather. He didn't talk to me for a year after I moved in with Dad. It was his way or no way. He gave me no way." Evan clunks the chair down on all four feet. It's the sound of finality.

COOKING LESSON

Violet is still in the kitchen sorting food. She hands a platter of pastry-wrapped hot dogs to my cousin Shelly, who passes them to everyone in the breakfast room. We're swapping family stories. I pick up a hot dog, peel away the soft layers of dough, and nudge Liz with my shoulder.

"Do you remember the time you invited Theo for lunch and wanted to make hot dogs and salad? You asked me how to cook the dogs and wash lettuce." I muffle a laugh.

"You were such a twerp," Liz says, taking over the conversation. "I invited my boyfriend, Theo, over for his favorite lunch—hot dogs and salad. Rinnie cooks, I don't. I asked her to help me, and she kindly gave me a cooking lesson."

"Did you see Theo at the funeral?" I interrupt. "He sat behind Uncle Matt."

"I saw him. He'll be here later," Liz says.

"That's nice of him," Shelly says.

"Oh, Mom loved Theo. They used to hang out even when I wasn't home," Liz says.

"But she didn't make hot dogs for him," I say.

"You twerpette," Liz starts the story, "Rinnie told me I had to wash the lettuce with soap and make sure it was absolutely clean because lettuce spiders bury their eggs in the leaves."

I interrupt, "And you did."

"Of course I did. I trusted you."

"Liz was brilliant the way she separated and gently buttered each leaf with a dip of detergent and her fingertips," I say. "I told Liz to cook the hot dogs for half an hour and turn them the whole time so they wouldn't burn. When I told Theo what Liz was doing, he rolled his eyes and paid me back with a knuckle rub to my head. That hurt."

"You deserved it," Liz says.

"Did Theo eat the hot dogs?" Sandy, Aunt Millie's oldest daughter, asks.

"He did." I say and add, "With a lot of mustard." A gurgle escapes my lips.

"Cuz, you have some 'naughties' in you," Sandy says. She thumps her hand on my back and knocks the hot dogs from my thoughts.

"It's amazing you and Liz never had any animosity between you," she says. "My sister and brothers would have destroyed me."

I reach for another hot dog, smile, and peel off the dough. Nah. We needed to stick together.

HISTORY

The high-pitched buzz of Gaga's doorbell sends Mrs. Peck scurrying.

"Hi. Are Rinnie and Liz here?" It's a familiar voice.

"In the breakfast room, dear," Mrs. Peck says. "You might want to wipe your feet on the mat before you come in."

It's my stepsister Alana. I wonder if Dad told her to stop by. Mom never got to know her very well. Sometimes I think I haven't either. In the beginning, our friendship bolted through the starting gate spurred by novelty for us both—new stepsisters, a new stepbrother, a new house—for them. It was exciting. Now, three years later, when I think of Alana, I think, *she has my dad.*

I nod and shake my head, empty out the past and replace "failure to bond" with a smile. It's time to say hello to Alana. It is nice of her to stop by.

ART IMITATES LIFE

The friction of Gaga's rubber-soled shoes against the linoleum floor and the scent of bath powder announce her entrance. "Dears, why didn't you sit with us at the dining table?" she looks at the three of us.

Because your sister, Millie, stole our place, I want to say, but Gaga wouldn't hear me. She's dedicated herself to ignoring the ugly.

"The table was full," I say.

"Well, I'm glad you all got to sit together."

Something green is stuck between her teeth. The sincerity of her blue eyes combined with the green between her teeth is reassuring. Some things *are* constant: Food nestled in Gaga's teeth proves it. She's still beautiful, I think. Gaga's beauty grows from the inside out. The warmth of her smile, like the smell of cookies hot out of the oven, engulfs friends and strangers.

"Family is the most important thing of all. Stick together," she says, looking at each of us. "You each have a gift to give the world."

Gaga's lipstick is the same color as a scarlet rose, her favorite flower. Gaga's focus on beauty shielded her from the thorns on her favorite rose, my mother. I know Gaga will miss Mom. I wonder if she misses Pop Pop.

"Sorry kids. I'm taking your Gaga with me." One of the ladies from Gaga's investment group puts her hand on Gaga's shoulder and steers her into the foyer.

I follow them, not ready to let go of the warmth Gaga offers. The dwindling crowd follows, and I detour to the dining room.

In the dining room, I look at the place where Mom sat every Monday night when we came for dinner, always by her mother, her protector. I look at the table with the pop art desserts. I'm in my Garden of Eden, and it's blooming with temptation. Mom's death has something to do with biting into forbidden fruit. Could her end be my beginning? She's gone. She can't call me whore or fat ass anymore or try to fatten me up because she thinks I am too thin. Never again will she scream, "You are the bad seed," even if I am.

The round cake with the hole in the center looks like I feel.

"I'm waiting for you," it says.

"I am here for you too," the apple strudel says.

I slice a thin piece of the round cake. A swirl of cinnamon weaves a wavy line across the spongy yellow slice. It dazzles like gold. My eyes are closed so I won't see my hand put the cake on my tongue.

The impulse drenches my mouth with desire. Lips, teeth, tongue, surge forward. The cake disappears. One bite is too many. A chunk of strudel tumbles down my throat, bits of apple fall from my lips. I reach for the lemon bars, a profiterole, brownies. *Come to me. Hug me.*

I'm grateful these are not imaginary pastries. I've starved a long time. There has been no sweetness. I'm caught in an avalanche and can't stop somersaulting.

PICTURE-PERFECT

"I'm glad the house is filled with people who care about Gaga," I say. The variety of black outfits is astonishing. "But I want to be alone with you guys," I say, putting my arms around Liz and Evan. My gaze flirts with the figures in the painting above the wing chair. Three well-groomed, buck-toothed children stare back. Dark-eyed Evan, curly-haired Liz, and fair-skinned me—before visits to Dr. Johnson for braces.

Evan pops some salted nuts into his mouth and snickers.

"That's the idea," Liz says. "No thinkee, no sadee."

"Do you think it'd be rude to go upstairs?" I ask.

"Yes," Liz says.

"Rude or not, I'm going for a walk." Evan stands, reaches into the candy dish, and fills his fist with cashews. "Emergency rations," he says. "Want to join me for a rush of Arctic air?"

Liz shakes her head. I want to go, but if Liz stays, I need to stay.

A shrunken lady with a black dress and a rainbow-colored hat hobbles into the room, arm in arm with Gaga.

"These are Rose's children," Gaga says.

We stand and introduce ourselves.

“My, you’ve grown up. I remember when the three of you sat for this picture. Your mother bribed you to sit still with cashews.”

It’s Mrs. Clark, the woman who painted our portraits.

“I don’t know how you captured the children, Julia, but I love it,” Gaga says.

“It’s like putting a jigsaw puzzle together, Eva.” Mrs. Clark uses the wing chair for support and straightens the picture frame. “I put irregular pieces together and create artistic harmony.”

“Did she just infer we’re odd?” I ask Liz.

“You are!” Liz mumbles and grins.

HOME COOKING

"I'm surprised there's no cheesecake on the sweet table," Sandy says. "Your mother adored baking them."

"Probably M.I.A. out of deference to Aunt Rose," my cousin Jeff says. "Everyone else's would pale in comparison. I'll never forget the Thanksgiving she brought cherry pies instead of cheesecakes. I'm sure the pies were delicious, but our side of the family was so disappointed we wouldn't even taste them. Your poor mother! But there wasn't as much to be thankful for without an Aunt Rose cheesecake."

"Mom took pride in her cheesecakes, that's for sure." The oohs and aahs quenched Mom's thirst for attention. A jumble of ideas flash through my mind, but like fireworks, dissolve before I'm able to grasp them. It's about Mom and thirst and . . .

"Please pass the pitcher," I say. Maybe watering my memory will help it grow.

"She was a fabulous baker," Sandy says. "You guys must have loved it when she made desserts, yummy beaters and bowls to lick." Sandy picks a corner off a brownie, leaving a trail from the tray of cookies to her napkin.

"Loved it? That's not the word I'd use," I say, pushing brownie crumbs into a tiny pyramid. "Dreaded it is much more like it."

Sandy's face goes blank. "What do you mean?"

"Mom believed in R and R—rules and rituals," I say. It's strange my cousin who's been around longer than me doesn't have a clue about life with Aunt Rose.

I begin. "First, Mom read the list of ingredients to Verna, who lined the ingredients up in a row, like foot soldiers. Then Mom inspected her troops, commenting on their freshness." She was a general contemplating her next maneuver.

"That's the sign of a cook who cares," Sandy says, shrugging.

"Mom could make cheesecake in her sleep, but she always insisted on having the recipe in front of her." I continue. "If Liz, Evan, and I even rolled our eyes, we got a dishonorable discharge and immediate dismissal from the kitchen."

"Wow! I always think of your mom being more like Betty Crocker," Sandy says. "You know, 'I love being in the kitchen and baking for my family—lick the bowl, kids!'"

"That's *your* mom," I say. "*My* mom baked three times a year and made a year's worth of desserts each time. She just acted normal in public."

My cousin crunches forward with her hands locked together between her legs. "What are you talking about?"

I think of Mom, in her beautiful, shiny, dignified casket, hugged by walls of wet earth. I wonder if she can hear me. When she gets to heaven, will she tell God I ratted on her the day of her funeral? I go on.

"When Mom made cheesecakes and they were in the oven, she ordered, 'Only tiptoeing! No noise until the cheesecakes are baked and cooled. They could fall.' Can you picture it—everyone in the house bound and gagged by cheesecakes? Mom shushing everyone for hours?"

"Come on! It couldn't have been that bad," Sandy says. "It's sort of funny, don't you think?"

"If you only knew," my raised eyebrows sigh silently.

Sandy places her elbows on the table and leans into them. "Hmmph," she says as though pondering Einstein's theory of relativity.

I want to lift my hands above my head and push the weight of memories away.

"I had lots to be thankful for the Thanksgiving Mom made cherry pies," I tell Sandy. "We did have lip lickin' good pie."

"Yeah, I'll bet," Sandy says.

I nod with a sideways sort of grin. Cherry-pie day cast its own spell. The air heaving with the scent of warm pastry and sugared cherries wrapped us in comfort. That smell would make an awesome perfume. I remember Verna stood at the breakfast table surrounded by mounds of white freezer paper. Next to her were towers of freezer paper-wrapped cherry pies. Verna and I carried twenty-eight pies to the basement and stacked them in the freezer, rearranging trays of pecan rolls. The freezer was Mom's monument to cherry growers everywhere and proof she could cook. Verna and I built muscles that afternoon.

"Wow, twenty-eight pies," Sandy's voice drifts off.

"If you only knew how funny it sort of was, Sandy, I could make you laugh till you cry."

TIME OUT

"Anyone want coffee?" I ask, squeezing past my cousins to get to the kitchen. Except for two women I recognize, but don't know, the kitchen is vacant. They smile at me, and I smile back. "Thank you for coming and helping us," I say.

"Are you Lizzie or Rinnie?" one of the women says. "Look how grown up you are."

"I'm Rinnie. Liz has curly hair."

"Lovely," her friend says. "I remember when you were no bigger than a minute. My, how you've grown. You look like your mother, same blue eyes. Tsk tsk." They shake their heads. "We were just off to join the others in the dining room. Call if you need anything."

Glug. Glug. Glug. The coffeemaker burps in response. China cups line the counter. The scent of hazelnut and coffee is so mouthwatering I swallow each inhalation. A tray of frosted raspberry-filled cookies is piled as high as the saucers. Before I realize it, my tongue caresses the roof of my mouth with a finger-full of frosting. Liquefied silk. Its long-forgotten pleasure dissolves into another time; a time of patting dough into circles with floured hands, a time of peppering dough with cookie-cutter shapes, a time in a happy kitchen with Verna, laughing and licking beaters. I remember her words, "Pat the dough nice and flat, cut a cookie just like that!"

I close my eyes and take a choppy deep breath. I want all the raspberry cookies. Gooey, flaky, chewy, crispy, crumbly. Anything but crunchy. Raw vegetables are crunchy. Thank goodness for coffee.

MAY I BE EXCUSED?

My brain is thick with other people's conversation. I excuse myself, and Liz joins me.

"Liz, I'm going upstairs. I need some alone time. If you need me, knock on the door."

"Are you OK, Rinnie?"

"Yeah, sort of overwhelmed. Mom's really gone." I start to go up the winding staircase.

"Rinnie. Things don't make sense to me either. Maybe we can talk later."

"OK."

I smile and thank God for my sister. What would I do without her?

BE CAREFUL WHAT YOU WISH FOR

I snuggle into the blue chair and watch the indigo lines of the cushion bend and sink beneath my body. I'm upstairs in the blue room. What's left of the funeral party lingers downstairs.

Liz, Evan, and I have named all twelve rooms in Gaga's house after colors. When Liz and I first began to stay here during exam week, I was in the ninth grade.

"Because I'm the oldest, I get first dibs on a room," Liz said.

She chose the pink room. Liz prefers the woven rug, thick with embroidered roses and ribbons of gold and green, to the plain carpets in the other bedrooms. A curved high-back chair covered in pink velvet soft as the satin-sheathed down quilts on the beds faces the doorway. Liz is queen of the pink room, and the chair is her throne.

Liz wants to be the queen. I don't mind. Her room is next to Gaga's, and Gaga snores.

When Evan spends the night, he stays in the caramel-colored room at the back of the house. It belonged to Uncle Matt. From the windows, the swimming pool, rose garden, and landscaped patio create a golden triangle.

My room is the blue room. Blue cornflowers sway in an imaginary breeze across the papered walls. The furniture is painted the blue of a summer sky at noon. Milky blue pleats of curtain blend into the walls. Only the carpet is white. I feel like I am wrapped in a cloud when I'm in this room—a cloud of tranquility.

The blue room used to be Mom's room. But now the photograph of her in her lace wedding gown, emerging like Aphrodite from a veil that billows on the floor, is the only reminder that she once lived here. I try to imagine her putting makeup on in this room, dreaming of boyfriends, travel, and one day having children.

What declares *my* existence in this room? Textbooks, the desk piled with exam notes, stacks of possible exam questions I wrote, hair clips, a blue tunic and white blouse in the closet, my favorite writing pen on the night table, peach body wash, zit medicine in the cupboard. On the wall hangs a picture of the Grand Canyon I painted in the eighth grade. Taped to my bedside table are two biology tests. *Excellent* reads one. *Superior work* reads the other.

I yawn and crank open a window to let in some fresh air. The smell of winter's dampness curls off the frost-brushed bushes below like smoke. It's the smell of wood snapping in fireplaces. But I think of the summer roses and smell Joy, Mom's favorite perfume. She was a Rose and a Gardener, but she didn't tend herself, and her thorns were sharp. Mom's presence in this room, like her Joy, is no longer.

It's quiet here. Peaceful. And an image of Gaga, Liz, and me at the breakfast table swirls in my head like the smells of the hot buttered toast and café au lait that swirl up the spiral staircase and wake me when I sleep here. At breakfast, Gaga sits between Liz and me.

"I'm glad you're here. Did you sleep well, dears?" she always asks.

I know the hiding places in this house, the contents of every closet, the boards that squeak in the attic, and which drawers stick when they open.

The giggle of two girls as they walk across the lawn draws my attention. Their blue and white uniforms label them as Cincinnati Girls' School students. "Everyone thinks we CGS girls are so smart," I say to myself. If they only knew how hard I work.

Mom's voice hijacks my thoughts. "You're impossible, Rinnie. . . . Stop asking so many questions. . . . You're driving me crazy. . . . Let the boys beat you in games. . . . Miss Smarty-Pants . . . you're not so great. Let me tell you something, you don't know it all. Your IQ is ninety-five. That's how smart you are."

Like a jockey's crop snapping horse flesh, the words smack. There's no rest. I gallop and gallop and run.

And when I stop, Mom is always at the finish line.

How many times did Liz warn, "Mom's on a rampage?"

Wasn't it last month Liz said, "Better check your room." I close my eyes to obstruct the thought, but I see my bedroom, the drawers upside down, empty. T-shirts, underwear, sweaters, pants, empty hangers, pencils, paper, erasers, pens, and markers strewn over the bed, the floor, and the chair like a poorly sewn patchwork quilt. I hear the conversation.

"You, too?" I ask Liz.

"Oh, yeah."

"What did we do this time?"

"We're unappreciative spoiled girls who make Mom spend money she doesn't have to keep us satisfied." Liz mimics Mom. "This will teach you to take care of your things. Put them away neatly or else!"

I remember wishing. I wish she'd die. . . .

I lay on the bed in the blue room, stiffly so my black dress won't wrinkle. Stiffly, like a corpse.

You didn't make her die, I tell myself. You didn't make her die.

HEAVEN

I close my eyes, and an image of hands fill the darkness—like the hands in the famous Durer painting Mrs. O'Claire showed in art class. Only these hands aren't praying. These hands are open, translucent, and the palms are the color of raspberries. They are Mom's hands, red from her grip on the hospital bed rails. Hands, afraid to let go. Afraid to lose control, afraid to lose life. My stomach muscles clench with sorrow, fist-like, then rebound and thrust pity and sorrow upward, into a reservoir that fills my heart and splashes over the boundaries of my world. It's difficult to stay afloat. I want to go back, but there is no back to go back to.

I look at Mom's photograph. Happy eyes stare into real life. The bride is radiant, expectant. I find a piece of myself in her face. It isn't the oval shape that is caressed by wavy hair, or her Greek nose, or even the freckles hidden beneath her powdered skin. I see her, I feel her, from the inside out. Disintegrated dreams and expectations, crumbled under her gown of hope.

I wear Mom's hand-me-downs: Demands to be heard, listened to, loved. My arms wrap around my chest and clutch fragments from our past.

"One, two, three, four, five."

Mom counts each stroke of color she brushes on her right eyelid. We're in her bathroom, and she's getting ready to go on a date. The left lid hovers over her bottom lashes like an aircraft carrier until called into service. One, two, three, four, five. Both lids are ready for takeoff.

I remember her insistence on perfection.

"Rinnie, do you think my eyes are even?" she asks me, her makeup consultant. I watch as she slides maraschino cherry-red lipstick over her thin lips. The lips that so often frowned in my direction. The bright color highlights her straight teeth. Even the nicotine stains don't mar Mom's beauty.

Warm air from a floor vent moves along my dark stocking-covered legs. Stocking-less, they are as pink and freckled as Mom's legs were in the height of summer. Summer meant swimming. The memory of her legs, smooth as ice cream, pumping me through the cold water, sails by. We almost played together. I swung on her legs, my seahorses, and Mom sat on the edge of the pool and talked to her friends.

"You're pretty like a mermaid," I said. But she didn't hear. She was being important. I want to sail with Mom one more time. I hold the memory close and we rock, nestled in the wave of a mattress sea. The sea is calm, but inside me, swells grow.

I whisper, "Mommy. Mommy." Sobs wring my body. "It wasn't supposed to be like this."

Tears trickle sideways from my eyes and into my hair, releasing the scent of shampoo—fresh, unblemished, succulent. I choke the smell in.

"God," I whisper. "I want to shampoo my life." A wad of sadness gathers in the back of my throat. I won't stuff it down. Not like the cinnamon cake, or the apple strudel, the brownies and frosted cookies. I won't make it a part of me anymore. I think of the words on the fortune I pulled from Mr. Algrin's cup. *Look for answers where the eyes can't see.* I close my eyes. Nothing is visible. And I rock on the bed.

CHANGE OF PALACE

Liz and I have been living with Gaga. Everything is different here. The air is fresher, the light lighter. I take deeper breaths. I think it's the same for Liz, but we don't talk about it. We just smile more and worry about different things.

Gaga found a position for Verna with the youngest daughter of Miriam Wallis, one of the women she plays golf with. Miriam's daughter has two little boys. It's too far to walk to the Wallis's, but I can ride my bike or drive if Gaga lets me use her car. It's different though. Verna isn't ours anymore.

NOTE to MYSELF

I place my hands below my rib cage, index fingers touch in the center. I flip my hands to feel my ribs from the back. I count each rib and relax. The measurement hasn't changed since my funeral binge last month. It's going to be a good day.

BREAKFAST

"Good Morning, darling," a voice coos from above. I rub my face in the downy pillow and take one last smell of last night's sleep.

"Morning, Gaga. Thanks for waking me."

"I love waking you girls, and I look forward to doing it until you both are away at college."

I love waking to Gaga's lilting voice, though I miss the sound of Verna's pebbles hitting my window. I miss hurrying downstairs to open the door for her. It was our ritual. Now there is a new one. Liz, Gaga, and I breakfast together every day.

"I'll be downstairs waiting for you," she says, scuttling off in her worn terrycloth slippers and wraparound cotton robe.

As usual, dressing's a breeze. It's the same look every day: white blouse, light blue tunic, white socks, and saddle shoes. I grab my navy sweater, standard issue with the uniform, and glance in the mirror. I know a ponytail is a good choice for my needs-a-wash hair.

The familiar smell of buttered toast and café au lait climb the stairs. I hurry to catch it.

The Asian men painted on the breakfast room walls still pull their rickshaws and the women still carry their umbrellas. There are three of us, though it's more like a gathering of old friends: the four-story tower of toast on a chipped plate, the half glasses of orange juice, coffee cups promising a warm start to the day. Liz and I have devoured skyscrapers of toast at this table. Gaga isn't Julia Child, but she does make the most delicious drenched-in-butter, thinly sliced, golden-brown toast. Sometimes with cinnamon and raisins.

"Mmmm." My mouth's watering. Gaga bites delicately into what I want.

"Have some toast," she says.

Liz carefully puts two halves together and bites along the edges.

"It looks yummy, but I think I'll make an egg white."

Her face changes tenor just a note, flatter.

"Rinnie . . . "

"Tennis," I interrupt and make up. "Have to stay in shape." I don't want to tell Gaga carbohydrates are fattening and butter abominable. I hope Liz will keep her mouth filled with food so she can't tell either. Gaga won't understand. Carbohydrates along with heath bars are her favorite food groups. The café au lait is compromise enough. I bring my egg to the table.

"That looks gross," Liz says. "It's so, so white."

"It's very tasty," I counter. "And full of protein."

I notice the tower of toast resembles rubble from a tornado. Little chunks of picked-at bread lie next to scattered crumbs.

"Better hurry or we'll be late for school," Liz says.

The anemic egg white looks up at me. "You're right," I say to no one. "It's very white."

NOTE to MYSELF

Buttered cinnamon toast, orange juice, café au lait, oatmeal raisin cookies at lunch, and bagels and cream cheese for an after-school snack taste a whole lot better than egg whites and plain vegetables. In two months, my body's become food rich from rich food, and my wealth is apparent even in a not-so-baggy-anymore tunic. In two more months, I'll be the wealthiest-looking girl at CGS.

NOTE to MYSELF

Mr. Algrin asks me if I want to talk about Mom.

I say, "Not really."

BINGE

I want to be alone. I just pigged out—again. I rock back and forth trying to pacify the ache in my stomach. Arm over arm, I feel like I'm on fire. Electrified. My mind speeds through every red-light warning: EXIT THE KITCHEN. LEAVE NOW.

<u>Victim count</u>: One. <u>Implements Engaged</u>: A dozen donuts, half a loaf of cinnamon bread, frozen cookies. <u>Methodology</u>: Biting, chewing, spitting out, biting, chewing, and swallowing. <u>Missing Evidence</u>: Statement as to why I stuff my mouth with things I don't like—ginger chews, root beer suckers, honey toffees? Why I cram stale potato chips and disgusting Fritos down my throat? <u>Theory</u>: Food doesn't talk back, it doesn't leave. It caters to me, withstands my curses, and is my voice when I can't speak. Food is my repellent to keep connections at a safe distance. It fills the gaps. Yea, though I walk through the valley of food I shall fear no evil. For thou shalt comfort me.

SHAME

POEM 1

A little winged thing,
You bore into my soft spot.
Deposited your eggs.
Covered them with secretions.
Suffocating malleable virtue.
How old was I?

POEM 2

S-Scornful, sarcastic, scarring,
H-Her gift to me
A-An alienating accessory,
M-Mea culpa
E-Eeeek.

POEM 3

Shame is the outfit
A child picks out, puts on, plays in,
While someone else
Shows him, shushes him, submerges him
In
Not good enough
Or
All wrong.
Who said,
"Clothing does not make the man?"

ELECTIVE

"Second semester, juniors get to choose an elective. It's the first time I've had a choice in my education. I'll be working in the pre-kindergarten two afternoons a week," I tell Verna.

We huddle in the enclosed alcove between the door to the inside of the Wallis house and the door to the outside.

"What do you know about little children? You never baby-sat a child in your life," she says. "But you was a good little kid so there's hope. I always said you were an angel—when you was asleep."

"The headmaster thinks it's a good fit," I say, tipping my nose a little higher than where it had been. I keep to myself that he's a dork and doesn't know me from a hill of beans. "What's important is that I interact well."

"You'll do fine, girl. I know you will." Verna steps closer to the door. I know she's checking to see if Mrs. Wallis is headed toward where we stand.

I'm finally not following in Liz's footsteps. She chose horticulture as her elective but never grew into it.

"I will never be Booker T. Washington," Liz fumed weekly. She did water the plants in the living room well. They're still alive.

Thoughts of returning to pre-kindergarten circle like pinwheels. Everything seemed pretty good then.

CUPCAKES

The hallways in the pre-kindergarten are mosaicked with children gathering flowers, leaves, and fruit. It's sweet so I decide to name the rooms after desserts. Mrs. Fox's room, my assigned room, is Cupcake. It's sandwiched between Sugar Cookie and Banana Pudding. All of them have windowed doors with yellow shades. When I walk into Cupcake, the scent of new linoleum and warm bodies greet me.

Pre-kindergarteners warble over the childish clang of metal cars and emergency vehicles. In a corner is a full-length mirror reflecting a crowd of kids in oversized hats and dress-up clothes that drag on the floor. Other children, carrying plastic baskets, shop inside a cardboard grocery store; still others huddle over stockpiles of wood blocks. They look like bear cubs guarding honey pots. A few kids sit on pillows. Their crossed legs balancing books spread open. I want to play in this room!

A stout woman, hair pulled back in a bun, wades through little people and waves me in.

"Welcome to pre-kindergarten! You must be Rinnie. I'm Mrs. Fox." She turns off the light. "Christopher, would you kindly keep your hands to yourself," she says. "Shawn, come stand next to me, please."

It takes less than a minute before all eyes are on us.

"I'd like to introduce Rinnie to everyone. Rinnie is going to help me teach this semester. Let's welcome her to our room with our class cheer."

Eighteen voices sing out of unison:

"We are the cupcakes, sweet and friendly, cupcakes.
Every time we pla-aay we learn to share and sa-aay,
May I help you, Please and thank you.
We are the cupcakes sweet and friendly cupcakes. YAY!"

Eighteen squirming bodies jump in place.

"Thank you, everyone. That was an exuberant welcome! You are excellent singers," Mrs. Fox claps. "Go back to your business. There's still time to play before circle. Rinnie will come by and introduce herself."

The kids scurry to play house, pour and sift sand at the sand table, play with puppets behind a makeshift wall of stuffed animals, shop at the grocery store, dress up, and guard their blocks.

A chubby girl dressed in green overalls tugs my uniform. "Will you tie my shoe?"

She looks like a brussel sprout. I look down at hair matted with curls, orangey-brown eyes, and a radish of a nose.

"Please," she adds, sticking her rhinestone-studded shoe on my leg, laces dangling on either side.

"Sure," I say. "What's your name?"

"Melissa."

I bend over, take the laces, and show her how to make them into two loopy bunny ears.

"Melissa, watch me cross one bunny ear over the other and push it under the first one. It's like a rabbit hopping into his hole," I say. "Look! He's popping back out." I pull the lace upward.

She smiles. "Do the other one." She sticks her left shoe out and unties the laces.

"Will you help me?"

She nods.

"I'll make one ear and you make the other," I say.

When the shoelace is tied, I say, "I like your shoes. The emeralds and diamonds are beautiful."

"I know. Look at my socks." She sticks one leg in the air and almost topples over.

"I'd like to have sparkly shoes and socks like yours. When they don't fit you anymore may I have them?"

She gazes at me. "You're silly," she says and hop-skips toward the grocery store.

"Silly is good. There isn't enough silly in the world," I answer.

SEDUCTION

Mrs. Fox is reading to the children while they rest. I gravitate to the easels and pick up a short-handled brush marinating in a jar of dense turquoise. It's just the right size for small hands.

I move the brush as if it were a feather tickling the paper. I can feel it as if I were the paper. The sensation is luscious. I think of silky maple syrup dripping over French toast. I make another stroke, only bolder and with yellow paint. I slide and twist the brush into wide curves back and forth, side to side, until the still-wet turquoise becomes luminous green. The colors are mouthwatering. I dip my finger into the red liquid and write my name. My first piece of pre-kindergarten art.

LITTLE BOOK of QUESTIONS

Newest Entries:

Is everyone teachable?

Are there "re-dos in life"?

When does art become Art?

A GOOD LESSON

Muted laughter catches my attention at the easel. Two boys fence with drippy paintbrushes and splatter the floor with orange and green drips that meld into brown. Plastic smocks protect their clothes, but their arms are zigzagged with orange and green brush strokes.

"Hey guys, not a good idea," I say, trying to disarm them without being gored with paint. "Whatever you get paint on, you'll have to clean up." *I sound like my mother.* "Why not use the paper. It's easier to carry home than the floor."

"Huh?"

"I want to show you something. By the way, my name is Rinnie."

I squat in front of the easel so we're all the same size. "Do you know there are art superheroes? Jackson Pollock is one of them, and he *loves* to paint by splattering colors all over his paper. He dribbles paint all over his work sort of like what you were doing with each other. Are you Jackson Pollocks?"

I get another odd look.

"I'm Luke, and he's Sam," says a mud-puddle brown mess. "Is Jackson Polk a grown-up?"

"Yes," I say, smiling. "Mr. Pollock is a grown-up that likes to make drippy paintings. I have a great idea!"

I tear paper from the roll behind me and double it over onto the already wet floor.

"Luke, you stand on this side of the paper by me. Sam stand across from Luke over there," I point to a clean spot on the floor. "Here, two for you and two for you." I hand them each two paint-soaked brushes. "Now dangle your brushes over the paper, move your arms, and see what happens. Ready, set, go!"

Luke rocks his arm slowly back and forth. Ribbons of paint stream from his brushes making long ticker-tape lines.

"My drips are red explosions. It's blood," Sam says.

"Time out," I say and have the boys change places. "Now paint on top of your friend's painting. Time in."

Mrs. Fox walks by. "Interesting approach, Rinnie. We have cleanup in ten minutes," she says. "You might want to start sooner."

She watches the boys, leans over, and says, "You redirected Luke and Sam in a way I haven't seen before. Very nicely done." She writes something on her clipboard then compliments the boys. Before moving on, she glances toward me and taps her watch.

Redirecting play—I'll read about that tonight. Whatever it is, it was fun.

OBSERVATION

Today in pre-kindergarten, the kids made Valentine's Day cards. Mrs. Fox and I had them finish the sentence, "Mommies and Daddies are important because . . . " and then we wrote their responses on the cards. We don't tell the kids what to write. They make it up. I'm beginning to understand what Mr. Algrin means when he says we are the authors of our lives. I watch the kids make life up every day.

Answers the "Cupcakes" gave include:

Daddy takes me to school when Mommy plays tennis.

Daddy works so we will have money for food and clothes and our dog.

Mommy is important because she loves me.

Daddy buys me candy.

Mommy is important because she helps me find Show and Tell.

Daddy is important because he calls the plumber to fix the toilet.

Mommy and Daddy are important because without them, we wouldn't have a Mommy or Daddy and that would be sad.

FIVE THOUGHTS THIS WEEK

I hate this feeling. My thighs are sequoia trees. Fat steamrolls my waistband. Blubber. Whale fat. I hate this. I hate me. I hate eating. I hate starving. Please, please, please. I'm on my knees. Make this go away.

I can hardly breathe in these pants.

A fold of skin blocks my stomach from touching my thigh when I bend over to shave my legs. I am disgusting.

I sit crossed-legged on the floor and run my hands down my sides, feeling the curve of each rib and then the flesh cushioning my once prominent pelvic bones. The edges are gone. I pinch the ripple of flesh. Desperation. It's Saturday. I want to wear my baggy tunic. Please, please, please make me stop eating.

It's easier to not eat. I promise not to overeat today. I promise to sit while I eat. I promise not to eat more than one serving of everything. I promise to eat slowly. I promise to chew twenty times before I swallow. I promise to stop when I am full. I promise to be good.

MAYBE I WILL . . .

Sandwiched between poster boards under my bed is a stack of paintings. Some I painted; a couple are presents from my pre-kindergartners. I wipe salty buttered popcorn bits and grease off my hands and pull the paintings out.

As I sort the pictures into two piles—paintings that awaken joy and ones that Freud would enjoy—I hear Gaga's voice mix with mine.

"Beautiful colors, like summer on paper, landscapey and lovely, bold and strong."

In Freud's pile, I notice that all but Sam's pictures in his signature red and black, and one from a girl named Tiffany—that she made the day we ran out of yellow and red—belong to me. Paper clipped together is a series I made when the pre-kindergartners focused on families and community workers. I pull the bundle out and lay each painting on the smooth, low-piled carpet.

My work has a theme, large clumped circles and a smaller one spun far from the rest. The backgrounds in my pictures are never still. The lines have a tempo—crescendos and decrescendos—that restrict any cadence of calm.

I then turn the paintings over, restack them, and place them back between the cardboard sheets. Be patient, I tell them. Until I'm ready to do something with the thought you hold in the back of my mind. I finish my diet Coke and scoot my makeshift portfolio under the bed.

SHOW BUT NO TELL

"I'd love to see your work, Rinnie, I'm flattered," Mr. Algrin says when I ask if he would like to see my paintings.

Mr. Algrin studies them as if they are authentic pieces of Renaissance art.

"I'm making up my life, with paint—like the kids," I tell him, hoping he will note my positive attitude.

"Ah, I see," he says. "Though I'm not so sure you are making life up."

"These are originals!"

Mr. Algrin looks at me and waits.

"I d-didn't copy anything." I know he means the paintings have meaning. I try to divert the conversation, but a "do and don't" duel jabs the inside of my head.

Tell him. Tell him what the symbols mean.

It's humiliating. Handle it yourself.

Now's your chance. He's offering to listen.

No! I don't want to.

Chicken.

It's too private.

Tell him.

Not now.

And I don't.

Mr. Algrin waits a long time and then some more. The clock ticks.

"As my mother used to say, 'You can lead a horse to water, but you can't make him drink,'" Mr. Algrin says.

"Hey," I say. "My mother used to say that, too."

"She was right. Your mother knew what she was talking about."

Mom was right? She knew what she was talking about? "How can you say that? Whose side are you on?" I hear myself yelp. "Is it right to be mean to children? Is it right to lie? How can you say that?" I'm on the attack. It's almost time for me to go, and I swoop up the paintings, crushing them in my arms. I'm sorry I brought them in.

Mr. Algrin stands up and extends his arms. "Whoa, there. We're a team. Remember? It's not about sides. Wrongs have been committed. You hurt, and rightly so."

I stand, tapping my foot in time to my anger.

"Breathe," he says.

I take a deep breath, a second, one more, and exhale fumes of frustration.

Mr. Algrin's voice is metered and steady. "I made an observation. It got linked to things you've experienced. The statement and your experiences are separate. It wasn't a judgment."

Maybe Mr. Algrin is right. I still want to shout or punch something to shut out my feeling of I want, I want, I want. It's gross, like a two-year-old having a tantrum and not knowing exactly what it is I want.

"This is so hard. I want a different life. No one else comes and talks to you week after week, month after month."

"You don't know that. That's why I was hired. People need to share, to know someone cares, to trust. It is hard—maybe the hardest work you'll ever do. Think about your name, Rin Tin Tin. Why did you choose it? Think about it," he says, opening the door for me to leave.

I want to slam the door so he'll know talking to him didn't help. But I don't because I'm a good girl, and he'd say the anger isn't about him anyway.

TELL

"Mrs. Fox says my pictures are expressive. She says they speak for me."

"I agree, and it's good to see you today," Mr. Algrin says in a fatherly way. "But that doesn't mean you get a pass. Here, with me, is where you get to share your thoughts."

It's strange that Mr. Algrin welcomes me back in his casual open way. I thought he'd be insulted after my last outburst.

I unroll a painting and lay it on the floor. Mr. Algrin swivels in his chair, and his eyes navigate through the islands of color.

"Tell me about your painting," he says.

I remind myself, I'm Rinnie, like Rin Tin Tin, the strongest, bravest, fastest dog in the world. I save people. And I begin.

"I call this *My Life*. The big dark circles represent me, my parents, and my siblings—real and step. They're purple and black because that's how I feel around them—bruised. The linked circles represent my activities: School, tennis, boys, art—that sort of stuff. The colorful swirls everywhere else are the things that happen in life, they're always changing. I can't control them."

"Change is certain. Change breeds change."

I want to tell him that sounds redundant, but he continues. "What would you like to control if you could?"

I want to say, "My life," but Mr. Algrin will say, "Life's a blanket. Look under the blanket."

So I say, "My family."

"That's a big one. How's it feel not to have control?" Mr. Algrin asks.

I stop to think. "Tense. Really tense." The dry sting that happens before tears bastes my eyes. "No matter how hard I try to make things good, to be good, I can't. I'm never enough."

Mr. Algrin says softly, "What do you do to try?"

YAH, Rinnie, I order myself to keep going. "I try to be the person people want me to be. Skinny and cute for boys, pretty and funny for Dad, competitive with Alana for Mom, attentive and obedient for Pop Pop, cheerful for Gaga. It's so hard." I take a tissue from the box next to me.

"You've got yourself entangled in a straitjacket of trying."

His voice is sad, and it pushes me to look away from him.

"It's OK to be sad. It's OK to cry," Mr. Algrin says. "Being all those things for other people doesn't leave much time for you to be yourself. It must be frightening and lonely to give yourself away piece by piece. It would make me want to run away."

"Have you?"

"Run away? No. I've tried it, but I'm always at my destination."

"I'm always at my destination, too," I say. "It takes so much control to hold on to all the parts. That's the problem. I used to be able to do it. Now, I can't control anything."

"I don't think whether you can control or not is the problem. I think it blocks out the problem."

"Then what is the problem?" I ask smartly.

"Try this on. Controlling is a means to an end. The end you're seeking hasn't paid off. Pursuing control isn't working. Ever hear, 'What you resist, persists'?"

"You're saying I'm resisting being happy?"

"I'm saying you're resisting being who you really are. Your interpretation of life is based on experiences that have skewed your vision."

"Is this like the *Mona Lisa* and the Kandinsky."

"Yes. This is exactly like the *Mona Lisa* and the Kandinsky."

I blow my nose and make room in my head for listening.

"You've shown me that there is an exception to what I just said. Times you act from your heart, that's not planned. Do you know what I'm referring to?" Mr. Algrin asks.

"When I'm with the little kids and when I paint?"

"Yes," he says. "Do you know why that is?"

"Because," I bite the inside of my cheek to help me think, "Because I feel free."

"And why do you do you feel free?"

I bite harder. "Because I'm not judging me, and they're not judging me."

Mr. Algrin springs from his chair. "Yes, Rinnie! It's because something in you has made it OK to be you. Like the paintings, there's more to pleasing than meets the eye. In art terms, you're using one-point perspective. Life needs multiple perspectives."

"I only have my own perspective. It's me that's experiencing things. How do I get other perspectives?"

"By doing what you're already doing: talking about your experiences, questioning what happened, considering circumstances and the circumstances of people involved in what happened. And by refusing to be at fault for everyone's bad behavior."

Mr. Algrin repeats each point pausing in between to read my expression.

"But a lot *is* my fault. It has to be. Why would people who are supposed to love and protect me knowingly hurt me? That's sick."

"Sick and egocentric," he says with a sideways shake of his head.

"Maybe, but my parents are educated."

Mr. Algrin chuckles. "Self-absorption is an open passport for anyone. Some, particularly in your family, Rinnie, go abroad more than others." He pauses. I watch the light in his face fade. "Everyone carries shame. Some of us just have to blacken others with it. That's when shame becomes destructive," he says.

Every one carries shame. Some of us just have to blacken others with it. I think of Pop Pop introducing Liz and me as his two morons: More On and More Off. We rolled our eyes at each other in embarrassment. It hurt. I think of Mom growing up with him as a father.

"Blackening others with shame is destructive," I say.

The words drift around me like aimless ghosts, and I wonder if I will be haunted by the darkness of my mother and father forever.

SWIRL

"Give me an example of a swirl," Mr. Algrin says.

"Being in the same class with my stepsister Alana is a swirl."

"Explain please."

I knew that was coming. "At school, Alana is Alana and not my sister. She has her friends, the loud girls, the ones who party and break rules. I have my friends. They're more, umm, individual, less lemming, more cat." I pause. "They act more independently. We don't travel in a pack. We don't leave people out."

Mr. Algrin tiptoes forward with his body. "So you and Alana don't speak or interact at school?"

"Not much."

"Ow, that must be uncomfortable."

"It's how it is."

"What about when you visit your Dad?"

"We have to talk then. Dad tells me to spend time with Alana until he's finished whatever he's doing."

Mr. Algrin raises his eyebrows.

"Usually we bake brownies and talk about assignments or tennis. We have the same coach. By the time the brownies are out of the oven, Dad's ready to do something. It's the weekend. The steps have their plans, and Liz and I have ours. Jake usually has his friend Rocky over, Amy plays with a neighbor who's her age, and sometimes Alana has a friend over, or she goes out. Evan practices his guitar. It's weird, trying to spend time with Dad and be a part of that family."

"It sounds weird." He fumbles for a pencil to write something down and hands me the cup filled with white slips of paper.

I take a slip of paper.

"No control," I say. "A swirl."

NOTE to MYSELF

Telling the truth to Mr. Algrin and myself is good. I haven't binged in almost three weeks—or starved.

P.S. I have my fortunes thumbtacked inside an empty picture frame in my bedroom.

MOM'S LAST WORDS

"Think about her last words. Paint them. Paint a picture of them and bring it to me next week."

I'm used to "Algrin Homework." It takes effort, but unlike in math, I usually feel better after figuring out what the factors mean. Mom's last words, "With you I created a monster," are words I don't want to think about. But I want change. I finger the slip of paper I pulled from his cup last week. It's a quote from President Franklin Roosevelt. "There is nothing to fear but fear itself."

PAINTING ONE

For a week, I think about colors and shapes, control and surrender, power and helplessness. I do my homework, work in the pre-kindergarten, and think some more.

I want to paint a monster. Disney monsters come to mind. Dragons that breathe fire and flash their tails in a fever of craziness. Eyes that eat you in one blink. Curved teeth so white, they blind their prey. Is this me?

I whip color across the blank sheet, forcing the brush to bend its tough bristles. Monster! Monster! Monster! I label myself, pounding an ache into my head. I unclip the wet page, ball it up, and toss it on the floor. Angry is how I'm supposed to feel. Angry. But I don't. My heart isn't spitting fire. Spines don't rise from my back. My eyes only eat what my mouth can't.

No, I am more subtle: a master of disguise, costumed in a tunic that signals "smart girl," a ponytail that suggests "innocence," and a big smile that communicates "happy."

"You are the bad seed. You are a monster," I say. We sink to the floor, sadness, emptiness, disappointment, and me.

"Paint them. Paint them." Mr. Algrin's words, like a chain tug me to a stand.

Slowly, I paint, thinking about my time with Mom, thinking about how she grew up, thinking about her life with Dad. I cover the page with self-doubt, fear, unhappiness, and swirls. When the paper can no longer absorb the wetness, I stop. I don't want my painting to fall apart.

TWO PAINTINGS

"Two stories, one girl," Mr. Algrin says, as we shift our gazes from one painting to the other.

"This one, the one with the wavy lines, happened first. But it's not the real first one. The real first one is the painting of elongated red ovals, belted with orange daggers that hide against the blue background, and a black dot. The ovals are supposed to be devouring the page. They are my mom. They are all women bigger than I am. I am the dot."

I grip my arms around me. They feel so thin. I suck in a long breath and heave it toward Mr. Algrin. My words come faster. I can't hide the wobble in my voice. "They can't be trusted. They're dishonest, cruel. I'm not safe in this picture."

"You're safe here, Rinnie." Mr. Algrin's voice is a gentle lullaby. "How old are you here?"

"Sixteen."

"I mean, how old is the black dot of you in the painting?"

"Oh," I say. "I don't know. I'm so little. Maybe I'm four."

"About the age of your pre-kindergartners, correct?"

I nod my head.

"What would sixteen-year-old Rinnie say to that fear-struck four-year-old girl?"

"I don't know."

"But you do. You've told me many times. When you've calmed a young kid, stemmed their tears, bandaged an 'owie.'"

I hadn't thought of those things. "I guess I'd kneel down and hug her. And tell her, very softly, that she's not alone, that I'll protect her, that I won't leave her. I'd tell her everyone gets scared and that it's OK to cry. Crying is a way to call for help."

Silence.

"Rinnie," Mr. Algrin whispers. "You are that little girl. Don't you think it's time to show her some compassion?"

I agree with the slightest nod of my head. I'm embarrassed that he said this.

"It's OK to cry. Crying is a way to call for help," he says.

Mr. Algrin is a good listener, and I cry.

I tug on the fringes of my relationship with my mother.

"May I have a tissue, please?" I blow my nose in a way that would make my mother frown. "She became all women. And all girls who are taller than I am," I say. The thought seems bizarre to me, as if I'm speaking in tongues, but the feeling is true.

"That would include classmates, wouldn't it?" Mr. Algrin asks. His question isn't really a question. "You've hooked a big catch. Will you reel it in?"

I look at the other painting on the floor and point to it.

"Lavender is self-doubt. Maroon is fear. Dark blue is unhappiness. The swirls are white, a combination of all colors, all feelings. The lines are wavy because I can't fit the feelings into a linear mold."

"Molds are static things," Mr. Algrin says.

"Yes. Comfortable and confining," I agree. A thought strikes at the feel of confinement . . . restriction. "Maybe I don't need a mold."

He smiles.

COURAGE

When I asked a question that Mom couldn't answer, she'd say, "Heaven knows." I squeeze my eyes tight and listen for angel's harps.

"Heaven," I say. "Where do monsters come from?"

"From one's imagination," comes the answer.

The sound is steady and firm like Mr. Algrin. It's gentle and warm like Verna, and it's encouraging and strong like Marie, the riding instructor at Camp Katawauk. Their friendship makes my search for answers possible.

CIRCLE TIME

I'm amazed the kids listen to me. When I'm with the kids, I feel like a bigger version of them. One of my favorite things is when a little body unexpectedly crawls into my lap and makes him or herself comfortable, like it's the most normal thing in the world. The poet Robert Browning must have felt this when he wrote, "God's in his Heaven, all's right with the world." I don't know about the God part, but I do know about the world of pre-kindergarten.

Today, everyone raised his or her hand to speak, no one had a time out, and no one needed to change clothes due to an accident. We got through show and tell, the calendar and weather, and a chat about Ben's cats throwing up. And there was still time for me to read a book about making soup from a stone. Maybe we can make stone soup for a snack one day.

Before circle time ended, Leah invited me to her fifth birthday party, and then the rest of the class invited me to their birthday parties. I feel like celebrating.

PRESCRIPTION FOR "HAPPY"

Go to pre-kindergarten.
Be goofy.
Play Duck Duck Goose.
Bring something for show and tell.
Bury treasure in the sand table.
Sing "Ring Around the Rosey" ten times.
Eat graham crackers (dip in milk first).
Glue, cut, paint.
Run around outside.
Get a hug.
Pass it on.

WATER TABLE

Kirk's waterlogged hands wrap around a large plastic milk jug. He insists I stand nestled behind him and watch as he tilts the jug just enough to spill the tinted pink water into a giant metal funnel. Each awkward pour splashes liquid from the container onto my clothes where Kirk's body is too slender to protect. Each swish of his smock greets my bare legs with a wet hello.

When I raise my arms to reach for the paper towels, Kirk grabs my sleeves and tugs, then pushes his body into my lowered arms. The sleeves of my sweater need to be pushed up before they are drenched. Once more, my arms brush up against thin but determined limbs. Kirk springs into action and pulls my arms downward.

"What are you doing?" I say with a tone of discomfort. The dampness of my clothes has filtered into my voice. I'm ready for a different learning center, but I can't move. It's a hostage situation. My right arm is slung over Kirk's shoulder and my left is being kissed.

I am twice Kirk's size yet his gesture knocks me off balance. How could such a little kid wield so much power? What strangeness? In pre-kindergarten, I'm supposed to be like Athena, Greek goddess of gardens. My job is to nurture young seedlings and appreciate their fragrance. But I don't have the right tools and the fragrance of kisses is questionable.

MONKEY BARS

The wind whistles through the playground equipment, chasing the squeals of the children.

Tyler and Luke are on the monkey bars. Several kids stand patiently on a merry-go-round while several others push to move it forward. Sam digs for China, his daily outside ritual. Other pre-kindergarteners ride scooters and tricycles, or run back and forth over the rubber hill that was installed a few days ago. Mrs. Fox watches from inside as she often does.

"I'm cold," whimpers a small voice from below. I turn away from the action and kneel to face cheeks, stained red from the chill.

"I think I know why, Lynnie. Someone's striped vest is open."

"Mine," she says proudly.

"Yep, it sure is. Let's button it. You button the red ones, and I'll button the blue ones."

As the last button moves into the vacant slit, a child's shriek falls over the playground.

"Oh my God!" the Sugar Cookie teacher cries. Her scarf stirs the words in the air. I run to where she's headed. Tyler's sprawled on the ground, howling. His pants are scraped and dirty, his cap by his ankles, his hands dimpled with flecks of gravel and grass.

"I only looked away for a moment," I said to the teacher who reached Tyler first. She removes her scarf and folds it to make a little pillow for Tyler's head.

"He's OK, startled and a little bruised but no breaks or sprains," she says after a quick examination.

"Tyler, I'm so sorry," I say. "I am so sorry." I take his red hands and brush off the gunk. "That must have been very scary." I give his hands a kiss, place his baseball cap on his head, and tell him I think he's very brave. Then I hug him. The fast beat of my chest melts into his.

To myself I say, "Thank you, thank you for having Tyler wear a sturdy coat today." It cushioned his fall. How could I have been so stupid to take my eyes off the climbers? How could I be so dumb? I know the rules: Safety First, Eyes Open, Be Alert. He could have hit his head. He could have died. Idiot! I hear Mom's relentless voice.

The sound of Tyler's shriek worms through my head the rest of the afternoon.

I don't even stay to paint. Mrs. Fox sees me pack up and approaches me

"Rinnie," she says. "I think you're hurt more than Tyler. Accidents happen. You can't control every facet of life—yours or anyone else's. It's OK."

"I didn't do my job. It was a mistake to look away."

"Rinnie, it was because you were doing your job that you didn't see Tyler. No one has eyes in the back of her head. I certainly don't. When I was student teaching, and I was a lot older than you are now, I lost track of one of the kids in my care on a field trip. He slipped into another room while the rest of the class waited in line, in a hallway, to use the bathroom. I was near hysteria with fear and guilt. I insisted the police be called. Thank goodness, a security guard heard his crying in an unused room and brought him to me."

"Really? Did that happen?"

"Really. It happened. And that wasn't my only mistake. My philosophy is making mistakes is the best way to learn. Just keep making new mistakes and learn from the old ones."

"I'll try," I say, as I open the door to leave. "And I'm really sorry."

NO THANK YOU

It's Tuesday. Mr. Algrin day. Instead of a painting, I bring a letter I wrote.

Dear Mom,

We received your gifts.

Evan has your marquis-cut sapphire ring and the matching double hoop earrings. He says they are his favorites of your jewels, and one day he might give them to his future wife. Your collection of handblown, artisan-crafted glass paperweights will grace the dwelling he'll call home. Evan loves the bronze sculpture of horses galloping and says it reminds him of not being allowed to sit in the living room because he might break something.

Liz, who would like to become an editor or a nurse, will wear the diamond helix necklace and the diamond encrusted ring you gave her, at her literary soirees—or maybe at the hospital. She will be the belle of her own ball. Her table will be set with your filigree silver knives, forks, and spoons, and she will serve from your silver tea set. She promises to make use of everything and to entertain at least as much as you did.

The diamond solitaire necklace you gave me is beautiful. I will keep it as a reminder of all that was good and beautiful about you. It is a precious stone in many ways. I promise not to lose it like the delicately twisted gold band that slipped off my finger when I was ten.

Your other gift to me is unnecessary. I'm giving the shame back. I don't need it anymore.

Wherever you are, I hope you are happy.

Thinking of you, Rinnie

"You have great style," Mr. Algrin says. "Build on it."

He hands me the cup with the paper slips. I take one and read it aloud. "I can't go back to yesterday because I was a different person then. Lewis Carroll, *Alice in Wonderland.*"

EVALUATION

"Working with you has been an exceptional experience," Mrs. Fox begins. "I've learned a few tricks, been reminded of some hands-on techniques, and have reveled in your enthusiasm."

I can almost feel the twinkle in my eyes. I want to believe her words.

"If all our student assistants could reclaim their four-year-old selves as you do, Rinnie, while using the knowledge of their sixteen-year-old selves, teaching would be so much more effective and fun for everyone."

I really want Mrs. Fox to stop talking so I can wallow in every single syllable. On her desk, the blunt tipped scissors, a crowd of crayons, swirls of silver glitter, a half-eaten package of chocolate marshmallow cookies, squares of blank newsprint, and a stack of picture books that bump into a purple stapler bridge us as much as the kids do. They are extensions of my ideas and our work together.

"Has anyone told you that you're a diamond in the rough?"

I look at her like I don't understand. My eyes amble about her face. Approval, comfort, and encouragement bloom like sunflowers. It's a face from which every child should pick blooms. Even me. I can tell when she clears her voice to speak that she knows I don't understand about being a diamond.

"It's clear when you play with the children that your inner child, little Rinnie, is alive and well. Equally as important is your innate ability to soothe a skinned knee, a hurt feeling, an unrealized fear. Have you noticed how the children seek you out? To them you are a playmate, a protector, a cheerleader."

"The kids are amazing," I jump in. "Being with them is like embracing a kite on a windy day. Their imaginations go every which way. I heard Sam and Ella comparing lunches today. Sam said he had a gorilla cheese sandwich and Ella had an egg salad sandwich without the salad."

"Yes. They do say funny things," she chuckles. "I want to show you something." Mrs. Fox sifts through the top drawer of her desk.

"Emily brought this in from home." She hands me a paper colored with markers. Five oddly rounded figures with long rounded arms and legs bob in the middle of the page.

"There are four people in Emily's family," Mrs. Fox continues. "Emily, her older sister, mother, and father. Do you know who the fifth person is?" She taps one of the distorted ovals.

"Her nanny?"

"It's you. Emily told me that this is her family and that 'Rinnie is with me because I love her. She's here for dinner.' You've become a part of her life. As you have with the other children."

A fog of feelings collects in the back of my throat and clogs any words from coming out.

"It's quite a compliment," she says.

"It is!" I say. I hope Mrs. Fox can't hear my disbelief.

"I thought you'd like to know. Take a look at this." Mrs. Fox maneuvers her hand over the scissors, around the marshmallow cookies, the picture books, and the stapler. She hands me a spiral-bound notebook. It's filled with things she's written down about what I've done with the kids. The list is long. I read a few lines.

Utilizes water table as a "pond" in which to fish. Rinnie attached a string to a drumstick and dangled a magnet from the string. The magnet is the bait and catches paper clips that are fastened to assorted objects in the water.

Cuts large letters from magazines. Spreads them on a table then has child locate the letters in his name. Child glues letters in proper order to paper, to make a name tag. Uses letters to spell other words. Also cuts jewelry out of fashion magazines. Uses tape to make bracelets and crowns for the children.

Fills empty water table with cooked spaghetti that has been dyed with food coloring—Tactile activity. Also places pasta on white paper in various shapes to make a picture. Starch makes pasta stick. Spells words with pasta.

I hand the notebook back to her.

"You'll notice in the coming weeks that I've incorporated aspects of your creative play into the curriculum for all pre-kindergarten classes. I've kept this notebook of your ideas. We'll continue to use them with your permission. I'd like to adapt your Rinnie-style storytelling techniques to promote pre-reading, deductive thinking, and social skills. You've been an asset to the class. And by the way, I hope you'll keep painting. As long as you have a paintbrush in your hand, you'll never be bored."

"I appreciate you letting me use the supplies."

"You were born to create, Rinnie. Don't ever forget that," Mrs. Fox says.

She gathers her coat, scarf, and canvas bag filled with books with photographs of bears, frogs, squirrels, and snakes on the covers. "If you decide to become a teacher, your children will be very lucky."

"What's the topic next week?" I ask.

"Animals that hibernate."

"It would be fun if the kids could wear their pajamas to school."

"Rinnie, that idea's a gem. See what I mean? A diamond in the rough."

"Thanks," I say. And I sparkle all the way home.

OPENINGS

"Mr. Algrin, I've been thinking about monsters. I think I understand what my mother meant."

"I'm all ears, Rinnie. I'd really like to hear what you have to say." He sits back in his chair so serenely, it's as if he's already heard what I have to say.

"Monsters are scary, right? OK. People are scared of things they don't understand. Scared of things they think will hurt them. Scared of things that question their value. Scared of things they don't want to know about themselves."

"This is a sophisticated conversation. How did you come to those conclusions?"

I grin and tell him, "I continued to do what you said I was already doing: Talking, questioning, and considering."

Mr. Algrin puts his feet on his desk, massages his fingers through his hair, and claps his hands together making a loud pop.

"You are Rinnie the Lionheart, you really are," he says.

"There's more," I continue. "I was a scared person—scared of not being good enough, of not being wanted, of being nothing. I don't want to be scared anymore. I'm not afraid to 'look under the blanket.' And I don't believe that I'm scary."

"No, you're not scary," Mr. Algrin draws the words out. "You're kind and fair, empathetic and industrious, but not scary."

"To Mom I was scary. I think she thought I had something she lost."

"What's that?"

"Potential. I remember one night when Dad tucked me into bed, he read the fairy tale *Sleeping Beauty*. When the story ended, he said that Mom and I shared many gifts. I thought he meant like Chanukah or Christmas gifts, and I told him I thought my gifts were just for me. Dad explained about inner gifts. He said Mom and I shared inner gifts: curiosity, courage, feistiness, friendliness, and that we were both beautiful. After their divorce, I think every time I went out with a new guy, had boys over, refused to cry when Mom went nuts, refused to compromise my morals—that made Mom sad and angry. My successes mirrored her losses. I became the big bad wolf—a monster."

"That's very astute and not easy to confront."

"There's one more piece. I'm a lot like my dad. We're both good athletes, detail oriented, artistic, practical, and we don't give up easily. I reminded Mom of him too much. He hurt her. He was a monster to her and that made me one, too."

"Did I mention that you are also perceptive?" Mr. Algrin asks.

I want to say perceptive and astute are redundant, but I don't.

"In a way, your mother probably did want your freedom and talent. She needed your unconditional love. She needed you to parent her. But that was impossible and not your job. She had a tough time, too."

"Pretty weird," I say. "I understand it here," pointing to my head, "but not entirely here," pointing to my heart.

"It'll take time. I have confidence you will."

He's so sure he makes me sure as well.

Mr. Algrin loses his informal air and locks his eyes on mine. He's so close I can smell the starch in his shirt.

"You can re-parent yourself, Rinnie. You can choose to love yourself unconditionally. It's your life. You get to write it. What do you want on your tombstone? *She never made a mistake because she was afraid to take a risk* OR *She celebrated every day and loved her life."*

"How do I start?"

"You already have. Baby steps. First one, then another. Remember the pebbles in the road, the easy ones to pick up? You're ready for stones, rocks, even small boulders."

I remember a saying from long ago, on one of Mr. Algrin's slips of paper.

I say the words out loud. "'Look for answers where they can't be seen.' I never understood this until now. The answers are tangled inside me, in the darkness, in the scary places. I'm not afraid to go there anymore. I'm not alone, am I?"

"You're not alone. You never have to be. Like you said, 'You don't give up easily.'" Mr. Algrin's face shines. "You're Rinnie from Rin Tin Tin: fast, smart, brave, and you save people. That includes you."

"I remember a dream I had as a little girl. There's a poem I used to hear in my sleep . . . a monster taunted me with a poem. It was a long, long time ago," I say.

"Can you recite the poem?" Mr. Algrin asks.

The words recall themselves from a curtained memory.

"If you ever, ever, ever,
Try to sneak away,
I'll be waiting in the night.
I'll be waiting in the day.
You never will escape me.
You never will be free.
You're my forever, ever, ever
You're the lock that fits my key."

Mr. Algrin is quiet. So am I.

"Forever, ever, ever." He chants the phrase like an evil spell. "It's chilling. What do you think the poem means?"

A belly breath speaks for me, and then I say, "I think it's about Mom and me. Mom needed a place for her pain. The place had to be well guarded, and it had to be malleable. It had to be strong to hold on to holding on. It had to be tough enough to endure. The place was the lock. Mom fit what she hated about herself and her life into the lock. The lock is a metaphor."

"Yes," he pauses. "Yes. Do you know where the lock is?"

I pause. "In front of you . . . I'm in front of you," I say. "I am the lock!"

Mr. Algrin swallows. I swear there are tears in his eyes.

"Mom was the key." I stop and wipe away my own tear. "We were miscast. Her key never fit my lock, did it?"

The thought reminds me of a drawing I made. "Remember the picture I drew of a faceless house?"

"I remember you wondered who would live in a house like that."

"I wrote a poem that goes with that house. I want to share it with you," I say. I close my eyes, slow my breath, and start:

"Whose house is this I'd like to know,
It's like a bride without trousseau.
It lacks both windows and a door
It greets the eye and nothing more.
Why build a structure blind and mute,
A non-fulfilling substitute.
For openhearted give and take.
Aborted life, a big mistake."

We both sit quietly, the poem still noisy in the air.

"No windows, no door, no chimney. No exit, no entry—by me or anyone else. I built that house around me. It seemed the safest way to exist," I say in a whisper. "I want more than to just exist. I'm drawing a door—and windows."

Mr. Algrin gets up slowly and stands next to me. He doesn't move and then he claps me on the back and says, "Good work, Rinnie."

I hug myself and laugh. It's an odd sound in Mr. Algrin's office.

It feels good.

EPILOGUE

My name is Rinnie Gardener. I am truly a gardener. I have planted seeds. I'm growing perennials. One perennial is hope, another trust, and a third freedom. My garden is big. There's room to grow many more things. I'm posting a sign in the garden that says "Visitors Welcome."

I think the growing season will be a long one. I know there will be freezes, insects, drought, or heavy rains. I also know there will be sunny days, filled with butterflies and fluffy white clouds. Fluffy white clouds tucked in a bed of blue sky. Tranquil. Almost as healing as painting.

ACKNOWLEDGMENTS

Thank you to Jane Resh Thomas for encouraging me to "just write." A thousand thanks to Alison McGee. To Andy and Cris, I can't imagine life without you. And to Brad, for encouraging me to illustrate children's books. If you hadn't, Rinnie would never have been born.